The Vizier's Elephant

The
Vizier's Elephant

Three Novellas by

IVO ANDRIĆ

Awarded the Nobel Prize for Literature in 1961

Translated from the Serbo-Croat by Drenka Willen

Henry Regnery Company • Chicago

A Gateway Edition

Contents

The spelling of proper names does not follow the accepted system of diacritical marks used in the Croatian Latin alphabet. Instead, a system of phonetic transliteration has been introduced, based on the method employed in translations from Russian and other Slavic languages using the Cyrillic alphabet. This should enable the reader to pronounce the words in accordance with regular English usage. The only exception to this rule is the town of Sarajevo, the pronunciation of which is well known despite its local spelling.

· The Vizier's Elephant ·

THE TOWNS AND CITIES OF BOSNIA ABOUND WITH STORIES. IN THESE tales the real and unrecorded history of the region, the life of the people and of generations long since passed, are concealed in the guise of unlikely events and under a mask of frequently improvised names. These are the oriental lies described by the Turkish proverb as "more true than the truth."

These stories live a curious, secretive life. They are like the Bosnian trout. In the brooks and streams of Bosnia there is a special sort of trout, whose dark back is broken up by two or three big red spots. It is an unusually gluttonous fish, sly and swift, rushing a hook cast by a skillful hand as if blind. But this fish cannot be caught, is even invisible, to people unfamiliar with those waters or that kind of fish. Strangers may wade forever in the stream, rod in hand, and not catch a thing, not even see anything but a black lightning-like streak that occasionally cuts through the water from rock to rock, resembling anything sooner than a fish.

These stories are like that. You may live in a Bosnian town for months and never hear one of them told truthfully and fully; on the other hand, you might spend a night somewhere by chance and be told two or three of these improbable tales, so revealing of the place and the people.

The citizens of Travnik, the wisest in all Bosnia, know more tales than anyone else, but they rarely tell them to strangers, much as the rich are loath to give away money. One of their stories is worth three of anyone else's; in their judgment, at any rate.

Such is the story of the *fil*, the Vizier's elephant.

When the news reached Travnik of the impending transfer
of their Vizier, Mehmed Ruzhdi Pasha, the Travnichani were
full of concern, and not without reason. Ruzhdi Pasha was
a jovial fellow, not given to worrying; lighthearted by nature
and sloppy in business, he was so good that neither Travnik
nor Bosnia felt his presence. But wise and shrewd people had
been uneasy for some time now, instinctively feeling that this
situation could not last. Now they were really upset, and on
two counts: because of the good Vizier who was leaving, and
because of the unknown one who was to replace him. And immediately they sought to discover as much as they could about
their new ruler.

Many a stranger wondered why the Travnichani made so
many inquiries about every new vizier, and ridiculed them for
it, attributing their curiosity to conceit and their habit of getting involved in important state affairs. But it was neither curiosity nor pride that led the Travnichani to inquire about the
most minute physical and moral traits and eccentricities of
every new vizier, but, rather, their long experience and dire
need.

In the long line of viziers, there had been many types, wise
and humane, careless and indifferent, amusing and sinful. But
there were also the evil ones, about whom stories were later
told which concealed the worst and the most important details,
just as people out of superstitious fear do not mention illnesses and evil things by name. An ill-tempered vizier was a
burden to all of Bosnia, but especially to Travnik, its capital;
for elsewhere in Bosnia he ruled with a stranger's hand,
whereas here he ruled personally, with his own hand, his unknown disposition, his retinue, and his servants.

The Travnichani would inquire right and left, spend

money, stand people to drinks, simply in order to learn some little thing about the man who was to be their vizier. Sometimes they would pay large sums to allegedly well-informed people, only to realize later that they were all frauds and liars. But they never considered the money wasted, for the lies told about a man are sometimes as revealing as the truth. Experienced and shrewd as they were, the Travnichani were frequently able to extract from the lies grains of truth of which the deceivers themselves had been unaware. If nothing else, a lie could serve as a point of departure for further speculation; and once the truth was known, the lies could be set aside easily enough.

The old Travnichani say, and not without good reason, that there are three towns in Bosnia in which wise people live. And they hasten to add that one town, the wisest of all three, is Travnik. As a rule, however, they neglect to mention what the other two are.

This time, too, the Travnichani had managed to gather quite a bit of information about the new Vizier.

For one thing, his name was Sayid Ali Jelaludin Pasha.

Born in Adrianople, he was an educated man; on completing his schooling he was to become an imam among the poor of Adrianople; but he left suddenly, went to Stambul, and joined the military administration. In Stambul he gained a reputation by skillfully tracking down thieves and dishonest merchants, punishing them severely and mercilessly. The story went that on one occasion he caught a Jew selling diluted and unusable tar to a military shipyard. Having investigated the matter and having received the professional opinion of two army quartermasters, he ordered that the Jew be drowned in his own tar. However, it did not happen that way. The Jew had been caught in the fraud, it is true, and had been asked to appear before a commission which was to examine on the spot

5

the quality of the tar. The merchant hopped about a wooden basin filled with tar, trying to explain his innocence, while Jelaludin Effendi sat motionless, glaring at him. Unable to remove himself from Jelaludin's gaze or to turn his own eyes away from him, no longer knowing what he was saying or where he was putting his feet, the unfortunate merchant slipped, fell into the basin, and disappeared quickly, proving the tar indeed too watery.

That was the way it actually happened, but Jelaludin Effendi had no objection to the more fantastic and horrible version of the story, nor to the circulation of so many other tales about his cruelty. He wisely calculated that he would gain the reputation of a "strong-willed man," and thus attract the attention of the Grand Vizier. And he was not mistaken.

All reasonable people, observing his work in the army, quickly realized that Jelaludin Effendi was not, in fact, overmuch concerned with justice, or with the inviolability of the state treasury, but that what he did was done out of an irresistible impulse and an inborn urge to judge, punish, torture, and kill, and that law and state interests served only as a pretext and a welcome excuse. The Grand Vizier in Stambul was doubtless aware of this trait in Jelaludin's character, but crumbling institutions and authorities, lacking new blood and inner strength, need exactly such people.

This was the beginning of Jelaludin's rise. From then on things took their own course, following the necessities of a weak and feeble society, in decline because of the very forces that had brought about Jelaludin's success in the world. His rise culminated in his appointment as the vizier of Bitol.

In Bitol a group of noble Turkish families had gained power, and governed there quite independently, each ruling its own territory; they warred among themselves and recognized no higher authority. It would seem that Jelaludin ac-

6

complished his task in Bitol to his superior's satisfaction, for a year later he was appointed vizier of Bosnia, where the decaying and downtrodden nobility had long since lost both the power to rule and the ability to obey. This proud but rebellious breed had to be subdued and conquered. Jelaludin Pasha was appointed to do just that.

"A sharp saber in a fast and unmerciful hand is about to descend on you," was the message sent to the Travnik nobles by a friend and informant in Stambul. He also described how Jelaludin Pasha had dealt with the Bitol nobles.

"As soon as he had arrived in Bitol, Jelaludin summoned the leading men and ordered that each cut an oak stake at least three feet long, write his name on it, and bring it to his quarters, the konak. As though spellbound, the nobles obeyed the humiliating order. Only one of them did not respond, determined to run away into the forest with several of his men rather than do such a shameful thing. But the Vizier's soldiers cut him to pieces before any of his relatives could come to the rescue. Then the Pasha had the stakes driven into the earth in his yard, until it looked like a little forest. Once again he assembled all the nobles in his yard and told them that now each one of them 'knew his place,' and that in case of even the slightest resistance in the district, he would impale them all on the stakes—which were arranged in alphabetical order."

The Travnichani accepted this story and yet again did not. In the past thirty years they had heard a great many black and strange reports and had seen even blacker and stranger things, so that for them even the strongest words had lost clarity and the power of conviction. To believe anything, they had to see it with their own eyes. They were full of these thoughts when, at last, the new Vizier reached Travnik.

There was nothing about the manner of his arrival that would justify the stories spread about him. Other horrible

7

viziers had entered the town boisterously, sumptuously, intending to frighten people to death by their mere appearance; but Jelaludin Pasha had entered the city at night, unnoticed, and was simply there in Travnik one morning in February. Everyone knew he was there, though no one had seen him as yet.

But when the Vizier received the town nobility and when they saw and heard him, there was yet another surprise. Contrary to reports, the Vizier was still a young man, between thirty-five and forty, with reddish-brown hair, pale skin, and a small head on a tall, thin body. His face was shaven, oval, and somehow childlike, with an inconspicuous reddish-brown mustache and rounded cheeks which evenly reflected light, like those of a porcelain doll. And in that light-skinned, fair-haired face, there were two brown, almost black, and somewhat uneven eyes, frequently shadowed by long, very light and reddish lashes, which gave his whole face a strange, stiff expression, as if it were breaking into a smile. But as soon as the lashes were raised it was clear from his dark eyes that the impression was deceptive and that there was no trace of a smile on that face. A tiny, pale mouth, a doll's mouth, opened only a trifle as he spoke, and the upper lip never moved, suggesting a row of bad and chipped teeth behind it.

When the Turkish nobles, the begs, gathered to exchange impressions and opinions after the first visit with the Vizier, many were inclined to judge this man (whom fate would not make an imam) a little less harshly; they underrated him and concluded that the advance warnings had been much exaggerated. But several more experienced and subtle men, who "knew the times well," kept silent, with a fixed look in their eyes, not daring, even in their own minds, to come to any full or final judgment, but sensing that into their midst there had come an unusual man and a villain of a very special kind.

8

Jelaludin Pasha arrived in Travnik at the beginning of February, and the slaughter of the begs took place in the middle of March.

By proclamation of the Sultan, Jelaludin summoned all the Turkish begs and all the distinguished leaders and town officials from all over Bosnia to an important gathering in Travnik. Exactly forty were asked to come. Thirteen did not show up, some out of shrewdness and because they sensed trouble, others out of traditional family pride, which proved this time to be as valuable as shrewdness. Of the twenty-seven, seventeen were executed on the spot, right there in the konak yard; the remaining ten were sent to Stambul the following day, linked together by a chain attached to iron bands round their necks.

There were no witnesses, and it is impossible to determine how so many experienced and distinguished people fell into a trap of this kind, to be slaughtered, like sheep, in the middle of Travnik, without any resistance or protest. The slaughter of the begs, carried out with deliberation and in cold blood before the Vizier's own eyes, with no respect for form, and in a manner never before employed by a vizier, appeared in the eyes of the people as an ugly dream and a form of black magic. From that time on, opinion of Jelaludin Pasha, who had become popularly known as the Jelaliya among the Travnichani, was uniform, a rare occurrence indeed. Prior to that, every evil vizier had been described as the worst of them all (which applied even to those who were not quite so bad). But of the present one they no longer said anything. For between the worst and this Jelaliya there was a long and horrible road, and along that road, out of fear, people lost their power of speech and memory, and the ability to compare and come up with a word that would best define Jelaliya, who he was and what he was.

The month of April passed in cold astonishment and mute anticipation of what would happen next, if anything could happen after this debacle.

Then, in the first days of May, the Vizier acquired an elephant.

When people in Turkey reached high positions and gained power and wealth, they often developed an interest in unusual animals, an interest resembling the passion for hunting, but a perverted passion that precludes physical effort. Thus, in the past, viziers had brought to Travnik a number of beasts never before seen here: a monkey, a parrot, a Persian cat. One of them even had a young panther, but it seems that the Travnik climate was not suitable to this kind of tiger. After the panther's initial outburst and a brief demonstration of his bloodthirsty nature, the beast stopped growing altogether. It is also true, of course, that the Vizier's retainers, who had nothing better to do, were in the habit of watering the animal with powerful rakiya and stuffing it with sweets of *esran* and *afion*. As time went on, the panther, by now a sickly beast, lost all his teeth. His fur lost its sheen and began shedding. Fattened and stunted, he lay in the yard unguarded and harmless, purring in the sun, while roosters pecked at him and unruly puppies abused him. And the following winter the animal died the natural and disreputable death of an ordinary Travnik tomcat.

Yes, in the past, too, fierce, eccentric viziers had brought with them strange animals, but judging by eccentricity and fierceness, this particular Jelaliya should have brought a whole herd of fearful beasts, such as are seen only in pictures or described in stories. Therefore, the Travnichani were little surprised when it was learned that the Vizier was expecting an elephant.

The elephant came from Africa. Young, snappy, and not

10

yet fully grown, he was but two years old. These details, as well as other information, had preceded the elephant into Travnik. Indeed, in Travnik everything was known: how he traveled, how he was looked after by his numerous escort, how he was transported and fed, and how he was received by the authorities along the way. And the Travnichani referred to him by the Turkish word *fil*, which means elephant.

The *fil* was on his way, lumbering along at a slow pace, even though he was still a young *fil*, no bigger than a good Bosnian ox. This whimsical baby elephant was causing a peck of trouble to his escort. Sometimes the *fil* refused to eat and simply lay in the grass, closing his eyes, hiccupping and belching, while his entourage was in a state of frenzy lest something happen to the Vizier's elephant; then he slyly opened one eye, glanced around him, leaped up, and, furiously wagging his short tail, broke into a run, going so fast that the guards could hardly keep up with him.

And then again he would refuse to move.

The guards pushed and pulled him; they tried to persuade him to move in all the languages under the sun, they baby-talked to him, they cursed him discreetly. Some even secretly pinched him in the soft area under the tail, but all in vain. Then they harnessed some oxen commandeered from the peasants to a special low cart called a *tehtervan*, and ended up by carrying the elephant in this manner through Bosnia.

No one could decipher his moods. And the Bosnians among the guards kept their jaws clenched tight lest they give away their thoughts about all the elephants and all the viziers of this world, and cursed the day they had been assigned to the bodyguard of this creature that Bosnia had never seen.

Every member of the elephant's party, from the highest ranking to the lowest, was worried and ill-humored. The thought of the Vizier's reaction to failure made them shudder

11

with fright; their only comfort was in the confusion and fear they themselves spread wherever they passed, as well as the booty to which they were entitled in the name of the Vizier's pet.

The scene was much the same in each town and village through which they passed. When the procession entered a Bosnian *kasaba*, which is to say a small town, the children would run out to meet it, laughing and gaily calling to one another. Older people would assemble in the square to see this miracle of miracles, but as soon as they spotted the somber faces of the guards and heard the name of Jelaludin Vizier, voices died down, faces froze, and everyone sought the quickest path home, trying to convince themselves that they had been nowhere and seen nothing. Local officials, army officers, *muhtars,* and police, whose duty compelled them not to do otherwise, paid their respects to the Vizier's pet with fear and awe. Not daring to ask why or what for, they ruthlessly and quickly extracted from the townspeople whatever the entourage demanded. Some of them approached the party with flattering smiles, not the guards alone, but also the young elephant; affably observing the young animal and not quite knowing what to say to him, they stroked their beards and murmured, but so the guards could hear them:

"Mashallah, mashallah! Knock on wood!"

But deep down in their hearts they feared lest something happen to the elephant while on their territory, and waited impatiently for the hour when this whole assemblage, together with the monster, would cross into the neighboring district, under someone else's jurisdiction. And after the procession had left, they heaved a mute sigh of relief and of long-accumulated disgust for everything, a sigh that the "sultan's men" occasionally heave, but in such a fashion that not even the black earth could hear it, let alone a live man.

And the people, too, the little men and women who were nothing and had nothing, could not speak publicly and freely about what they had seen. It was only behind the closed doors of their homes that they made fun of the elephant and sneered at the expense and care with which, like a relic, the Vizier's animal was being transported.

Only the children, ignoring every warning and propriety, talked freely, made bets about the length of the elephant's trunk, the thickness of his legs, and the size of his ears. On playgrounds, spotted with grass that was just beginning to show, the children played "the *fil* and his escort." One child is the elephant; he walks on four legs, swaying his head, on which a trunk and big floppy ears are to be imagined. The others are his escort, ill-natured and boorish servants and guards. One of the boys plays the role of the local judge, and with a great deal of true fear and false charm approaches the would-be elephant and, stroking his beard, murmurs:

"Mashallah, mashallah! What a pretty animal! Yá, yá, God's own gift!"

And he acted so well that all the children roared with laughter, including the would-be elephant.

When the *fil* and his party approached Sarajevo, they were received according to the venerable customs applied to traveling viziers, who, on their way to Travnik, did not enter the town itself, but stopped at nearby Goritsa for two nights at the most, while the city of Sarajevo sent up everything that was desired, food and drink, candles and fuel. The *fil* and his party spent one night at Goritsa. But the citizens of Sarajevo showed very little interest in this strange beast. (Many of their families were in mourning following the recent slaughter carried out by the Vizier.) The proud and rich Sarajevo citizens, who were suspicious of the Vizier and of everything connected with him, sent a messenger up to inquire how large the party was so that they might deliver whatever was needed. Nothing for the elephant, however, for this was what they said: "We know what the *fil*'s Vizier eats, but we do not know what is fed to the Vizier's *fil,* and if we knew his nature we would send what is necessary."

So from town to town the *fil* crossed half of Bosnia and finally arrived in Travnik without major mishaps. The elephant's reception by the town fittingly demonstrated the people's feelings about the Vizier. Some turned their backs and appeared as though they knew nothing and noticed nothing; some hesitated between fear and curiosity; others tried to devise ways of showing such esteem for the Vizier's elephant that an impression would be made on the right people. And lastly, there were the poor, who did not care much about viziers or elephants, and who viewed this as they did everything else, from only one standpoint: how they could acquire, at least once in a lifetime, if even for a short time, everything they or those close to them most needed.

The few exceptionally eager citizens who wanted to please the Vizier by greeting his elephant hesitated to do so, and most of them ended up by staying discreetly at home. For one never knows what turn things may take, they thought, and what harm and disaster may come of it. Who can anticipate and guess the disposition and willfulness of the Sultan's men? This may explain the absence of large crowds and the emptiness of the streets the day the *fil* entered Travnik.

In the narrow Travnik *charshiya,* the town's market street, the *fil* looked much larger than he really was, and much more awesome and outlandish, for as people watched the animal, they were thinking not of him but of the Vizier. And many of those who merely caught a glimpse of the *fil* in the procession, adorned with fresh green branches, afterward vied with each other, at coffeehouses and at home among the women at their spinning, in telling lies about the fearful appearance and the unusual qualities of this creature of the Vizier's. Now this is not surprising, for here, as elsewhere in the world, the eye easily sees what the mind imagines. And then again our people cherish more and like better their own stories about reality than the reality about which the stories are told.

No one could gather any information as to how the *fil* was accommodated at the Vizier's quarters, the konak, or how he had spent his first few days in Travnik, for even if there had been someone with the courage to ask, there was certainly no one with the courage to answer.

But what the Travnichani cannot learn legitimately, they know how to make up, and what they are not allowed to say, they whisper bravely and with persistence. The *fil* grew in the people's fancy, acquired nicknames that sounded neither pretty nor polite, even when whispered, let alone when written down. Even so, the *fil* was not only talked about, but written about too.

The priest of Dolats, Fra Mato Mikich, wrote to his friend the Father Superior of the Guchegorski Monastery, informing him of the elephant's arrival, but mysteriously, and partly in Latin, using quotations from the Apocalypse about the great beast. (*"Et vidi bestiam . . ."*) At the same time he sent his regular report on the situation at the konak, in Travnik, and in Bosnia.

"As you know," Fra Mato wrote, "some of our people, witnessing the slaughter of the Turkish begs, believed that some good might come of it for the rayah, for our fools think that someone else's misfortune must necessarily mean their good. You can freely tell your people—so they will know now, since they had not known before—that nothing will come of it. The only news is that 'a beast has acquired a beast' and that idle people tell tales about it and talk nonsense. As for reforms and improvements, there are none and there never shall be any."

And, carefully mixing Latin words with ours, as in a code, Fra Mato ended his letter: "*Et sic Bosna ut antea neuregiena sine lege vagatur et vagabitur forte* until the day of judgment." (And thus Bosnia, disorganized and lawless as ever, wanders and will wander until the day of judgment.)

And indeed, days went by, but there was not a word from the konak on any subject, not even the elephant. Ever since the gates closed behind the *fil*—that monster of the Travnik tales—he sank into the great konak, vanished without a trace, as though he had become one with the invisible Vizier.

The Vizier hardly ever left the konak. The Travnichani saw him only on rare occasions; this simple fact was in itself frightening, gave rise to various conjectures, and became another means of spreading fear. From the very start, the *charshiya* had been extremely anxious to learn a few more details about the Vizier, anything about his way of life, his habits, his passions, his likes and dislikes, so as to gain access to some door through which he could be approached.

The only information a well-paid informant from the konak could give them about the reserved, silent Vizier was that so far as the passions were concerned he had none. He lived modestly, smoked a little, drank even less, ate with moderation, dressed simply; he sought neither money nor fame and was neither lecherous nor avaricious.

Like most truths, this, too, was difficult to believe. On hearing the report, impatient Travnichani mockingly asked: If the man who lives at the konak is such a lamb, who was it then that slaughtered so many people in our Bosnia?

Even so, the report was correct. The Vizier's only passion, if it can be called that, was collecting pencils, fine paper, and inkstands.

16

In his collection was paper from all over the world—China, Venice, France, Holland, Germany. There were inkstands in different sizes, made of metal, jade, and of specially treated leather. The Vizier himself did not do much writing, since he was not particularly skilled in the art of calligraphy, but he passionately collected samples of beautiful writing and kept them folded in leather cases or in round boxes made of fine wood.

The Vizier was particularly proud of his collection of *kaléms,* those pencils used in the East in place of a quill. They were made of reed grass, most often of bamboo, pointed and split at the top in the shape of a pen.

Sitting there, absent-minded and still, the Vizier would roll the pencils gently from one hand into another—pencils of all kinds, colors, and sizes. There were pale-yellow pencils, almost white, reddish and purple pencils, and others black and shiny like tempered steel, all of them in natural hues; some were slim and completely smooth, like metal strips, others were thick as thumbs with knotty joints. Many reflected the strange play of nature; a *kalém* would end in a shoot shaped like a human skull, while the knots at the bamboo joints resembled human eyes. The whole Turkish Empire, Persia, and Egypt were represented with at least one sample in this collection of over eight hundred *kaléms,* of which not one looked like any other. None of them were of the ordinary kind bought by the dozen, and some were wholly unique in color and shape; the Vizier kept those wrapped in special elongated boxes of Chinese lacquer.

In a large room, enveloped in a deep silence, one could hear nothing for hours but the shuffling of paper and the tinkling of the *kaléms* in the Vizier's hands. He measured them and compared them to one another; he wrote stylized letters using oversized initials in different colored inks; then he would wipe and clean the pencils with special sponges and put them back in their places in the large collection.

It was in this manner that Sayid Ali Jelaludin Pasha passed the long hours in Travnik.

And while the Vizier spent whole days over his pencils, completely immersed in this innocent occupation, the whole of Bosnia was asking with hidden fear and unacknowledged concern: What is the Vizier doing and planning? Everyone was inclined to believe the worst and to see in the Vizier's constraint and silence a vague danger aimed at their families and themselves. And since everyone had a different picture of the Vizier, everyone imagined him at a different job, and it was always huge and bloody.

But the *kaléms* were not the Vizier's only entertainment. Every day he paid a visit to the elephant, examining him carefully from all sides, tossing some grass or fruit to him, quietly calling him funny names, but never touching the animal with his hand.

Such was the information the *charshiya* had about its invisible Vizier; too little for the *charshiya*. His passion for pencils and paper was neither credible nor quite comprehensible. His possession of the elephant was more understandable and somehow more familiar. Especially since the elephant soon began to appear before their amazed eyes.

· II ·

Before long the *fil* was indeed taken out; this had to happen because once the elephant had recovered from the effects of the long journey and had begun to eat well again, the konak became too small for him. Everyone had known that it would be impossible to keep a young elephant in a stable like a calf, but no one had realized that the animal would be so restless and moody.

It was easy to get the *fil* to take a walk, since he craved open space and greenery, but it was difficult to look after him and restrain him. On his second outing he suddenly started running across the shallow river Lashva, lifting his trunk high up for joy, splashing water around him on all sides. And then later, running along the garden fences, he would press his trunk against the pickets as if to determine how well they had been hammered together; and reaching high up into the trees he would bend and crush the branches. The servants chased after him, but by this time he had gone back into the Lashva and was playfully sprinkling them as well as himself with water.

A few days later the servants concluded that the *fil* should be taken out on a leash; of course a pretty one and in good taste. Around his neck was placed a firm collar made of leather lined with red cloth decorated with glittering spangles and tinkling bells. Long chains were attached to each side of the collar, which were held by two servants. A tall, imposing mulatto with slanted eyes strutted in front. He served as a kind of coach or trainer to the young elephant, and was the only one who, with a movement of his hand, a cry, or a glance, could exercise any influence over him. The people called him Filfil.

At the start the *fil* was taken to the hills around the konak, but later these walks were extended until at last he was led through the town itself. The first time they marched the *fil* through the *charshiya,* the townspeople behaved as they had on the day of his arrival in Travnik; they were reserved, frightened, but seemingly indifferent. The walks grew more frequent and soon became a regular event. In time the *fil* familiarized himself with the *charshiya* and began to display his real nature.

The moment the *fil* and his party appeared at one end of the *charshiya*, there was excitement and alarm. Dogs, the numerous *charshiya* dogs, became restless and confused as they sniffed the strange beast, who was outside of all their experience, and left their positions around the butcher shops. Those which had grown old and fat withdrew silently, but the younger, thinner, quicker ones barked with venom and violence through the fences or some hole in the wall, as though to deafen their own fear. The cats, too, were nervous, crossing the street and crawling against the walls and up the vines, climbing onto the wooden balconies or even up to the roofs. The hens, which were gathered around the market place, pecking away at their share of the oat sacks spread out for the village horses, clucking and fluttering, flew across the tall fences. Quacking, the ducks waddled awkwardly, falling off the walls into the stream.

The peasants' horses were exceptionally terrified of the *fil*. Otherwise patient and enduring, these small, brown, hairy Bosnian ponies, whose soft eyes seemed to peer through their forelocks with quiet joy, simply lost their senses as soon as they so much as caught a glimpse of the *fil* or heard the tinkling of his bells. They snapped their harnesses, threw off their loads and packsaddles, and ran, kicking violently with their hind legs at the invisible enemy. The desperate peasants ran, too, calling their giddy horses by name, hoping to calm them down and halt them. (There is something very painful in the image of a peasant who, with his legs and arms outstretched, runs out and stands in front of his raving horse and, with that little bit of reason he possesses, tries to be wiser than both his witless animal and those maniacs who had out of sheer insolence taken the monster into the *charshiya*.)

The town children, and in particular the little gypsies, ran from the side streets and, hiding at the corners of the houses, watched the strange animal with fear and sweet excitement. And with every day the children grew more daring and more enterprising; they shouted, whistled, and pushed each other, laughing and screaming, out into the main street and into the path of the elephant.

Concealed behind the wooden grilles of balconies and windows, women and girls watched the *fil* in his red adornment, accompanied by the strong well-dressed men of the Vizier's retinue. Three or four of them would flock together behind a grille, whispering, making jokes about the unusual animal, tickling one another, and giggling under their breath. Mothers and mothers-in-law would not let their pregnant daughters near the window for fear the children they carried might take after the monster.

But it was even worse on a market day. In their panic, horses, cattle, and sheep almost broke their legs. Peasant women from the nearby villages, in their long white dresses, with white kerchiefs handsomely wound round their heads, fled with long strides into side streets, crossing themselves and squealing with fear and excitement.

Swaying and tottering, the *fil* moved ponderously through all this commotion while his escort pranced around him, jumping up and down, laughing and shrieking. All this was so new and unusual that at times it seemed as if everything was moving to the accompaniment of some strange inaudible music and that the *fil*'s procession was accompanied not by little bells and laughter and the screeching of his guards and the gypsies, but by drums, cymbals, and instruments of unknown shape and origin.

The *fil* stomped with his heavy, strong legs, shifting his weight from one foot to another with a light, quiet rhythm, like any other young creature which has much more energy than he needs to carry and move his body, so that all the surplus turns into whimsy and play.

Having already made himself at home in the *charshiya,* the *fil*'s insolence daily grew more pronounced, and he carried out his intentions with all the more cunning and persistence; no one as yet could suspect or anticipate those caprices, so full of devilish slyness and almost human malice (at least such was the interpretation of the excited and offended *charshiya*). Now he would upset some poor devil's basket full of plums, and then he would fling his trunk and knock down all the pitchforks and rakes which a peasant had propped against the wall to display them for sale at the market. The people got out of his way as though before the inevitable, swallowed their rage, and quietly suffered the damage to their goods. The pastry cook Veysil tried to defend himself. The *fil* extended his trunk toward the circular board on which the cakes were displayed, but Veysil was faster and he threatened the animal with a heavy rolling pin. The elephant indeed withdrew his trunk. But then that Filfil, who was tough and strong, with long arms like a monkey's, ran over and gave Veysil a slap on the face the like of which no one in Travnik could remember. By the time the pastry cook had regained his senses the *fil* and his escort had already disappeared, and Veysil found himself surrounded by men splashing him with water. There were four thick bruises on his cheek as well as a bloodstained mark from the ring Filfil wore on his middle finger. And everyone said that judging by what could have happened the pastry cook had fared well.

In fact, the *fil*'s retinue plagued the *charshiya* more than the *fil* himself, senseless and strange animal that he was. The *fil*'s chief keeper, that Filfil, whose real name no one knew, with his long arms and his inhuman face, was always there. Then there were two soldiers as escort, and an idle courtier or two from the konak who came along to enjoy the spectacle of the frightened crowds, the chaos, the general confusion, the comic scenes and the laughter they inspired. The *charshiya* had known well and for a long time the special fury of low-ranking and subordinate officials in this land of unstable laws and evil masters. Indeed, the old Travnichani used to say: Evil masters are bad enough, but even worse are their servants and bootlickers.

The animal was not restrained in any way; on the contrary, he was encouraged and incited to disorder.

The idle and the gypsies would get ready early in the morning for the *fil*'s procession, to enjoy the jokes and the misadventures that followed. And they were never disappointed. One day the *fil* paused, wiggled a little, as though in thought, and then approached the shop of Avdaga Zlatarevich (a small merchant, but a respected citizen), leaned with the rear of his body against a wooden post on which the front of the shop rested, and scratched himself violently and for a long time. The wooden shop rocked and the joints creaked. Avdaga vanished through a little door that led into the storeroom, constructed of stone; the retinue stood and waited for the *fil* to finish scratching himself; the townspeople laughed. The following day, angry and bitter, Avdaga retreated into his storeroom well before the *fil* arrived. The elephant went directly to the front of his shop, approached the same wooden post, but instead of scratching himself, spread his hind legs a little and passed water, loudly and plentifully, in front of Avdaga's very door. Then he shook several times, exercising the muscles of his back, raised his ears playfully, and continued on his way with his slow solemn stride.

The gypsies, following at ten paces, giggled and made rude remarks, and the guards patted the elephant on the behind.

There were days when the *fil* went through the *charshiya* and nothing unusual happened; and there were days when they took him to another part of town instead. But the people of the *charshiya* were so accustomed to the excitement and to the *fil*'s tantrums that they told stories about him even when nothing happened.

The idle ones, who were there day in and day out to watch the elephant, talked and talked.

"The *fil* wasn't around yesterday," said one of them.

"He wasn't here, but do you know what happened in the gypsy quarter?" said one Karishik, an alcoholic and a gossip.

"What, what happened?" asked two men, forgetting that Karishik had established for himself the reputation of being the greatest liar in and around Travnik.

"A pregnant gypsy took one look at the *fil* and miscarried right then and there, that's what happened. It doesn't matter whether I tell you or not, but that's what happened! A woman with child in her eighth month stepped out to rinse a pot, when for some reason she looked up the alley and saw the *fil* heading straight toward her. And the woman dropped the pot, and as she screamed "Ou!" she folded up like a Turkish lantern. And there was a pool of blood right there. So both she and the premature baby were taken into the house. The woman did not come around, the child did; it was alive and healthy—but dumb, not a peep out of it. Fear made it dumb! Yá, that was it, my brother!"

All Karishik's stories ended with this "yá, my brother," an expression that served as a kind of trade-mark for each one of his stories and lies.

The idle dispersed and began to spread the story, most of them neglecting to mention that it originated with Karishik the gypsy. And the *charshiya* sizzled, anticipating the next day's visit by the *fil*, or at any rate some new story about him, true or false.

It is not difficult to imagine how Travnik shopkeepers and merchants felt; they were the calmest, most dignified business-men in Bosnia, serious, stiff, conceited, and proud of the clean-liness, tranquillity, and order of the community.

And the troubles with the *fil* grew; what is more, no one could see an end to them. Who can tell what goes on in the mind of an animal, even our Bosnian animals, let alone one brought from the alien outside world? Who could guess just what tortures the *fil* may have endured? But the *charshiya* was not in the habit of philosophizing about the problems of others, but confined its thought to matters concerning its own order and interests. While the empire creaked, groaned, and was bursting on all sides and Bosnia was living from hand to mouth, slovenly, full of fear and apprehension, and while the begs were in mourning and devising means of avenging them-selves, this *charshiya* could think of nothing but the *fil*, and saw in him its chief enemy.

Out of tradition as well as conviction, these people pro-tected animals, even the harmful ones, fed dogs, cats, and pigeons, and never even killed vermin. But this rule did not apply to the Vizier's elephant. They had designs on his life and hated him as one hates a human enemy.

But as the days and weeks went by the *fil* grew bigger and stronger, ever more frisky and restless.

At times he would race wildly through the Travnik *charshiya,* just as he had raced, when still a suckling, over the African plain, through the lush, tough grass that whipped him from all sides and awakened his young blood and bound-less appetite; he raced as though looking for something, and not finding it, he would wheel about and demolish everything

25

within reach. The *fil* had a craving for something; perhaps for playmates of his own age and strength. His molars began to grow, increasing his restlessness and creating an irresistible urge to gnaw at things, bite whatever he could reach; and the *charshiya* saw in this behavior the spirit of the Jelaliya as well as hundreds of other machinations.

At times the *fil* romped tamely and cheerfully, paying attention to no one, touching nothing, playfully whacking himself on the head with his own trunk. Then again he would pause in the middle of the *charshiya* and, standing still, his trunk hanging limp with sadness, his eyes downcast, he would look lost and discouraged. Even so, the men standing in front of the shops would nudge one another mischievously.

"Do you know who this *fil* reminds me of?" asked a silversmith of his neighbor.

"Who?"

"Of the Vizier! His spitting image!" the silversmith went on with conviction, although he himself had never had the courage to look up when the Vizier rode past his shop. And the neighbor, without looking at the animal, concluded that this was indeed possible, and, spitting to one side, mumbled something ugly about the Vizier and the *fil*'s mother.

Such was their hatred! And when the *charshiya*'s hatred is centered on one object it never abandons it, but concentrates on it with increasing intensity, and as time goes on the hatred changes its form and shape, outgrows its origins entirely, and develops a life of its own. The original object becomes secondary, leaving only its name; the hatred crystallizes, feeds on itself according to its own laws and needs, and becomes powerful, cunning, and passionate, like some evil love, finding new food and encouragement in everything, creating sources of ever greater hatred. And once the *charshiya* begins to hate someone, he has to fall, sooner or later, under the invisible

and malicious burden of the hatred; there is no salvation for
him, unless he were to raze the *charshiya* to the ground and
destroy the *charshiya* people root and branch.

Their hatred is blind and deaf, but it is not dumb. They do
not say much while in the *charshiya*, for a Jelaliya is a Jelaliya,
but in the evening when they get together in front of their
houses, the tongues loosen, the imaginations surge. And the
weather helped it along. Autumn was advancing. The nights
were still beautiful. The dark skies were rich with low stars
which were constantly breaking off and falling, and meteors
streaked the horizon, each one shaking the whole sky like a
sheet.

On the steep hillsides fires were burning. The last of the
preserves were being put up for the winter. People moved
around and sat by the fires, working or talking. And everywhere there were jokes and storytelling, and fruit and nuts,
coffee and tobacco, and almost everywhere—rakiya. But there
was no fire and no gathering at which the talk did not come
around to the Vizier and his elephant.

"Look, we've had enough of this!"

Most of their conversations began with these words. Many a
time over the years and centuries had these words been heard
in the Travnik *charshiya*. There was no generation that had
not had enough, and several times in a lifetime at that. One
could not determine with certainty at what point, indeed, they
had had enough and at what point they had the right to utter
these words, which are like a deep sigh or a silent cry forced
through the teeth, always relentless and true for those who
utter them.

The same problem was discussed in different ways around
different fires. There were some fires around which young men
sat, talking chiefly about girls and courting, games and tavern
exploits. There were other fires around which the petty crafts-

men and merchants of the *charshiya* were gathered. And, lastly, there were the small groups of big landowners, rich businessmen, and those of good family.

Two young men were sitting around one of the fires. The host was Shecheragich, and his guest, Gluhbegovich. The host was a youth of about twenty, hunchbacked and sickly, the only son in his family. His guest was of the same age, but tall, strong, and straight as an arrow, with sharp, blue eyes, above which met straight, thin brows like metal strips bent and sharpened at either end. The young men, although different in so many ways, were inseparable friends and liked to get away from others to talk alone and freely about all the things that delighted and tormented people of their age.

Today was Friday. The rest of their friends had gone to town to whisper with girls across a fence or through a crack in the gate.

While the two young men were sitting, quietly talking and smoking, several little girls were moving around by the cauldron in which the preserves were boiling. A servant was busy stirring it.

Gazing at the fire and somehow all immersed in himself, the hunchbacked youth was saying to his friend:

"They talk of nothing but the Vizier and his *fil*."

"Well, people have had enough!"

"It bores me though to listen to the same thing over and over again: the Vizier—the *fil*; the *fil*—the Vizier. And when I think about it, I somehow feel sorry for the beast. What harm has he really done? They caught him somewhere, across the seas, tied him up and sold him, and the Vizier brought him here to suffer in a foreign land all alone. And then again, I think: The Vizier, too, came by force; he, too, was sent here by others, who never asked him whether he liked it or not. And whoever sent him had to send someone to calm

28

down Bosnia and to put it in order. And so it seems to me everyone is being pushed around according to some kind of need and somebody else's will; nobody is where he would like to be and where he is liked."

Gluhbegovich interrupted him:

"You've gone too far, my friend! It's no good your thinking. By the time you find out who sent whom where, the *fil* will be sitting on top of your head. So don't try to find out anything, just defend yourself and strike when you can and whom you may."

"Eh," sighed the hunchbacked youth, "if everyone were to strike whomever was in his way and whomever is closest at hand, then there would be no end of it; the fight would go on forever."

"Let it! What do I care about eternity?"

Shecheragich said nothing, but withdrew ever farther into himself and gazed at the fire even more intently.

The talk around the fire bore no consequences for either the town or the *fil*, nor could it, for talk does not get anything done.

At a nearby fire there was a different crowd and different talk. This was a big gathering. About a dozen small merchants were sitting around drinking rakiya, some passionately and quietly, others prudently and protesting all the while. The talk went on, evolved, turned into jokes, into biting waspishness, formal monologues, long boasting, and complex lies, into short lightning-fast truths. Rakiya stirs in people unprecedented feelings and all kinds of thoughts, devises new words, engenders bold decisions, which here, between the gay fire and the darkness enveloping the sleeping and hushed world, seem natural and easily realized.

"Well, friends, my cheeks burn from that monster of the Vizier's, my own and those of all the *charshiya*. I'm sick of this life," Avdaga Zlatarevich was bitterly saying under his breath.

And instantly an almost inaudible but lively talk began, with everyone participating, everyone expressing his anger in his own way, according to his own temper, income, and the degree to which the rakiya had influenced him. Some were quarrelsome and aggressive, bold in word and fearless in proposal, others cautious in speech and more inclined to indirect means of achieving their aim, without noise and fanfare.

A short aga, red-haired, bony, sharp, and belligerent, with a bristling, short mustache, agreed with everything that was said, trembling with shame at the thought of what they had to endure in their own town and on this earth. And he cursed Travnik and whoever put it on that spot. "One should set fire to it," he said, "so that even a mouse in the wall will burn up." He cursed all of Bosnia up and down. "In truth, it is not like other countries," he said, crimson with rage. "There is no one who has not trampled on it; only an elephant was missing, and now here he is. They brought him over so this wonder, too, could be seen. Ah," he said, "I'll take a gun, and when he approaches my shop, I'll empty twenty drams of lead into his forehead, and afterward let them impale me in the market place."

Except for one hoarse mumble of approval, offered by a man who was not sober when he arrived, the small aga's outburst was met with complete silence. They knew well both the man and his threats. He had already emptied the same twenty drams of lead many times, and those at whom he aimed his fire were still healthy and alive, eating bread and being warmed by the sun. They also knew that the Travnik guns do not trigger lightly, but when they strike home, they do it discreetly.

But this did not stop the little aga, who went on making threats. Others joined him, abusing Bosnia and the Vizier, but more quietly and with less precision, until at last the time

30

came for hatching plots. Many proposals were put forward. Some favored immediate and violent action, although they were not always sure what they had in mind. Others advocated a moderate, cautious approach, to be followed at some future date; in the meantime, Travnik must wait and endure.

"How long are we to wait?" someone broke in belligerently. "Until the *fil* grows big and starts entering our houses and attacking our women? Do you know that an elephant lives to be over a hundred? Ah?"

"Maybe an elephant will," said an elderly, pale merchant calmly, "but his master won't."

Some of the merchants greeted this remark with significant nods, while others, the quarrelsome ones, were silenced for an instant, and the talk again turned to plotting.

But no serious or worthwhile solutions could be reached, not even at a gathering such as this, with its loud boasting and whispered threats. All that came forth were bold proposals, which delighted their authors and sometimes those to whom they were addressed. On the morrow, in the clear light of day, no one would ever think of carrying them out. The following evening the game of fancy and taletelling would start all over again. If someone were by chance to call attention to last night's proposals he was never taken too seriously; his reminders served only as the basis for fresh stories. This is how the story of Alyo and the *fil* evolved.

One September night it was particularly warm and clear. The women were stirring the preserves, the men were sitting by the fire with their coffee, rakiya and tobacco. Each word they pronounced was sweet to them, all they could see with their eyes and touch with their fingers was dear to them. Life was neither easy nor free and certainly not secure, but one could embellish it richly, talk about it wisely and so cleverly.

It was unusually noisy around one of the fires. A dozen or

31

so shopkeepers had gathered there, petty businessmen, and, for that very reason, the most belligerent.

Alyo kept a small but well-known silk-goods store in the *charshiya*, in which he wove cords, knitted ribbons, and sold silk bags and sashes. Alyo's family, the Kazazi, goes back to a big and powerful, now extinct, family of the Shahbegovich. But through various circumstances, they became landless, turned to handicraft and trade, and for more than fifty years have been members of the silk, or *kazazi*, guild. Thus they acquired the name Kazazi. They were known as good men and skilled craftsmen. Our Alyo also enjoyed this reputation, but he was a little eccentric and a law unto himself. Tall and husky, he had a ruddy face with black eyes and a thin uneven beard. He was known to be a great joker, naïve and simple, clever and resolute, a man who dared say what others would never say, and do what others would never dare do, and no one ever quite knew when he was jesting or when he would allow others to jest with him, when he used his wit to express a truth or when he played with the truth simply to be witty.

A long time ago, as a young man, he served under Suleyman Pasha during the Montenegrin campaign. He was as well known for his wit as for his courage.

Alyo had hardly sat down when they greeted him with questions.

"Alyo, here we are arguing as to what is the worst and most terrible thing in the world, what is the best and the sweetest."

"The worst thing is to be in the Montenegrin mountains on a windy night, with a unit of Montenegrins in front of you and another in back of you."

Alyo said this offhandedly, without thinking, as something he knew by heart, but then suddenly he paused, grew silent, and looked pensive. They insisted that he answer the second question too, but he gave them a roguish look with his black, shiny eyes, and then said quietly:

"What's the sweetest thing? . . . What's the sweetest thing? . . . Tell me: what is the sweetest thing? Only a fool can ask such a question; every sensible person knows what the sweetest thing is. That's known; you don't ask what it is. Come on, don't be silly."

But after these first few innocent jests, the talk again turned to the *fil*. The usual complaints, threats, boasting. Someone proposed that five *charshiya* men be chosen to go before the Vizier to complain openly of the *fil* and his retinue.

Tosun Aga, a small, sickly tailor, gulped down his cup of rakiya and, breathing violently (the rakiya breath inspires strong words), said:

"Here, I shall be the first to go!"

He was a shadow of a man, a sinful soul and of doubtful reputation, possessed by a vanity that dominated every feeling, including fear. In the strong light of the fire, he looked even more pale, worn, and weak, with very little life in him.

"Come on! If you are the first to go, let me be the third at the very least," said Alyo laughing.

Others gulped down their rakiya and began vying with one another.

"Count on me!"

"Me too!"

Thus they showed off for quite a while and competed with sharp words. They dispersed late that night with definite plans and solemn oaths that the five chosen men meet the next day in front of Tosun Aga's shop to go to the konak and ask permission to see the Vizier, to tell him the whole truth, the real feelings of the *charshiya* concerning the *fil* and his ruthless keepers, and to ask him kindly to remove this burden from their backs.

33

That same night many a boaster lay awake, wondering with fear whether it was possible that he, while drinking and talking, had promised to face the Jelaliya, or whether it was just a mad dream.

· III ·

When dawn broke the next morning and the appointed hour came, only three of the five men showed up in front of Tosun Aga's shop. The other two were not to be found anywhere. On the way to the konak, one of the three got such cramps in his intestines that he turned aside into one of the dense gardens along the route and vanished without a trace. Only Alyo remained, and with him Tosun Aga.

They walked slowly, each with the same thought in his head: that they should turn back from this dangerous and senseless journey. But since neither was willing to give expression to this thought, they went on. So, full of suspicion about one another, they reached the bridge on the Lashva, on the other side of which stood the konak. Tosun Aga hesitated and stopped, while Alyo went on toward the bridge, where he had planned to pause, leaving them free to reconsider a decision that might well cost them their heads. Loud voices awakened him from his meditations. The two sentries standing at the other end of the bridge yelled something in chorus. At first Alyo thought they were telling him to clear away from the bridge. Very pleased, he was about to turn back when he saw them waving their arms and calling to him:

"Hey you!"

"Come here!"

The guards had been reinforced, as though someone had been expected. The two clean-shaven sentries walked over to meet him. Alyo was terrified, but he had no choice: and since he had no choice, he quickly and amiably started toward them.

Harshly, they asked him where he was going and what he was looking for. Alyo replied in a natural and innocent tone that he was on his way to see his friends, the Halovichi, concerning some plums, but he had been talking with a neighbor, whom he met along the way, and thus talking, he reached the konak without knowing it. And he smiled at himself and his absent-mindedness with a broad and ridiculously good-natured smile. The sentries looked at him dubiously for a moment or so, and the elder of the two said in a milder tone:

"Go on your way!"

Relieved of his initial fear, quite calm by now, Alyo felt a curious desire to talk with these good youths, to jest in the face of the danger that had passed him by.

"Well, well, boys, you take good care, and be obedient! God give long life to your master!"

The Jelaliya's soldiers, hardened and veteran killers that they were, looked at him with a smile on their dull faces.

Going up the hillside, by the outside wall of the Vizier's garden, Alyo turned back once again to smile at the soldiers, who were no longer looking in his direction. At the same time he cast a glance toward the other bank of the Lashva, from where Tosun Aga had vanished, abandoning his friend and betraying all the oaths of the night before.

Climbing along a bumpy path bordered with fences, he reached the top of the hill, where he found some flat ground under a tall pear tree whose leaves had already turned. There he sat down, took out his tobacco, and rolled himself a cigarette.

Beneath him, the konak was hidden in the valley, on the right bank of the Lashva. Travnik appeared as a crowded heap of black and gray roofs above which deep blue and white smoke writhed from the chimneys, two or three joining into one, expanding, shrinking, and disappearing under the heavens.

It was only then, after the first puffs of his cigarette, that he calmed down a little and realized how he had been deceived that morning and how badly the *charshiya* had treated him, exposing him alone to that terrible place. They had left him to attack that which, all things considered, bothered him the least, and to defend what they themselves could not defend.

From the small clearing, in this odd, slanted perspective, he saw his native town with new eyes. It was many years since he had been anywhere else but in his shop at this hour of the day, and just as many years since he had climbed this hill or been in these parts. They looked remote and unfamiliar, and thoughts continuously surged into his head, new and unusual, and so powerful that they dominated all his feelings. Time passed swiftly and imperceptibly. He sat there through lunch and for the rest of the afternoon. Who could tell what thoughts swarmed on this mild September day in that Kazazi head in which customarily jest and reality replaced one another like flood and ebb, wiping out one another, leaving no trace. He thought intensively, as never before: about what had happened that morning, about the *fil*, the *charshiya*, Bosnia, and the Empire. His was not a head accustomed to clear thinking, but today, here, a flash penetrated his brain, a weak and short flash of insight into the nature of the town, the country, and the Empire in which he, Alyo, lived, as well as thousands of others like him, a little crazier or a little cleverer, a little richer and a lot poorer. What lives they lived! Thin, undignified lives lived madly and paid for dearly, and when one comes to grips with it, it isn't worth it, brother, it isn't worth it. And these thoughts reduced themselves to one proposition: Men have neither courage nor spirit.

The human being is cursed with fear, and is therefore weak. Everyone in the *charshiya* is frightened, some more, some less. But there are hundreds of different ways in which people conceal their fear, justify it before themselves and before others. And a man shouldn't be that way, shouldn't! He should be proud, fearless, and aware of his strength at all times, not allowing anyone to take advantage of him. For if he accepts the most minor insults, just once, and does not flare up (because there is no fire in him) he is finished; everyone will bully him, not merely the sultan and the Vizier, but the Vizier's servants, elephants, and every animal down to the nit. Nothing can come of this Bosnia so long as it is ruled by a Jelaludin. Today it is Jelaludin and tomorrow someone else, worse and blacker than he. But one ought to strike the evil against the ground, stand upright and not let anyone get anywhere near you. Anyone! But can this be done? In this *charshiya,* in which you cannot assemble five men who will say one straight word to the Vizier's face? Nothing, nothing can be done! And that's the way it has been for a long time: those who are hardy and proud quickly lose their bread and freedom, and those who lower their heads and give themselves up to fear lose so much of themselves, fear eats them so that life loses its value. And those who chance to live in Jelaliya's times have to choose one of the two. That is to say, those who are able to choose.

And who can?

There you are: and he who has such thoughts, he, too, what can he say for himself? He has always stressed his courage, and boasted that he was fearless enough for three men, for ten, for half of Travnik, and the brave half of it too. Others also praised him. So? Last night by the fire he was fearless, and now he thinks he is just as fearless. But where was his courage when he was talking to the sentries, when everything deserted him except for his mad fear, and his legs just barely carried his behind up the hill? Had not the truth remained the truth, and right remained the right, in spite of the four miserable effendis who deserted him? No, no, there is neither blood nor strength left in Travnik, or in its *charshiya*, and the little breath that remains to them is wasted in jests and mockery, and the cunning required to outfox one's neighbor, cheat the peasant, and make two pennies out of one. That's why they live in such a way and that's why their life is no good, no good at all.

Alyo considered these thoughts and many others for a long time, and left them all unresolved, in their own blind alleys.

He was awakened from his thoughts by the sound of sheep bells. Shepherds were taking their flocks down the hill and back into town. In the twilight he slowly walked down into town himself. As he descended the hill, the surge of his confused thoughts subsided, and he was again the old Alyo, a *charshiya* man who liked to jest and mock, and with each stride a desire was crystallizing in his mind: to return insult for injury, to make fools of the *charshiya* men, as their empty praise and great cowardice warranted. At this thought his face lit up with his old roguish smile. Making his way through side alleys in an effort to reach his house unnoticed, he was busy devising a joke with which to avenge himself and make fools of everyone.

At home his wife and children met him with the tearful joy that follows great distress. He ate well, slept even better, and when he left the house the following morning there was not a trace of yesterday's grievous thoughts in his head; instead, he carried with him a complete story, worked out in every detail, describing his trip to the konak and his encounter with the Vizier.

Alyo Kazaz's absence from his shop the day before had been immediately noticed by the *charshiya* merchants as they opened their doors for business. A little later they learned that Tosun Aga had come back more dead than alive from the Lashva bridge, and that Alyo himself had disappeared among the konak sentries. In a state of great agitation, Alyo's neighbors kept glancing over at his shop, while others sent their apprentices to find out what was what.

The *charshiya* closed down that evening full of apprehension about Alyo. Their relief was therefore considerable when, the following morning, Alyo passed by, healthy and smiling, opened his door as usual, and calmly began unrolling a length of yellow silk across the store. And whereas yesterday they had been full of foreboding about Alyo's fate (that is, about their own too), today they claimed they had known all along that it would end well, since, as a rule, crazy heads stay safely on crazy shoulders. Curious, idle men walked up and down in front of Alyo's store. He cheerfully exchanged pleasantries with them all, but they got nothing from him except his innocent, sly smile. And so the whole day passed. The *charshiya* was dying of curiosity, but Alyo kept quiet. It was only in the evening that he told one of his neighbors, softly and in confidence, his story of the day before.

"I can tell you everything," whispered Alyo, "because I know you won't repeat it. To tell you the truth, I was uneasy when I tangled with the sentries and saw that Tosun Aga had slipped around the corner. But I saw that there was no way out. I pretended that I was minding my own business and was on my way to see my friends, the Halovichi, but they wouldn't hear of it. We know everything, they said: you were on your way to the konak, so the gates of the konak have been opened for you. And they took me to the konak, through one gate, and then through another, and then into a large dark room. I looked around and around, and would have given a lot to have been elsewhere. There I was left alone. I waited and waited; all kinds of thoughts came to my mind, and I kept asking myself whether I would ever see my house again. I saw two or three doors, but they were all closed; a light, as strong as the sun, broke through the keyhole of one of them. I tiptoed toward this door and bent down to peep through; I had hardly fixed my eyes against the keyhole when the door opened, and I staggered on all fours into a bright spacious chamber. Once I was up again there was a sight to see. A rich spread and every comfort! The whole place smelled of amber. There were two men in cloth dolmans and heavy armor, and, between them, a little farther back, the Jelaludin himself. I recognized him instantly. He asked me something. But, confused as I was, I listened but didn't hear a word. Again he asked me who I was and what I wanted, his voice soft as silk. I started stammering something, as though with someone else's tongue: 'That, you see, because of the *fil*, you see, we had agreed to come, you see, to plead . . .'

" 'Who else is with you?' asked the Vizier with that same voice, as if speaking from a distance, and yet looking me straight in the eye.

"I froze, the blood inside of me growing numb. I turned around to see if at least that stinking Tosun was behind me, although I knew well that there was no one, that they had all betrayed me and left me in that terrible place, and that I had to account for everything myself. And something happened inside of me. I pulled myself together, looked straight at the Vizier, and then, bending my head and with a hand on my chest (as though I had rehearsed it for a long time!), I began to speak openly:

" 'I have, noble Pasha, been sent by the whole *charshiya*, not to disturb you (who would even dare think of such a thing?), but to ask your minister to communicate to you our wish and our entreaty: this *fil* of yours is the pride and ornament of our town, and our *charshiya* would be happy if you obtained one more of the same, so that we could be proud before all of Bosnia. And the beast would no longer be alone like this, and without a companion. And we have already become so fond of him that we do not love our own pets as much as we love him. You see, that's what they sent me to tell you and ask you in the name of the whole *charshiya*, and you know best what can be done and how it should be done. But as for us, the *charshiya* men, I can say that it would be no burden to us if you were to get three or . . . four of them. And we beg of you not to believe other words which you may hear, for they are spread only by false and evil people, with whom we from the *charshiya* have nothing to do, and will have nothing to do. And forgive me, noble Pasha, for having unintentionally appeared before your eyes.'

"Thus I talked, not knowing where it all came from. When I was through, I fell to the ground, kissed the Vizier's sleeve and hand, and he said something to one of the retinue, I didn't hear what, and disappeared somewhere. But he must have said something good, for those two could not have treated me more courteously as they escorted me back into the dark room and into the yard. There I saw all of the Vizier's retinue gathered, ten or twelve in all, smiling at me, as though I were a judge. Two men approached me and put a half-peck of good tobacco into one hand and a bagful of sweets into the other, and so they took me to the gate like a bride.

"Ah, my man, when I saw the bridge and the Lashva it was as though I had been born a second time.

"That was how I saved my head. Ah, man, if it had been up

41

to the *charshiya* and those who had started out with me, the door of my shop would never again have opened, nor would the sun have been warming me this morning. Only don't tell anyone about this, not on your life . . . you know how it is."

"Of course I know; don't worry. But what do you think, do you think the Vizier will really get another elephant?"

Alyo shrugged and spread his arms.

"Well . . . ! God only knows, and let the *charshiya* worry about it. After this experience I don't think I'll occupy myself with either viziers or elephants for the rest of my life."

"Ay, ay," sighed the neighbor as he tried hard to drag another word or two out of Alyo, but Alyo only smiled and lapsed into silence.

When he had finished his story and parted company with his confidant, Alyo knew that it was as good as having let loose a public crier down the *charshiya*. And indeed, before twilight there was no shop in which the story of Alyo's visit to the konak, down to the minutest detail, was not known.

During those autumn days Alyo's story was told and retold many a time in shops and around the fires. Some upbraided him as a crazy and spiteful man who had made fools of the whole *charshiya*; others expressed their admiration for him and blamed those who initiated the plot and then deserted Alyo at the last moment; and still others kept an aloof silence, asserting that such conduct was hardly surprising when tailors and other such people mix themselves in public affairs and even lay petitions before the Vizier.

The Kazaz story spread quickly and, going from mouth to mouth, was changing in both form and content. And Alyo himself would say nothing, neither black nor white, yes nor no. In the evening, when he stopped by a fire, he would respond to questions with only a smile, stroke his beard, and say:

42

"The *charshiya* taught me a lesson, and I thank her this way."

And he would bow deeply with a hand on his chest.

Men were indignant, believing Alyo to be a buffoon with whom one could not talk seriously, and they said this bluntly when he was not around.

While the small merchants of Travnik sat around the fire arguing about Alyo and his adventure, a richer and more distinguished group sat nearby, around another fire, debating these issues in their own way. These were the *charshiya* leaders.

Here there was no rakiya, no laughter, no mirth, but, rather, measured talk in which pauses, meaningful looks, and the mute tightening of the lips told more, much more, than words. These men were older, gray-haired, calm, and, without exception, rich.

They, too, were preoccupied with the *fil*, but they talked in general terms, using gentle words which in themselves meant nothing and which gained significance only with the expressions and glances that accompanied them. These gestures were the real language of the upper rank of the *charshiya* men.

These were the people among whom, without threats or oaths, the real decisions would be made regarding the *charshiya*'s defense against the *fil*. Only here, among the old and the rich *charshiya* men, could this question be solved, if there were a solution. For this problem could be solved only through cunning, and cunning goes with wealth; it precedes it and accompanies it forever.

Thus the people of the *charshiya*, gathering in their shops, in their gardens and around their fires, jested and made up stories, cursed the *fil* and the man who brought him to Travnik, brooded and complained, went on dreaming up plans of murderous action.

Curses, complaints, and whispered plans cannot be confined to words for long anywhere, let alone in Bosnia. For some time all this talk seemed empty and vain; words and words and the helpless waving of arms and the twitching of jaw muscles from invisibly clenched teeth. Even so, one day, no one knows when or where, all this condenses, takes shape, and becomes a deed. It is frequently the young who possess the energy and the daring to give expression to the more careful plans and thoughts of their sober elders.

Walnuts began to ripen, and it turned out that the *fil* was very partial to the fresh, juicy Travnik walnuts. He shook the branches, and the walnuts, on striking the ground, freed themselves from the dry, cracked deep-green rind; then he would pick them up with his trunk, crack them in his large, hidden mouth, masterfully spit out the shell with some saliva, and, with delight, chew up and finally swallow the milky kernel.

Young boys would throw walnuts in the street; the *fil* would carefully pick them up, comically bending that large head of his. And then an unusual thing happened. One of the children split the walnut shell, took out one half of the kernel, and placed in the shell a live bee instead. Then he glued the two halves together so that the nut looked whole, and threw it in front of the *fil*. The elephant cracked the nut and at that instant began swinging his head, producing strange sounds, and tearing himself away from his escort. It was only after he had reached the Lashva and had relentlessly lapped up a great deal

44

of water that he calmed down a little. His retinue believed that a horsefly had stung him.

This cunning, cruel trick proved ineffective. More often than not, the *fil* would crush both the nut and the bee and swallow them without batting an eyelash. But this was only the beginning. In hatred men become persistent, evil, and inventive.

The adults took a keen interest in the children's games, but did so carefully and inconspicuously. They started throwing apples into the alleys through which the elephant passed, not just any old apples, but beautiful, big golden and green apples. However, out of some of them the Travnichani had cut a piece, scooped out the core, poured powdered glass and arsenic into it, and then fitted the piece back into the apple so that it looked whole. The glass had been ground into a fine powder, and the arsenic was used in small quantities. From their shop doors and closed windows the people kept an eye on the *fil*, watching for the effects of the poison, which, they were told, was slow but so potent that it could do away even with large animals. But the Travnichani found out how difficult it was to poison an elephant; his ability to withstand any kind of poison was phenomenal. Despite the constant exposure to poison, the *fil* continued for some time longer to enjoy himself in the Travnik *charshiya*. However, when the winter came, he began to lose weight and to experience various disturbances of his stomach and intestines.

The Travnichani were no longer allowed to throw fruit and nuts to the *fil*, and after some time his walks through the *charshiya* stopped altogether. He was taken out briefly onto the slopes around the konak. There he would cheer up a little. He trampled the snow carefully and solemnly, felt it with his trunk, lifted it to his mouth, and then threw it angrily high up into the air. Even these outings grew shorter, for the *fil* would return to the stable well before his escort was ready to take him back. There he lay in the straw, wailing softly, lapping up increasing amounts of water.

The *charshiya* was more anxious than ever to find out what was happening at the konak. They were unable to learn much directly, but after paying huge sums of money to a reliable informant they were told the following: first, that the *fil* lies flat on his back at all times and that he "flows both from the front and from the back"; second, that servants at the konak were debating "how much an elephant's skin was worth"; some claimed that it would fetch a thousand groschen, but others noted that it would take at least a year to tan it. The *charshiya*, which had a sharp sense of what really mattered, quickly grasped the meaning of these details; they gladly paid for this good news, went on waiting quietly, exchanging hopeful glances. And they did not have long to wait. One day a rumor spread through the *charshiya* that the *fil* had passed away.

"The *fil*'s dead."

Inquire as you may, you will never be able to discover who first uttered these words. When I describe this announcement, you will, I am afraid, immediately picture a scene of clear and animated talk, full of victorious exultation. But the *charshiya* people have never expressed themselves in this manner, and certainly not at the time of the *fil* and the Jelaliya. They are incapable of such expression, would not even know how to go about it. Born and reared in dampness and in drafts, in this town enclosed by mountains, over which a vizier had presided with his power and retinue for as long as the people could remember, forced to live with a dread whose origin and title changed but whose nature remained constant, they were burdened by heredity with the hundreds of *charshiya* proprieties, which never yield to time. And when it happens that there is a feeling of triumphant fervor in their hearts, it rises to a certain height, in some even up to their throats, and then it returns to where it came from, to lie down forever, next to so many enthusiasms, protests, which some time ago had also risen and, unexpressed and unheard, had fallen into that same graveyard.

It was in this manner and in this tone of voice that someone somewhere whispered that the *fil* was dead, and like underground water from an unknown spring, which can be detected only by its sound, these words began flowing through the *charshiya*, from throat to throat, from mouth to mouth. It was in this way that the news broke, and these permanently clogged Bosnian throats and permanently restrained lips spread the news through the whole town.

"The *fil*'s dead!

"Dead?"

"Dead, dead!"

And so this word sizzles through the *charshiya*, like a drop of water falling on red-hot tiles, and everyone knows everything and asks and says no more. One evil had gone underground.

But while the *charshiya* was speculating as to where the *fil* might be buried, and nervously anticipating the Vizier's reaction to it all, another informant, more reliable than the reliable one and much less expensive, sold the *charshiya* a second report on the *fil*'s health, this time the true one: the *fil* was alive and recovering rapidly. Several days before, the elephant had indeed reached the point of succumbing, and then one of the Vizier's servants had cured him with a concoction of horse basil, bran, and oil. And now the animal was better, and was on his feet again. At the konak, servants and officials were rejoicing, for if the *fil* had been dying of poison, they had been dying of fear. And it was this news—the news of the rejoicing at the konak—that was given to the *charshiya* by the man whose truth was cheaper than lies.

It can happen, of course, that the *charshiya* is fooled.

The bad news spread through the town almost as rapidly as had the good news, without a word, without a whisper. People looked at one another, lowered their eyes and pouted their lips slightly.

"Alive?" some of the younger men asked in bitter astonishment, and the only response they received was a peevish and reproachful gesture of the hand, with heads turned the other way.

Indeed, the elephant was alive. Around the beginning of March he left his spacious stable for the first time in several months. The *charshiya* delegated an emissary, a man of seeming innocence but reliable and sharp, to go to the konak to appraise the situation. And he saw the elephant and discovered that he had lost weight, had shrunk almost in half, his head had become smaller and more angular, his bones could be seen beneath his skin; his eyes had withdrawn into their enormous sockets so that they seemed even larger than usual; his skin looked like an oversized dress; his thin hair seemed even thinner and in places had turned a yellowish gray. Servants circled around him excitedly, but he lay as if unaware of their bustle, turning his back to the already warm spring sun, swaying his head constantly and slowly, sniffing the pale yellow grass among the scattered patches of the fast-melting snow.

As spring came to Travnik, the *fil*'s outings grew more extended. He was recovering slowly but visibly. Quivering with a redoubled hatred, the disappointed *charshiya* was awaiting the day of the *fil*'s complete recovery and the resumption of his walks with God knows what new madness and mischief.

The elephant's guards, and in particular his mulatto

48

trainer, had assumed from the very start that the *charshiya* people had systematically and maliciously poisoned the *fil*. It was with an air of triumph that they took the elephant on walks again, and they cast bloody glances at the *charshiya*, devising their own methods of revenge. During the winter, while the *fil* was still ailing, the mulatto had tried to persuade the Vizier to punish the *charshiya*, if for no other reason than to forestall punishment of his own servants. But this was of little concern to the Vizier. His thoughts had for some time been quite elsewhere, on the other side of the Empire, for it was not the *fil*'s life that was now at stake, but his own.

Jelaludin had fulfilled his irresistible desire to rule, to judge, to punish, and to kill. And if all of the complex problems of Bosnia and of the Ottoman Empire could have been solved through force, blood, and intimidation, his reign would have been a successful one. But for the solution of the Empire's problems, other qualities were needed, qualities that would not be found anywhere in the Empire, and particularly not in Jelaludin.

And when force turns out to be helpless, and is incapable of solving the tasks set for it, then the force itself must turn against the tyrant. This has always been the case in the Ottoman Empire, especially in 1820, when Jelaludin was the Vizier of Travnik, and when the Empire was breathing with only one third of a lung and was under attack by a hundred enemies, inside and outside.

These complex forces were now at work on the Jelaliya himself. He was one of those tyrants who, at bottom, are nothing more than paid assassins, and can therefore be employed but once; if that one job does not work out properly they themselves are destroyed by it.

The Jelaliya had understood none of this at the start of his career; and even now it was not altogether clear to him.

It was, however, obvious that his tactics had not destroyed the power of the Turkish nobility, nor had they pacified Bosnia, and that he himself, after having exhausted the only resources at his command, had no other means to deal with the situation. A new plan of action and, with it, a new vizier would have to be found to rule Bosnia. And it followed that if a new vizier was to be appointed, there was not much room left on earth for this one, and that a grave, or an exile equivalent to it, was awaiting him.

This much the Jelaliya could see, for such was the information he had.

Without roots, without special connections in Stambul, self-centered and eccentric, Jelaludin could not entertain hopes of a return from exile and a re-establishment of his position, as had sometimes happened in the case of other viziers. In his situation, exile meant the end of everything, a slow, ugly, undignified dying away. There was no doubt in his mind that a sudden and voluntary death would be preferable. By nature a tyrant and tormentor of men, he could not live without the power to do violence to others, nor did he have the strength to endure violence himself.

In March a special emissary arrived from Stambul with an edict announcing that a new vizier had been appointed to Bosnia, and ordering the Jelaludin Pasha to hand over his authority to Chehay Pasha, to withdraw to Adrianople, where he was to await further orders.

The emissary told Jelaludin privately, and with an air of certainty, that he would in time be appointed the new governor of Rumelia and that in the meantime he would be sent to put down a rebellion on the island of Morea. He congratulated Jelaludin on these appointments. He said all of this quickly and mechanically, as if it were a lesson he had learned.

It was not difficult for the Jelaludin to elicit, through liquor and bribery, a confession from the emissary that he had been specifically ordered to offer the Vizier these confidences. In fact, another man with a "strong hand" had already been appointed governor of Rumelia. So it was a trap. The Jelaliya realized that the decisive moment had come, and that Travnik was the last point in this world to which his subconscious urges were to bring him.

Then it became clear how close the thought of death had always been to Jelaludin; not only other men's deaths but his own as well.

Carefully and conscientiously he recorded his will, dividing his possessions among his associates and assistants, all murderers like himself. He put aside a considerable sum of money for a mausoleum to be built above his grave, and provided for even the most minute expenses of his burial. He even specified the inscription to be engraved on his tombstone, the *bashik*, which began with the words from the Koran "He is alive and eternal." With his own hands he burned his rich collection of *kaléms*, the pencils made of reed grass, placing them one by one in the fire which had been blazing in his chambers during the past few March days as if it were the middle of winter. No one in town knew of these events, just as no one had known or could have anticipated that he had left a volume of verses, a valuable calligraphic work, to his secretary, Omer Effendi. The collection contained thirty-two of the most beautiful songs of Persian and Arabian poets, and these songs shone and resounded with roses, hyacinths, wine, maidens, fountains, flutes, and nightingales, glorifying the black earth and the burning sun "which generously offer all these things to a man, and then takes them away from him, only to give them to another man."

After he had accomplished all of this the Vizier withdrew into his bedchamber, ordering his servants to awaken him an hour later, in time for the midday meal. Then he took a spoonful of white powder in a glass of cold Travnik water, drank it as one would bitter medicine, and faded away from this world just as quietly and unobtrusively as he had entered Travnik some time ago.

Just before noon, the muezzins began intoning the midday prayer from the minarets of the Travnik mosques. The townspeople quickly gathered that they were not hearing the usual noontime prayer, but a *Jeneza,* a prayer for the deceased. And, judging by the length of the prayer and the ardor of the muezzin, they concluded that the deceased was some powerful and rich man.

The news of the Vizier's death spread quickly—the first news about the Jelaliya which provoked no comment from the *charshiya.* He was buried in this atmosphere of silence on the same day. All the *charshiya* men attended the funeral, silently and piously, saying neither good nor bad about the Vizier at that time or thereafter. (This was a victory that needed no exultation.)

It did not trouble them that Jelaludin would be buried in Travnik; he would rest in peace in their city, two yards under ground, immovable and helpless, becoming smaller every day, slowly losing all resemblance to a live man.

The new Vizier, Chehaya, arrived at the konak on the day of the funeral, as Jelaliya's retinue was rapidly dispersing in all directions, fearful of punishment and anxious to cover their traces.

In his will the Jelaliya had left the *fil* to the mulatto who had taken care of him all these months, that very Filfil whom the *charshiya* hated more than the elephant himself. The Vizier had proposed that Filfil take the elephant back to Stambul, and had left the funds needed for such a journey. But it was not easy for Filfil to carry out this mandate, since it was difficult enough for him to devise a plan to save his own skin. In times like these it was not easy to smuggle a needle out of Bosnia, to say nothing of an elephant that no longer belonged to a vizier. So it happened that the hated Filfil fled from Travnik the very night of his master's death, and the *charshiya* men had no trouble breaking into the konak, where they slipped the *fil* a dose of poison far stronger and more reliable than the powdered glass that had been buried in the apples.

Four days after the Jelaliya's funeral the *fil*, too, died. He had abandoned his straw resting place by the door, and had withdrawn into the most remote corner of the stable, where he was found the following morning curled up and dead. And they buried him immediately, but how and where no one inquired, for when the *charshiya* was rid of an evil they did not mention it for some time. Only later, when it has been transformed into a tale, do they start talking about it again, but as of something long since passed and distant that can be told with jests and pleasure in the midst of fresh misfortunes.

Thus the *fil* lay underground along with the Vizier. There is room here for everyone underground.

The spring came, the first one without Jelaliya. Fear changes its shape and worry its name. The viziers replace one another. Life goes on. The Empire approaches its end. Travnik was withering, but the *charshiya* lived on like a worm in a windfall apple. The news had it that Ornosbeg Zade Sherif Siri Selim Pasha had been appointed the new vizier over Bosnia. The first rumor that reached them had it that he was a good and learned man, a Bosnian by birth. But some people in the *charshiya* shake their heads worriedly:

"If he is good, why such a long name?"

53

"Ah, brother, who knows what's on his mind, what he'll bring with him?"

So the *charshiya* lives in anticipation of fresh news and reliable information. The people suffer, whisper, protect themselves, and if they cannot do it any other way, they do it through stories in which their unclear and indestructible desire for justice is perpetuated, for a different life and better times. The masons are constructing a mausoleum over Jelaludin's grave. And the stonecutter is engraving the inscription on the Vizier's *bashik*, made of soft stone. He has already completed the first sentence of the inscription. And the story of Alyo and the *fil* has spread all over Bosnia, and has grown in the course of it.

· Anika's Times ·

DURING THE SIXTIES OF THE PAST CENTURY A STRONG DESIRE FOR knowledge, and the better life that education brings with it, penetrated even the most remote regions of Bosnia. Nothing, not even the mountain Romaniya or the river Drina, could prevent this desire from reaching Dobrun and enlightening its parish priest, Father Kosta Porubovich. And Father Kosta, a man already advanced in years, casting a glance at his only son, Vuyadin, a pale and timid boy, came to the conclusion that at any price his son must get an education. Through some friends, merchants in Sarajevo, he managed to send him all the way to Sremski Karlovtsi "to catch at least a year or two of theology." He caught just about that much, for toward the end of his second year Father Kosta suddenly died. Vuyadin returned home, was married off, and settled into the priesthood in his father's parish. In the first year of marriage his wife gave birth; true enough it was only a girl, but they had many years ahead of them, and it seemed certain that the Porubovichi would sustain the priesthood at Dobrun for many a generation to come.

However, all was not well with Father Vuyadin. Nothing specific could be discovered, nor was anyone sure that there was something wrong, but everyone sensed a certain strain between the priest and his parishioners. This strain could be attributed neither to the youth nor to the awkwardness of Father Vuyadin, since as time went on the tension grew rather than diminished. Vuyadin was of fine stature and handsome, like all the Porubovichi, but lean, pale, and unusually subdued, and, in spite of his youth, there was an aged, gray quality in his voice and eyes.

Around 1875, only a few years before the Austrian occupation of Bosnia, Father Vuyadin suffered a great loss: his wife died while giving birth to their second child. From that time onward he grew ever more remote from the world. He sent his little girl to his wife's relatives at Vishegrad, and he lived alone in a big house next to the Dobrun church with but a single servant. He performed the rites regularly, attended funerals, officiated at baptisms and weddings, read prayers when requested to do so, but he did not chat or drink with the peasants in the churchyard, or jest with the peasant women, or argue with debtors over their taxes. The townspeople, who were in any case suspicious of a silent, morose man and decidedly favored healthy, talkative priests, simply could not get used to Father Vuyadin. They would have forgiven him any other failing more easily. The women, who in these villages determined a man's reputation, good or bad, said of Father Vuyadin that there was a thundercloud over his forehead; they disliked going to church, and always brought up that "wild Father Kosta."

"Dull and lost, that's what he is," the peasants complained, forever comparing him to his father, the late Kosta Porubovich, who had been fat, cheerful, but wise and eloquent, on good terms with the peasants and the Turks, with the humble and the strong. Father Kosta's funeral had been a great common sorrow. Older people could even recall Vuyadin's grandfather, Yaksha, called Jakon, or Deacon. He, too, had been quite a different man: a Haiduk in his youth and proud of it. When they asked him why he was called Deacon, he would reply cheerfully:

"Ah, my son, when I was only a deacon I joined the Haiduks, and since every Haiduk must have a nickname, they started calling me Haiduk Deacon. So that name stuck with me. But later on, as years went by and honors struck me as arrows strike a horse, it was embarrassing to be called a Haiduk. So 'Haiduk' fell off me like a tail falls off a frog, and I remained simply Deacon."

He was an old man with thick hair and a big beard which

grew sideways and did not go gray but remained reddish and unruly until his death. Wild, headstrong, and cunning, he had true friends and fierce enemies among Christians and Turks alike. He enjoyed drinking and had an eye for women until his old age. Even so, he was much liked and respected.

And so it was that, hard as they tried, the peasants could not figure out why Vuyadin was the way he was, and not like his father or grandfather. In his lonely life as a widower Father Vuyadin was sinking lower and deteriorating further. His beard grew thinner, the hair on his temples white, his cheeks fell in and somehow turned gray so that his large green eyes and ashen brows no longer stood out on his face. Tall, straight, and stiff, he spoke only when absolutely necessary, in a deep voice without color or animation.

As the first priest with even a smattering of education in the more than one hundred years in which his family had served the Dobrun church, Father Vuyadin realized full well the extent of his awkward nature and manner. He knew what people were looking for and what sort of priest they wanted, and understood that what they sought was the exact opposite of what he could provide. This knowledge tormented him, but it also stiffened him, and in contact with the parishioners his conduct became all the more rigid. Little by little this rigidity transformed itself into a deep, uncontrollable disgust for these people.

The general weariness of a widower's life, as well as its many renunciations, rapidly widened the rift between Vuyadin and his flock. Long before he lost his wife he had suffered because he could not approach them, warm up to them, mix with them. Now this suffering was intensified; he was forced into a position of deliberately concealing many things from them, and in the process grew increasingly distant. Even before, every look and every word had been a torture, a burden, and a painful combat. Now it had become a danger, too, and the fear that he would give himself away made him even more insecure and suspicious.

So his loathing for men grew, settled in him and, like a hidden spleen, poisoned him with a hatred both incomprehensible and unconscious, but real enough nevertheless. This was the secret life of Father Vuyadin. He hated himself and his torment. There were days when, downcast and grayish, he would stand by the window, hidden in the shadows for a whole hour, lying in wait simply to get a glimpse of village women passing by on their way to the river to wash their laundry. And when he had spotted them and seen them disappearing behind the willows, he would turn away in disgust and walk back into the stuffy, half-empty room, giving the women most disgraceful names. This irrational hatred would rise up into his throat, he would lose his breath and with it his speech. He spat loudly, unable to find other relief or expression. Then, in the stillness of the stifling summer air, he would regain his senses, and, catching himself in this last violent gesture, would recall his terrible curses and freeze in terror. A shudder would race up his spine and into his skull, and he would be seized by a chilling thought: He was losing his mind.

These fits were tearing his whole being apart, and it had become almost impossible to carry on his own daily life, to say nothing of his duties as a priest. Less than half an hour after this seizure, he was supposed to talk with the peasants; and there he would sit, pale, with a fixed look and a hollow voice, trying to answer their numerous questions, arranging days for baptisms, prayers, and consecrations. And the difference between these two men—the one lying in wait in the shadows of his room, and the other, Father Vuyadin, giving advice to the peasants in the churchyard—was such that he was bending under it. The inner pain was producing convulsions; he would bite his mustache and run his fingers through his hair, possessing barely enough self-control to prevent himself from falling on his knees before the peasants and breaking into a scream:

"I am losing my mind!"

And while he was talking with the peasants he was constantly reminded that they were comparing him with his late father and all of his relatives. And he began to hate his father and all of his relatives.

Everything that happened to Vuyadin only increased his hidden bitterness and hatred. Every day spent in loneliness and every contact with men only strengthened a hatred that was becoming identified with his own body, with all of his movements, desires, and thoughts. The hatred grew larger and overshadowed everything within him, forming the substance of his life, more real than anything else, the only existence in which he moved. Bashful, like many descendants of good, old families, honorable and straight by nature, he concealed his condition as well as he could. Constantly torn between the two realities, he made superhuman efforts not to lose sight of the reality that others see. But the day would come when that inner life would assert itself and Father Vuyadin would cross over to the other side, to that strange land to which for years his whole inner life had urged him: into the sphere of open madness, visible and clear to all.

This was indeed what happened in the fifth year of Father Vuyadin's life as a widower. Early one morning he went out into the fields and stood around watching the men at work until lunchtime. On his way back, he was surprised to see, in a clearing among the fir trees at the foot of a cliff, a group of strangers. There were five in all: an engineer, two Austrian officers, and two women. A little distance away grooms were watching the horses. A rug was spread out and the strangers

61

were sitting on it, the men bareheaded, with their jackets un-
buckled, the women dressed in light frocks that dazzled the
eye with their whiteness. Father Vuyadin paused a moment,
and then quickly climbed a little way up the nearby cliff and
leaned against a twisted, half-fallen fir tree. He was perspiring and his heart was beating. Concealed behind the tree, he
fixed his eyes on the strangers below him, whom he saw from
an odd, slanted perspective. The sight perplexed and excited
him, like an image in a dream. And as in a dream, the sight
seemed to suggest unlimited possibilities, the more implausi-
ble the more likely. The strangers were eating and, in turns,
drinking from a glittering metal cup. This, too, excited him.
At first he was frightened that they might discover him, fully
aware, as he still was, of how embarrassing and ridiculous it
would be for the strangers to find a priest stretched along a
twisted fir tree gazing so intently at these two women. But little by little the last residue of propriety and embarrassment
abandoned him altogether. He did not know how long he had
been there absent-mindedly stripping the bark off the fir tree
with his fingers; it might have been for hours. At last, one of
the women, who seemed to be the younger of the two, rose
and started up the hill with the two officers. She passed directly underneath him, so that he could see the top of her
head. As she climbed, awkwardly using a walking stick for
assistance, her hips were swinging, and on her white face,
chapped from the wind and riding, red spots were visible, as
sometimes appear on the faces of healthy people after food
and drink in the fresh air. The other two were stretched out
under the fir tree, having covered themselves with the rug on
which they had been sitting.

As though the scene had come to an end, the priest suddenly
regained his senses, pulled himself together, and started on
his way home, carefully avoiding the couple lying under the

fir tree, and full of anxiety that he might be noticed by the three strangers still climbing up the hill.

It was well into the afternoon. In answer to the inquiries of his servant, Radivoy, Father Vuyadin mumbled something quite incoherent, lacking even the concentration to offer a plausible excuse for his tardy appearance at lunch. Walking through the empty house, he felt an immense heaviness; the earth and the day itself weighed on him like lead, and life seemed to him like embers and hard wood, without sap and without sweetness. His fingers were sticky with resin. He felt a violent thirst. His eyes were tired, his stride heavy. He ate his lunch and then fell into a heavy sleep.

When he awoke, he felt even more inert. He could just barely recall his encounter with the strangers in the woods, as though it were some distant pain. He left the house, and, taking a short cut up the cliff, reached the pine wood. He looked down; there was not a soul left at the clearing in the fir trees. The sun had set. Scattered paper and ripped tinfoil lay in the grass, glimmering in the twilight. In the soft earth he could discern the traces of women's shoes, deep and oblique and, to his eye, incredibly small. He followed the traces that mingled with men's footprints and those of horses' hoofs, at times losing them and then spotting them again. Absorbed and bent over, he walked as though searching for something he had lost. Blood rushed into his head. The approaching darkness further obscured the path and the footprints. He arrived at a crossroads where the trail ended and a road began. Here they must have mounted their horses, thought Vuyadin. The scene was deserted. It was already quite dark. In the still bright skies a diagonal wooden post, used as a landmark in the daytime, was outlined. He rushed down the bumpy road, staggering along the fence that followed the road, feeling the burnt edges of the field that crumbled under his feet. The night was clear, but the heat had not relented. Breathing was difficult; the air was stifling, as if there were an iron vault above his head in the dark. He crossed a trickling stream which, however, offered no coolness or freshness. He found himself suddenly in his own plum orchard, not far from his house, whose contours could be seen in the dark. Stupefied and exhausted, he slipped to the ground. He rested a short while, and then, abruptly, the image of the women he had seen that day was before him again, and with that image a question: Did I really see them, or have I merely imagined it? This question, ordinary and simple at first, slowly began to torment him. Excited, he jumped up. Was it real or wasn't it? Yes, it was; it was. And he was about to slump down into the grass again, but he paused and looked around.

It was dark, the dull and heavy darkness of the village, in which a sound can be heard across great distances, but lonely and awesome like the last spell of the dawn. And again the question rose with a painful throbbing in his temples: Were the women real or had he made them up? He shuddered each time the question renewed itself.

Terrified, he started back toward the crossroads. He stumbled in the dark and finally reached the wooden post and took hold of it with his hands. He bent down and began feeling for footprints in the clay, slightly moist at that spot near the swollen brook. He knelt down, running his fingers across the earth once again, trembling with fear, and burning with the desire to find out whether the day's images derived from fancy or reality. He could gather nothing from the touch of his fingers.

"I saw them! I saw them!" he mumbled to himself, as he raced down to the clearing; and there, too, he feverishly ran his fingers along the ground, trying to penetrate the dark with his eyes, hoping to catch sight of the paper wrappings he had seen, or thought he had seen, in the twilight. At last he had to give up the search. He walked slowly to the plum orchard, as though doomed, his confidence in his own senses shattered. He lay face down on the coarse, warm grass for a long time, his arms spread as though crucified, nailed down by the immense weight of his own muscles and bones. The sound of voices startled him and broke his half-conscious dreams. A fire was burning on the threshing floor of his neighbors, the Tasichi, and peasants were gathered around it. In the glow of the fire, the shapes of men and women could be seen, milling about and again disappearing in the dark. The voices were alternately high and low, but he was too far away to catch the words.

The Tasichi were about to spread the wheat on the floor. During the great heat waves, when the daytime breezes were so slight that they could not scatter the chaff, threshing was often done at night. A breeze invariably blew in from the mountain glades around nine o'clock.

To one side a fire was going. Young girls were holding aloft burning torches to provide light for the workers, long white sleeves hanging down their outstretched arms. They were motionless, except for the movement required, every so often, to switch the torch from one hand to another. The peasants were flinging the grain into the air with their shovels, and in the red glow Vuyadin could see the grain fly up and fall to the threshing floor, like heavy rain, while the chaff sailed slowly away and, carried by the wind, dispersed and was lost in the dark.

Father Vuyadin's excitement, which had been growing in him all day long, was stirred up again and reached a new peak. He trembled and stammered aloud:

65

"They won't keep quiet, even at night, but wiggle about in the dark, swinging their torches and waving their sleeves and skirts."

A whole series of images came before him: the foreign women whom he had watched when hidden behind the fir tree; the twilight; the tottering search for the footprints that vanished in the dark; and now the hollow night and the fire which illuminated the forms of men shoveling and women gliding along and waving their arms. Thus, his whole secret existence appeared before him, full of that suffering and torment which had turned into hatred. Gone was the last trace of the other existence: Father Vuyadin performing services in the church, listening to the peasants, going to town on market days while women and frightened children make way for him and kiss his hand. There was nothing now that could restore this existence and prevent him from giving expression to those desires to which everything had been driving him. Mumbling to himself like a man who was being pursued, he crossed the plum orchard with almost unnatural speed, and, racing through a dark corridor in his house, found himself in a room overlooking the churchyard and the Tasichi threshing floor. Knocking against furniture as if unaware of its presence, Father Vuyadin felt his way to the wall where his hunting rifle was hung, loaded at all times. Seizing it instantly, and without even placing it properly against his shoulder, he fired in the direction of the illuminated threshing floor. There was something pleasing in the pull that wrenched his arms as though the rifle were about to leap out of his hands. Even the recoil that struck him violently against the chest was comforting. It was only after he had fired a second barrel that he heard shrieking, followed by long cries. The torches swayed and then fell, the workers fled, leaving only the fire on the

66

threshing floor. Male voices could be heard, but above all the wailing of an old woman tore the darkness:

"Yovan, my son, they are killing us!"

The shots fired at the Tasichi threshing floor that night signaled the decisive breakthrough of Father Vuyadin's secret existence. He looked around in the dark, and found a huge knife on a shelf; clutching it firmly he fled into the night.

He waded across the river Rzav, which at that time of the year is quite shallow. Reaching the other side of the river he sat down, breathless and exhausted, in the sand among the young willows. Still mumbling to himself, he cooled his chest and forehead with water, as though he were dressing a wound.

The following day the news spread through the villages that, in his insanity, Father Vuyadin had fired several shots at the Tasichi and then fled into the woods on the other side of the Rzav. The story was hard to believe, and no one could either understand it or explain it, especially among the townspeople, who had more respect for Father Vuyadin than did the peasants. Although the peasants accept everything much more coolly and simply, they were perplexed by what happened, and even pitied him in their own way. Meeting on their way to the market, peasant women would pause, ask about each other's health, and then mention Father Vuyadin, crossing themselves and begging the great and merciful God to protect them and their own.

Vishegrad was full of gendarmes at that time, sent to round up the Nevesinye rebels. Before long they were all combing the countryside, tracking down Father Vuyadin. Peasants told the gendarmes that they had seen him in a certain forest, in rags, barefoot and hatless, with a knife in his hand, prowling like a beast of prey. But by the time a patrol arrived there was no trace of the priest. He had fled into the mountains, where, frightening off bands of shepherds, he would warm himself by their fire. One such fire, which could be seen from afar, betrayed him. When the gendarmes arrived just before dawn, they found him asleep, the fire having nearly gone out. They were forced to bind him since he resisted capture.

The next day the gendarmes walked Father Vuyadin through the town. His hands chained behind his back, he strutted unnaturally fast. His bare head was thrust back so that his long, grayish hair fell down his shoulders. He clenched his lower lip with his teeth and his eyes were half shut. On that face, turned up to the heavens, there was nothing insane, only a deep martyr-like pain. It was only when he lowered his glance that his bloody eyes betrayed a dull look without understanding. Everyone pitied him. The women wept. The authorities were embarrassed.

The gendarmes had been reluctant to bind him, but when he was released from chains he had put up resistance and tried to run. So he was dispatched to Sarajevo in chains. There, in a large hospital on the Kovachi, in a half-darkened room, he lived for ten more years, unaware of himself or of this world.

With the unfortunate Father Vuyadin the Porubovichi family came to an end. A stranger came to the Dobrun parish. And when Father Vuyadin finally passed away at the Sarajevo hospital he had been long forgotten. Among the peasants he was mentioned only in passing. ("That happened during the summer Father Vuyadin went mad. . . .") In the town, on the other hand, Father Vuyadin's fate caused more of a stir and occupied men's minds and thoughts for some time to come. For them it represented some hidden curse, an affliction so unexpected and curious that in commiserating with the unfortunate priest they had forebodings about their own fate and the fate of those close to them. Everyone sought a cause and an explanation for this misfortune, hoping in this way to set their minds at rest, to dull a painful memory. But in spite of their efforts, they could not recall anything in Father Vuyadin's life that might explain his strange end. Vuyadin's fate continued to confront them, stark, simple, and inexplicable; a cheerless child, a lonely youth, an unhappy man.

At last, the memory of Vuyadin and his affliction began to fade, even among the townspeople, but it would continue to evoke memories of other disasters and other times long since forgotten. In talking about the Porubovichi family, for example, they would not confine themselves to Vuyadin and his father and grandfather, but would go back to his great-grandfather the famous Dobrun priest Melentiye, and, through him, to Anika's times.

Mula Ibrahim Kuka was the first to mention Anika. He was a man who liked to appear scholarly and mysterious, but was in fact an idle, kindly fellow and an ignoramus who lived on the reputation and income of his grandfather, the renowned *mutaveliya* Mula Mehmed, a wise and learned man who lived to be a hundred and one. Among the collection of books and papers left by Mula Mehmed there were several yellowing volumes in which he had recorded everything that took place in his town as well as world events of which he had any knowledge. Floods, crop failures, wars near and distant were recorded here, as well as eclipses of the sun and the moon, mysterious signs and phenomena in the skies, and everything that in those days excited the *kasaba* and the people in it. Next to a report that in a town in Germany the devil was born (and since he turned out to be only a foot long he was stuffed into a bottle for all to see), there was an item about a Christian general by the name of Bonaparte who had crossed into Misir with the extraordinary idea of waging a war against the Sultan. And a few pages farther on there was a description of how the rayah had risen in the province of Belgrade, and how, incited by evil people, they committed rash deeds. Next to this item there was the following entry:

"That same year a young woman, a Christian (God confound all the infidels!), was overtaken by evil, and created such commotion and gained such strength that her evil reputation spread far and wide. Numerous men, both young and old, had gone to her, and many a youth had gone afoul there. And she placed both authority and law under her feet. But someone was found to deal with her, too, and she was crushed according to that which she deserved. And people were again put straight and were mindful of God's commands."

Mula Ibrahim read this entry to the people gathered in a coffeehouse, and the elder men tried to recall what they had heard, a long time ago, in their childhood, of Anika's times, of Anika's warfare with the Christians and all the secular and spiritual authorities, and especially of her struggle with the Dobrun priest Melentiye. Much of this had long ago been forgotten, but when her story was brought back to light it was much discussed, and, indeed, the expression "Anika's times" was later used as a point of reference in conversation.

This is what happened.

· I ·

In the *kasaba*, where men and women resemble one another like sheep, it happens sometimes that chance will bring a child, as the wind brings seeds, who is depraved and stands out from the usual order of things, causing ill-luck and confusion, until it is cut down itself and the old order re-established.

Anika's father was Marinko Krnoyelats, a baker in Vishegrad. As a young man, he was well known for his almost feminine good looks, but he had aged quickly and let himself go before his time. One day—he must have been about forty at the time—he was out in his plum orchard when he came upon a peasant who, with his son, as it happened, was stealing plums from Krnoyelats' trees. And picking up a wooden stake, Marinko killed him, right then and there. The child ran away. The police seized Marinko that same morning. He was sentenced to six years in the Vidin prison, near Sarajevo. Travelers reported that they had seen him there with other prisoners, hauling limestone to Zhuta Tabiya, their chains rattling.

Marinko spent four years in the jail in Vidin. When he came back to Vishegrad he brought with him a new wife. His first wife, with whom he had had no children, had died while he was serving his sentence. He took up his baking again, and lived quietly, as he had done before the disaster.

His second wife, called Anja, was much younger than he; bent at the waist, she had a tired, still expression in her eyes, and something foreign in her bearing. The townspeople neither liked her nor respected her. It was generally believed that Krnoyelats had found her in the prison, and they called her Vidinka, after the prison. It was in vain that Marinko tried to prove this story false and to convince them that she was the daughter of a baker for whom he had worked after leaving jail.

This woman was Anika's mother. Marinko had had another child with her, a boy, older than Anika. He was pale, thin, and tall with sweet, smiling eyes, but quite feeble-minded. They called him Lale. He spent his childhood next to his mother, and later worked with his father at the ovens; he

71

never went out with other boys, never drank, smoked, or looked at girls.

No one could quite recall the date of Anika's birth or the manner of her upbringing.

Next to her withdrawn, unsociable mother, she grew up a tall and thin girl with large eyes full of distrust and pride, with a mouth that looked too big for her small face. She grew, but only upward. Her mother tied a scarf around her head in such a way that no hair showed at all, which made the child look even thinner and more peculiar. Stiff and angular, the little girl walked with her head down as though ashamed of her own height, her lips defiant and tight and her eyes lowered. It was not surprising that so little attention was paid to the Krnoyelats girl, who was not much to look at, rarely went out, and even then only on brief trips to her father's shop.

A long and damp winter that had begun very early was capped by an unusual Epiphany, without ice or snow. The procession had to wade through mud. The church banners glistened and the people's eyes blinked in the premature, unhealthy sun. The water from which they drew out the cross was green and quivering, as in the springtime.

As the procession entered the church there was another surprise: Krnoyelats' daughter. Although still slender, the thin little girl had changed considerably over the winter. Her skin was milk-white, her bearing straight, and she was generally filled out; her eyes had become larger, her mouth smaller. She wore a satin pelisse of unusual cut. Townspeople turned to look at her, wondering who this young girl was and why she had come to church alone. Indeed, it seemed as though she had arrived from another town, from a strange world.

Anika slowly walked through the crowd with a new stride, looking neither around her nor at any of those who were staring at her, but straight at the gate of the churchyard toward which she was heading. At the gate she almost collided with a handsome young man, a certain Mihailo Nikolin, called Stranats—that is, Foreigner. The two were a trifle embarrassed (he more than she) by the manner of their encounter, but they proceeded to cross the doorstep, one next to the other, almost simultaneously.

The Sunday following the Epiphany, Anika and Mihailo met by the same church gate. But this time it was not by chance; Mihailo had waited for her and approached her directly. If the townspeople had been surprised by Anika's sudden transformation, they were equally surprised by Mihailo, who had never gone out with girls, but who now not only waited for Anika but escorted her home as well. The *kasaba* could not stop talking about Krnoyelats' daughter, who had so unexpectedly become a young woman, and had done it so well that she stood out, in most striking fashion, from all the other women of the town.

Anika's first appearance among the townspeople confused her as much as it did them. She began observing everything around her with new eyes. And as though she had become aware of her body for the first time, she began caring for her looks and preening herself.

The spring started out slowly and timorously that year. When the weather was good, Anika went into the yard, breathing deeply, her eyes blinking. Walking tired her, but when she went back into the house her room seemed so cold and dark that, shuddering, she went right out again. And when the sun set behind the wall of the yard and the shadows deepened, she raced up the hill to higher ground to catch the warm sun once again. On chilly days, when the skies were dark and sleet was in the air, Anika stayed in her room, lit the stove, and sat down next to it, staring into the fire. She unbuttoned her dress and placed her hand a little below the armpit, where a young girl's breasts begin to separate from the ribs. The skin is tight there and particularly smooth. She would press that spot for hours at a time and watch the fire and the little openings in the stove that are like eyes; and all the while she was saying something, as if conversing with the objects in the room. But when her mother called her to do something, and she had to withdraw her hand, button up, and step out of the house, she was startled, as though a trance had been broken. And when she came back and again sat by the fire, she could not settle down for quite a while; it seemed to her that she would never again be able to find that spot on which she had held her hand; it was as though not long ago something precious had been snatched from her by the wind and carried away.

So Krnoyelats' daughter lived immersed in thoughts about herself, taciturn, indifferent to everyone, but growing shapely and more beautiful every day. The girl's time passed swiftly and mysteriously: the summer, the autumn, and again the winter. On Sundays and holidays Anika went to church, accompanied by a pale, fragile girl from her neighborhood. At first Mihailo met her regularly in the churchyard and exchanged a few words with her. But in time, other young men approached her. The following winter the beautiful and tall young woman, who had by now completely outgrown the timid, skinny Krnoyelats girl, had become the chief object of men's desire and women's gossip.

That same winter Marinko died. His son, Lale, took over his father's business and continued working. Although young and feeble-minded, he proved himself a good baker and kept his father's customers.

Anja, who had lived like a shadow until that time, grew thinner and even more bent. Her daughter, whom she had never liked and with whom she did not get along, had reached the age when girls become self-centered and withdrawn, without consideration for their parents or their surroundings. With her husband's death, Vidinka's only link to this town had vanished. She ceased talking almost entirely. She did not weep. She observed everything around her with a detached look and passed away that same year, quietly and unobtrusively. Anika was not even given a chance to put away the mourning clothes she had worn for her father.

Their aunt, Plema, moved in with them, so the girl was not alone. Plema was the late Marinko's half-sister, an old, half-blind widow who had had a turbulent and unhappy youth, but a youth now so distant that no one, including herself, could recall just what was involved. So, there was Anika, with her half-witted brother on one side, and her half-blind aunt on the other. The death of her parents had created a vacuum around her. The mourning clothes only served to emphasize her great beauty and curious disposition.

She was a head taller than her brother, and was still growing and developing. Indeed, she was constantly changing. Her look became free, her dark eyes acquired a purple tone, her skin became whiter, her movements slower and more natural. The *kasaba* speculated about Anika's future marriage. So did the young men at church. She watched them all indifferently and listened to them quietly, but said little herself. And when she did speak it was in a subdued, husky voice, almost without opening her full but pale lips. Her frequently monosyllabic statements left not even the slightest echo behind them, but faded away and perished immediately after they had been spoken. It was her appearance rather than her voice or what she had said that left the strongest impression.

75

And the more curious and mysterious she became, the more the *kasaba* talked about finding a husband for her. Mihailo's name frequently came up.

Mihailo had come to the *kasaba* six years earlier as an apprentice to Master Nikola Subotich, after two years spent tending the Subotich store in Sarajevo. Master Nikola traded in cattle and hides, and since he had a great knack for business, he would have been among the most prosperous of merchants had it not been for two passions that undermined him: loafing and gambling. He could not settle down anywhere. While still young, he was left a widower and never remarried. A man of great courage and uncommon strength and intelligence, he had had a good deal of luck both in business and in gambling. Among his lucky strokes was the decision he had made eight years earlier to hire Mihailo as an apprentice, and later as a partner, with a salary of three groschen. While Master Nikola was constantly on the go, risking his luck at cards, which leaves one empty-handed in the end, Mihailo ran his house and kept his store at Vishegrad, working steadily and dividing the profits honestly. Such steadfast behavior had finally gained for Mihailo the respect of the *kasaba*. Initially, of course, the townspeople had received him as they did any stranger, with hostility and mistrust. But he had acquired the two things that make it possible to maintain oneself in the *kasaba*: property and position.

He lived in his master's house, which was kept by an old woman who had been Master Nikola's housekeeper since his marriage. Capable and literate and devoted to his work as he was, Mihailo not only assumed a larger part of his master's work, but the responsibility for it as well. His work habits aside, it seemed as if he were doing his best not to distinguish himself in any way from the townspeople. He did everything the other youths did: went out, drank and sang with them. Efforts were made to marry him off, but he refused all offers, either by jesting about it or through silence. Therefore, it had been a great surprise when, two winters earlier, he had started seeing Anika; but it must be said that it was an even greater surprise when, that spring, he suddenly stopped seeing her altogether. The *kasaba* speculated about what had happened between Krnoyelats' daughter, who was such a mystery to them, and Mihailo, about whom they also knew very little. And they were left guessing. Not a soul in this stale *kasaba* ever succeeded in finding out what had separated Mihailo and Anika, for none of them could have imagined what was concealed behind the quiet and diligent façade of Master Nikola's partner.

Mihailo's family was from Sanjak, but his grandfather had left Sanjak and moved to Prizren. The family had been gunsmiths for generations. At Prizren, Mihailo's father acquired a substantial fortune following this craft. One of his brothers had been a priest, and since Mihailo was literate and liked books, they wanted him to follow the same line. Besides, after four generations of working as gunsmiths, the family was living in comfortable circumstances and sought a certain refinement befitting its wealth. However, Mihailo's father had died while still a young man, so Mihailo went into the gunsmith trade together with his brother.

They worked and lived together. Mihailo's brother was twenty-three years old, but he neither sought a girl for himself nor would he allow his younger brother to marry before he did. Since Mihailo strongly desired a woman he suffered a great deal, but he was too embarrassed to come into conflict with his brother over such a thing. In a state of constant torment, he stopped one day at Krstinitsa's roadside inn, called a han in this part of the country. He was on his way back from his small estate at Lyubizhda.

It was still hot and there was no one at the han except for Krstinitsa herself, a buxom redhead of about thirty. While they were talking, she came very close to him. His whole body quivering, Mihailo extended a hand which met with no resistance. At that moment her husband, Krsto, showed up from somewhere. He was a sickly, morose man, completely dominated, as it turned out, by his healthy and alert wife. She whispered to Mihailo that he should come back the following evening. That night he slept little. When he arrived at the han, breathless and agitated, the following evening, he still could not believe that this was possible, that it would really happen. And, indeed, when she greeted him and showed him the way to an isolated room, it seemed to him as though an insufferable burden had been lifted and that God's whole beautiful world had opened before him.

Twice again that month he went to Krstinitsa secretly at night, and returned unseen into town. He never gave a thought to Krsto, who, it is true, was only a shadow of a man; nor did he pay any attention to what Krstinitsa said about the future, her terrible fate, about the pity God would take on her, and how He would free her from this burden at some point.

When Mihailo arrived at the han for his fourth visit he did not find Krstinitsa at her usual place by the fence. After a short wait he heard sounds of a violent quarrel coming from the same isolated room in which he and Krstinitsa had spent nights together. He stiffened with fear, but somehow made his way to that room, and, opening the door, saw Krsto and Krstinitsa wrestling with each other. Krsto was holding an ax in his right hand, but his wife had clasped him in such a way that the hand holding the ax was completely rigid and help-less. Panting from their exertions, both were uttering abuses and fragmentary sentences from a quarrel to which this strug-gle was evidently the climax. Aghast and astonished, Mihailo reached the doorstep just as Krstinitsa somehow managed to bring her husband to the floor. She fell with him, not releas-ing even for a split second the hand in which he held the ax. She fell on top of him as the snow plunges or the water breaks, aiming herself at him like a rock hurled from some-where, and pressing him with her hands, chest, knees, with all her strength and weight. Krsto thrashed his legs frantically in an effort to free himself, and she spread over him even more firmly, so that she was holding him down with her whole body, even with her chin. Unwilling to remove from him even the smallest muscle and thus relieve the pressure, she cast a glance at Mihailo and yelled under her breath, as though to preserve her energy:

"Legs! Hold his legs!"

Had he sat on Krsto's legs? And had he let Krstinitsa pull the knife attached to his belt? This was the eighth year that Mihailo had asked himself this question, every day and every night, as he ate and as he slept. And more often. And every time, after an emotional turmoil, he would reply to himself that such a thing was beyond belief, because one must not do such a thing, could not do it. And then a darkness would come over him and in the darkness he would tell himself the truth: that he had done it, that he did sit on Krsto's legs, that he had felt her pulling out the knife and heard her stabbing Krsto three, four, five times, at random, as a woman would, between the ribs, in the sides, the hips. Yes, he had done that which was beyond belief, which it was impossible to do. And this horrible and shameful deed stood before him at all times: unchangeable and irremediable.

After Krsto's murder he had dashed outside and had sat down on the trough in front of the han. The bubbling of the fountain in the stillness of the night sounded to him like thunder. He had placed his hands in the cold water.

Still trembling, he had pulled himself together, and suddenly understood what he had seen and heard inside the han. This horrible deed! So this was the true meaning of his month-long passion, of that vast happiness that had swelled inside him and had been spilling over, without a moment's anticipation of evil. And, strangely enough, instead of thinking of the horror and disaster that had taken place before his very eyes and in which he had had a share, his thoughts had reverted to his month-long happiness, wishing to deform it and shame it. For suddenly it had become clear that, from the very beginning, it had all been just as horrible, shameful, and merciless as the final deed itself. There was not a trace left of the thirst for love and happiness which had surged in him for a whole month. He was now involved in a larger event, in which he was an element without meaning and imperceptibly small, and yet the cause and the instrument of the final tragedy. Between Krsto and Krstinitsa there were big accounts of which he had known nothing, and which they had been disentangling for a long time—and now everything had been abruptly cut off, ended. He felt betrayed, shamed, robbed, permanently crushed, as though he had been caught in a trap, dragged there by a husband and wife, each for different reasons, as part of a deep and ancient hatred which was greater and stronger than all three of them. That was his happiness.

He was startled by the sound of Krstinitsa's voice; she was calling to him, almost in a whisper, from the half-opened door. He rose and walked over to her. She held on to the door with one hand and held out his knife with the other, saying in a factual, dry tone:

"I've washed it."

Clearly aware of what would follow if he accepted the knife from her hand, he stepped abruptly to one side, and with a powerful blow of his hand struck the woman: she let go of the door and fell back into the room with a dull thump. He left the door of the han half open. Inside a candle was burning quietly, casting a faint light on Krstinitsa, who was lying unconscious next to Krsto, whose dead body was already covered with a rush mat.

Mihailo quickly reached the road. The fountain was bubbling noisily and the trough spilled over with a splash.

Mihailo reached town before dawn, intending only to change his clothes before giving himself up to the authorities. But when he reached his house, walked through the yard and into his room, looked over the familiar objects in it, and realized that everything was exactly as it had been when he left for the han the night before, a new conviction rapidly took shape: that he should not report himself to the authorities, for in arresting him they would be taking an innocent man. He was guilty, to be sure, and in a most serious sense; but he was not guilty of the crime that would be charged against him. The gendarmes would be incapable of making this distinction, and he would be forced to defend himself from them, to strike and kill once again if necessary. A fever of excitement overtook him, shattering his strength and dimming his eyesight; but his decision not to report himself and to resist arrest was clear and unequivocal. He made up his mind to flee town immediately.

This unhappy young man, whom his father had intended for the priesthood, judged himself and others that morning, and was great in his misfortune and just and infallible in his judgment. But if he was infallible in his judgment of men, he

81

was less so in his judgment of time. Measuring everything by what was going on inside himself, it seemed to Mihailo that time had passed much more slowly than it had in fact.

He was changing his clothes and making hasty preparations for his flight when his servant, Yevra, entered his room to tell him the strange story she had heard in the *kasaba,* which, it turned out, had already opened to business. Apparently that very night a band of robbers had attacked the Krstinitsa han, killing Krsto and wounding Krstinitsa. In spite of her condition, Krstinitsa had been able to describe the attack in some detail, including a reference to the "Greek bandits" who were involved.

It was too late for Mihailo to leave town unnoticed; he decided to stay at home a little while longer to await confirmation of Yevra's story, which had come to him like a miracle; and if he should see a policeman or any authority at his gate he would flee through the garden toward the willow thickets.

Later in the day he made a cautious trip into town, firmly determined to kill or to be killed if any suspicion were cast on him, or if a policeman should so much as approach him.

With his hands on a knife hidden in his pocket, his teeth clenched, desperately controlling his trembling hands, Mihailo walked through the streets, wondering why the rest of the world did not hear the loud beating of his heart. He listened to everything that was said about the attack on Krstinitsa's han with seeming calm. He even summoned enough strength to add a few comments of his own. For days he lived without sleep and without food, prolonging his life by the minute.

Eventually it became clear that Krstinitsa would stick to her story about the unseen robbers and that no one doubted her testimony; she was in mourning for Krsto, but continued to run the han. She brought her widowed sister to the house so as not to be left alone. It was only when the danger had passed that Mihailo felt his strength giving way, and he fell ill.

But he did not disclose anything, not even during the period of his most acute fever. In three weeks he was on his feet again. He came to accept the fact that Krstinitsa was not going to tell the true story of Krsto's death. And it was with a peace of mind, surprising even to himself, that he started making preparations for his departure—slow and cautious preparations, so as not to arouse suspicion. His brother was by nature a greedy person, which eased Mihailo's departure. By leaving the shop to his brother, and taking only a small portion of his share in ready money, he was able to obtain his brother's approval to go into the world. Indeed, he had worked everything out so carefully that when his departure from town finally occurred it aroused neither suspicion nor surprise.

But as soon as he had passed the first hill, and was out of sight of his own fields and hayloft at Lyubizhda, his courage failed him and he lost his peace of mind once again. He believed that he was cursed and felt like a pursued beast. He traveled on side roads, took short cuts and detours, stopped only at little-known inns, and crossed and recrossed his own path—all to throw his imagined pursuers off his trail. But as the real danger disappeared, another danger began growing in him, and a game of infected fancy and disturbed conscience was taking root. He passed near the town of Nova Varosh, where he had relatives, but he did not stop. It was not until he reached Priboy that he went into a han for the first time to buy bread and tobacco.

Moderate by nature and brought up strictly by his father and elder brother, Mihailo had smoked little before; but from that time on he smoked constantly and passionately. He discovered that this permanent little flame before the eyes was a blessing and that the same purple smoke which tickles the eyes and the throat made it possible for a man to shed a tear without weeping, and, in exhaling the smoke, to sigh without sighing. So this flame shone before his eyes or burned between his fingers for many years to come. The smoke, always the same and yet forever varied, helped prevent his thoughts from reverting to what he feared most, and in exceptionally tranquil hours guided him into a state of complete oblivion and forgetfulness; it fed him, like bread, and comforted him, like a a friend. At night he would dream about smoking as others dream of encounters with those they love. But when his dreams turned into nightmares and he thought he saw Krsto's body or Krstinitsa's eyes, he would awaken with a cry, seize tobacco as one would a pistol, or as those who do not sleep alone would seize somebody's hand. And as soon as the flint had ignited in the dark, and the tobacco had caught the sparks, he would relax and with the invisible smoke he would blow away the burden from his agitated mind.

He continued his journey, avoiding Vishegrad, which was much too near his home. On the slopes of Mount Romaniya at the great Obodyash han, he met Master Nikola Subotich, who frequently traveled on the road between Sarajevo and Vishegrad. Subotich employed Mihailo as a herdsman, his first real pause since his wanderings had begun. Unaccustomed to the hard life and rough customs, he had to endure a great deal, but all this vanished before one great and singular blessing: that he was once again hard at work with other young men, in the fields or in market places swarming with people.

He spent two years in Sarajevo and on various side trips for Subotich. And it was at this point that, as we have seen, Subotich singled out Mihailo from the other young men and put him in charge of his interests in Vishegrad. At first he found this town forbidding, bounded as it was by two rivers and closed in by the mountains. Its people struck him as a scornful and mistrustful lot. But as time went on he grew accustomed to their ways, until he developed a real fondness for the town and its people, almost as if they were his own. In the process his secret torment seemed to have diminished, and life was easier.

On meeting Krnoyelats' daughter, Anika, last year, new prospects suddenly opened up for him, prospects which until then had not existed and for which he had not dared hope. For the first time in several years a whole day and a night passed in which he did not feel that black and horrible thought spinning through him, the thought in which Krsto's murder and a desire for his own death had become one and the same obsession. The very idea that something in this world might restore to him the freedom he had enjoyed before that dawn at the han was enough to lift him from the earth.

But when the time came for him to go beyond these hopes and dreams, insurmountable barriers seemed to arise before him, of whose nature only he was aware. Shaken and cut down so early in his life, he could not find a way to this girl: he would approach her genuinely and cheerfully, and then, suddenly, he would panic and retreat. The happiness and joy he felt with Anika was not enough to free him from the terror of the earlier experience. He yearned for Anika's smiles and hungrily followed all of her movements and expressions, carefully measuring them later in his solitude. He was searching for some resemblance to Krstinitsa, frightened at the same time that he might find it. This, of course, poisoned all of his pleasures, and even began to alter his appearance; it was the cause of his strange behavior toward the girl herself.

So a whole year passed. There was no true understanding between them, and yet there was no break either. Meanwhile, Anika was growing more beautiful and more unusual and was greatly admired. Under such circumstances, the break was

85

inevitable; it came the following spring, on quite an insignificant issue.

One day Aunt Plema called at Mihailo's, and told him that Anika wished to see him. He thought it unsuitable for him to visit a girl's home, but nevertheless he agreed to go.

Krnoyelats' house was quite luxuriously furnished; more so, at any rate, than other houses in Vishegrad. It was not so much its wealth but something foreign and outstanding in its color, furnishings, and carpeting. In this setting Anika seemed to him even taller and more extraordinary. She explained that she had asked him over to find out what plans he had made for St. George's feast day. There was a curious lack of proportion between her hollow, deep voice, her grave and milk-white face, and this trifle about which she was inquiring. Mihailo's confusion grew. However, they agreed to meet and he promised to go to the feast "with God's help."

"I shall be there too, with God's help and if I'm not married by then," added Anika.

"I don't see how you could get married within the next few days."

"There are many things I can do."

"No, I don't think you can. I don't think you can."

"You think not?"

This last phrase, strangely uttered, forced Mihailo to look her in the eyes.

These eyes, always deep, were now as though illuminated from within, clear and opaque all at once; they flashed with the color of blood, and the passion of tears, and their expression became sharp, clear, and hard. Mihailo stared straight into those eyes, dazed by their light, and full of disbelief, waiting for their color to change or fade away, like an illusion. But the look grew sharper and clearer, and the glow more intense. A thought flashed in Mihailo's mind and instantly took

86

shape, and he wanted to scream, to yell. Anika's look was familiar to him; he had seen it some time ago, at the han, and in the dreams of his long unhappy nights. It seemed to him that he was gazing at Krstinitsa's animal-like eyes, full of horrible and unknown intentions; and he wanted to run away, although one could never run far enough. He thought he might break the hold of her eyes by an abrupt movement and a violent scream, as he had so often done when confronted by this image in those sweaty nooks in haylofts and roadside inns. But the spell could not be broken, and as he stood there, swaying back and forth between dreams and reality, Anika's question rang again and again in his ears, with a hundredfold din.

"You think not?"

Anika and Mihailo continued to stare at each other, with the intensity of lovers in their first few days, or as two beasts that collide in the dark of the forest, seeing only each other's eyeballs. But even the longest look of love comes to an end. Tearing his eyes away from hers, Mihailo glanced at Anika's strong and beautiful hands, with their fine skin and rosy nails. Finally realizing the full extent of his horror, he was forced to give up any hope of release from it. And so he began to retreat, like a trapped beast.

With great effort he produced a smile designed to delude his enemy, and managed to control himself sufficiently not to run out of the house and slam the door. Instead, he took his leave and walked out with an easy stride, in spite of his deadly fear. The door closed behind him; somehow he crossed the yard, and walked to the town square, deserted at this time of day. The fountain was bubbling quietly. Mihailo approached the stone trough and, sitting down at one end, placed his hands under the stream of water, regaining his senses and calming down.

87

He spent the next few days struggling with his thoughts, as though with shadows and apparitions. For one whole year Anika had been the core of all his hopes; now he was losing these hopes, and he felt as if he were losing life itself.

When Aunt Plema called on him once again to ask him to come to Anika, he replied that he could not do so. The day before the feast of St. George she came to inquire whether he would accompany Anika to the feast. "I cannot," he replied, anticipating some terrible reaction, as one awaits a blow. (Like a man who is seriously ill, he could think only of himself; it did not occur to him to wonder, and he could not have guessed, what was going on in Anika's mind during those days.)

Events developed quickly, with deeper and more serious consequences than anyone could have predicted.

St. George's feast day that year was remembered in town as the day on which Anika "announced herself." By the time of the feast of St. Elias, only two months later, her banner was completely unfurled. Anika opened her home to men. She hired two women, village tramps, whose names were Yelenka and Saveta, as her companions. It was in this manner that the reign of Anika Krnoyelats began—a reign of a year and a half in which Anika devoted herself to evil and disaster in much the same way that other people might occupy themselves with children, bread, their homes. She ignited men, set them afire, not only in the *kasaba*, but in the whole district of Vishegrad. Many details have been forgotten, and many a misfortune was never revealed, but it was not until Anika's times that the people of Vishegrad discovered what powers an evil woman possesses.

Little by little the yard in front of Anika's house came to resemble a camping site. No one could keep track of the many who came at night; young and old, bachelors and married men, neighbors from nearby Dobrun and travelers from distant Focha. And there were others who, bereft of shame or reason, came in full daylight and sat in the yard or, if allowed, in the house, or simply wandered about with their hands in their pockets, glancing from time to time up at Anika's window.

One of the most desperate and ardent of Anika's visitors was a certain Tane Kuyunjiya, a thin man with very wide eyes on a worn, tired face. He would sit on a crate behind the kitchen door, saying nothing, waiting patiently for Anika, looking up only when Yelenka and Saveta entered the kitchen. Going past him as though he did not exist, Yelenka and Saveta received their guests and proceeded with them to their rooms. When they threw him out of the kitchen, he would seat himself somewhere in the yard, bashfully smiling at Yelenka as she chased him out.

"Ah, let me be, *bona*. What am I doing to you?"

He would wait in the yard for hours, with a mournful expression, as though he found it hard to sit there for so long. Occasionally he would rise and leave without a word, only to come again the next day. At home he was scolded by his wife, Kosara, a robust woman of peasant stock with eyebrows that ran together.

"Have you been sitting in the bitches' yard again, you ugly duckling? You should have stayed there!"

"Eh, I should have stayed there," he repeated sadly, and his thoughts went back to the yard he had just left.

This indifference drove Kosara insane and she started a dreadful row, but Tane only waved his hand, as though awakened from a dream.

Some of Anika's company were quite mad, like Nazif, a big and retarded youth from the house of a beg. He was a quiet fool, deaf and dumb. He would pass under Anika's window

89

and call to her in his unintelligible language at least twice a day. He offered her a handful of sugar, and she jested with him about it.

"That isn't enough, Nazif, not enough," Anika called from above, smiling. Somehow or other the idiot understood what she had said, ran home, stole some money from his brothers, bought two half-pecks of sugar and returned to the window. Grinning with happiness, he offered her his fortune in sugar. Anika roared with laughter and indicated to him, through signs, that he had still not brought enough, and he left mumbling sadly.

From that day on he came every morning, carrying a basket filled with sugar, as well as additional amounts under his wide sash and in his pockets. Anika soon grew bored with the joke. The madman's persistence angered her, and she sent Saveta and Yelenka to chase him away. He defended himself and then left muttering incoherently, only to appear bright and early the following day with even more sugar. They chased him away again. All day long he carried the sugar around the town, twittering and murmuring. Children followed him, teased him, and stole the sugar from the basket which he clutched so passionately.

There were, of course, men who, lacking the courage to come in the daytime, waited for night to make their regular appearance, although many of them had no prospects of even entering Anika's house. They would simply sit there, on the trough by the fountain, waiting and smoking all night long. A man could arrive at night unseen by anyone; and he could leave in the same way. On the following morning a small heap of wood shavings and cigarette butts would appear where he had been sitting. He must have been an unhappy young man, God only knew which one; Anika certainly did not know him, and he knew her only by sight. For they were not all there just to see Anika. Some came simply because they were drawn to evil things, others because they had been from birth lost and tormented. Everything that was questionable, and contrary to God's will, assembled around that house and in that yard. The circle of men around Anika's house was rapidly expanding, and in time embraced not only the weak and the wicked, but the healthy and the wise too.

In the end, there were but few young men in the *kasaba* who had not been to Anika or who had not tried to approach her. First, they went to her stealthily, at night, obliquely and individually. They talked of her as of something shameful and horrible, but at the same time distant and almost beyond belief. But the more they talked and gossiped about her, the more comprehensible her evil seemed. At first they pointed a stern finger at those who went there, but in the end it was those who did not go to Anika's who attracted scorn. Since only a small group of men managed to reach Anika at first try, and the rest had to content themselves with Yelenka and Saveta, envy, male pride, and vanity began taking their toll. Those who had been rejected came again, hoping to make up for the double humiliation of having gone and been rejected all in one night; and those who had been received once could no longer stop themselves, but as if under a spell went back again and again.

The women of Vishegrad were unanimously and savagely against the disgrace of the house in the Meydan and fought Anika defiantly, ruthlessly, as women will, without much reflection. But their struggle was not always easy or safe, and it was in such a struggle that the Ristichi household was ruined.

The old Ristichka, a rich widow with the ability and resolution of a man, had successfully married off all her daughters as well as her only son, a small fellow with rosy checks and a quiet disposition, a clever merchant who always sought the company of older men, made money, and looked after his family. The wife his mother had found for him was a beautiful, quiet girl from a rich family in Focha. They had two children.

The trouble began at a funeral repast the previous winter, when the women were complaining about Anika and their men. Old Ristichka, having emptied a glass for the soul of the deceased, remarked loudly and defiantly:

"By God, I say, don't let them go. I have a son, too, a good man. But so long as I'm alive he'll never cross that bitch's doorstep."

The very next day these words were reported to Anika, as was everything said about her, and a day later Ristichka received a message:

"Within the next month your son, the good man, will come to me with all of his Saturday earnings in his hands; and you will then discover who Anika is."

A certain restlessness and concern crept into the Ristichi house, but this did not stop the old woman. She went on upbraiding Anika, who was, at this very time, at the height of her powers. On the following Saturday the young Ristich, drunk and half carried by his companions, called on Anika with his Saturday earnings, deep in the pockets of his trousers. He lay in front of Anika's door, thrashing his feet, scattering money around, frantically calling out to Anika and his mother at the same time. Yelenka and Saveta hovered over him and invited the curious to come in and take a look. At dawn Anika ordered Saveta to arrange for two young Turks to escort him home.

When the old Ristichka had realized that her son was late for supper, she had made the rounds of the town. Finally understanding that he had, indeed, gone to Anika's, the old woman went home, collapsed in the middle of the parlor, foaming at the mouth, and never again regained consciousness. Her daughter-in-law, a slender, pale girl, with dark hair and large eyes, walked into the main room and, kneeling down before the sanctuary lamp, swiftly crossed herself several times and began cursing Anika:

"I pray to God, woman, to see you mad, driven about in chains; I hope to God to see you become leprous, your whole body covered with sores; tired of yourself; desiring death, but death not wanting you! Amen, oh, great and only God! Amen. Amen."

Then and only then she broke into tears, which surged forth with such power that she was blinded, lost her balance, and crumpled, falling to the floor with all her weight. Groping with her arms, she knocked down the sanctuary lamp and the light went out. Later in the night she arose and slowly began putting the room in order. She washed the floor, wiped the oil that had spilled on the rug, prepared another lamp and lit it, crossed herself three times in front of it, and bowed without out a word. She looked at the child who was sleeping in the crib. Then she went over to the sanctuary lamp, sat down under it, and, with her hands neatly folded in her lap, waited for her man.

Everything is known in the *kasaba*, even things one says to oneself; there is no secret of either the soul or the body. The news of the young woman's curse reached Anika the following day. In the afternoon, Anika's servant, a one-eyed gypsy, called on the daughter-in-law and handed her a kerchief full of silver and copper coins. As soon as the gypsy woman had handed over the kerchief, she retreated into a far corner of the yard where, full of foreboding, she repeated a message her mistress had given her. Even to a gypsy this was a terrifying task.

"Anika sends you this. 'Let Ristichka count the coins in the

93

company of her son and daughter-in-law; his earnings are all there, not a penny is missing. She returned to you your man, and she is returning his money as well. She took out only enough to pay for what she had given him. The curse means nothing to her.' "

Next to the women of the town, who all hated her with equal venom, Anika's greatest foe was Master Petar Filipovats. His son Andriya was among those who called most frequently at Anika's house. The eldest son in the family, an awkward and pale youth, always sleepy and seemingly lost, he showed, however, great energy and persistence in his passion for Anika. He stopped coming home altogether because his father tried to kill him one night, and would surely have done so had not his mother hidden him and saved him. Now he slept in the hayloft, and his mother stealthily sent him food. And all the while she prayed to God and wept, but in secret, for Master Petar had threatened to throw her out of the house too after thirty years of married life, if she uttered but one sigh or shed one tear for the renegade.

The people who truly hated and condemned Anika congregated in the shop of Master Petar Filipovats. They might take a smoke or exchange a few words about something else, but they would invariably return to their major concern: the girl from the Meydan. In this connection they recalled the story of Tiyana, often told them by their elders.

Some seventy years earlier there was a shepherd's daughter, by the name of Tiyana, who was well known for her beauty. Casting aside every scruple, she had played havoc with the *kasaba*. Such was the race and the fight to get her that during a great church fair all the *charshiya* shops had remained closed, which had happened before only in time of plague or flood. The Sarajevo silversmiths and the Skoplye merchants came with copper dishes, and left with her both their goods and their earnings, departing as naked as rifles. Nothing could be done to destroy her. But one day she vanished as abruptly as she had appeared. One of Tiyana's first admirers was a certain Kosta, called the Greek, a rich young man with neither mother nor father. He wanted to marry her, they said, but Tiyana would not hear of it; instead she gathered around her more ruffians than ever, Turks and men of every faith. The Greek withdrew and disappeared from the *kasaba*. It was later learned that he had gone to the Banya Monastery, had become a monk and was pining away. And they forgot all about him. But exactly a year later, when Tiyana was in full swing and both God and men had had enough of her, that same Kosta suddenly turned up again. His face was overgrown with hair, and he had lost weight and was dressed in a costume half-monk and half-peasant. He had neither the sack nor the stick of a monk; instead, there were two little pistols tucked in his belt. He barged straight into Tiyana's house, burst open the door of her room, and fired several shots at her. But she was only slightly injured, and fled into the street. Running up the Meydan, she lost her slippers, ducats fell from her neck and pins from her hair. She ran toward a woodland below the old town. Reaching a ditch, she dropped into it, utterly exhausted. The monk overtook her and killed her.

There she lay, all day, her hair spread about her, still holding onto a whip, her mouth wide open; and it almost seemed as if she were watching over the shepherds some distance away. A great black wound could be seen in her blue silk garment. At twilight two gypsies were sent from town to bury her where she had been killed. The slayer himself disappeared into the forest. No one looked for him. But three days later he was found, his throat slashed, on the mound over Tiyana's grave.

While men sat in their shops recounting the past and women were weeping in their homes over current domestic tragedies,

95

the game of feminine evil that Anika was playing went on. It was at this time that Anika began her fight with Melentiye, the Dobrun priest, over his son, Yaksha, called the Deacon.

· II ·

Anika's reputation had spread far and wide. But it had never occurred to Yaksha Porubovich, the son of the Dobrun parish priest, to visit her. He preferred rakiya to women, and better than rakiya he liked his freedom and the right to loaf.

Yaksha was twenty years old, the tallest and the strongest youth in the *kadiluks* of Dobrun and Vishegrad. He had even gone to Chayniche to wrestle with a certain Nejo, called Kuryakovich, and had pinned him down.

Fair and red-haired, with green, bold eyes, Yaksha was the very opposite of his father, who was a tall, thin man with an ashen face and a black wrinkle between his brows; he had been gray-haired since his youth. The priest was one of those people who was as much a burden to himself as he was to others, who seem to carry inside themselves from birth to death a heavy thought. His son, Yaksha, on the other hand, took after his maternal grandfather, a certain Milisav, from Trnavtsi, a rich man, jovial and kindly.

The priest dearly loved his only son and was greatly upset by his wild and restless behavior. Yaksha had been a deacon for one year now, and his father had pressed him to get married so that he could enter the priesthood. But Yaksha did not care too much for the ministry, and he would not hear of marriage. The priest's wife, a good, dark, worn old woman, thrifty to the point of stinginess, now defended the son and then again supported the father. And she wept for both of them.

That winter Yaksha had decidedly calmed down a little. He was at home more often, and even allowed his parents to talk about his future marriage, although he himself never said a word. They were expecting a visit from the Bishop of Sarajevo in the spring, sometime after St. George's feast day, and it was the priest's hope that by that time his son would be married and that he could be ordained by the Bishop himself. Toward the end of the winter, Yaksha came to Vishegrad on business.

He arrived during the big fish runs at the end of February, when thousands of fish come down the Rzav in three great swarms, each one separated by a few days. One such run occurs early in the morning, usually just before dawn, and lasts until noon, drawing everyone down to the river, nets in hand. The children waded in the shallow waters, catching fish in pots or in their bare hands.

These three days have become an early springtime holiday; the homes all smell of oil, and so much fish is consumed that people become tired of it and its price drops precipitously. The last catch, in fact, is usually bought in bulk by neighboring peasants, who take it to their villages, where the fish are stretched out and dried.

Riding along the Dobrun road that morning, Yaksha saw the Rzav before him with fishermen and children scattered along it like ants. The sun shone brilliantly, the earth smoked, the fish glittered.

Yaksha quickly finished the work that had brought him to Vishegrad and was planning to return to Dobrun before dark. But some friends asked him to stop by at a coffeehouse where several merchants' sons were snacking on fish and drinking a mild rakiya. They were jesting with Gaziya, one of Vishegrad's best fishermen and, like all fishermen, a drunkard. Gaziya stood in the middle of the café, holding a soaking net from

97

which a heavy lead weight was hanging; the water dripped onto the floor next to his bare feet. He had sold all of his catch. Wet up to his waist, he was shivering slightly and emptying one glass of rakiya after another. They asked him how the catch had been this year, and how much he had caught and sold, but, like most real hunters, he superstitiously evaded questions of this sort.

"I hear you've made a pretty penny and are preparing to buy a gift for Anika," one of the young men taunted him.

"I, a gift for Anika? My turn will never come—because of you gentlemen!" he protested, rolling a cigarette, and transferring his weight from one foot to another.

The truth is that he was one of many who tried in vain to reach Anika, and they teased him so that they themselves could start talking about her.

Gaziya paid for his drinks and left the coffeehouse, still shivering with cold, and muttering:

"That's for you, gentlemen. Such goods are not for me. I live on water."

And they went on talking about Anika.

Yaksha saw her that same night. He did not go back to Dobrun again. He spent whole nights with Anika, and it seemed that she received only him. The *kasaba* talked of nothing but the priest's son. Women turned their heads away from him, and men spent their time giving him counsel, gossiping about him, and envying him.

In vain the priest sent messages to his son, threatened and implored. Seeing that he was getting nowhere, he decided to go to Vishegrad personally. That did not help either. Then he turned to the Kaymekam, the Mayor of Vishegrad. His name was Alibeg.

The son of the rich and respected Jevad Pasha Plevlyak, Alibeg could easily have resided at a more distinguished place, or occupied a higher position, but from his mother, who was descended from the renowned Mehmed Pasha Sokolovich, who built the Vishegrad bridge, he had inherited a great and noble indifference to all things, especially to profiteering and speculating. Twenty-five years ago, when the *kasaba* was enjoying a sudden boom and a brief period of well-being and plenty, Alibeg was appointed police commissioner of the *kasaba* at the age of twenty-one. In those days a great deal of trade passed across the Vishegrad bridge, and the town was full of goods, money, and travelers; therefore a large police force was needed, in the command of a strong and incorruptible person such as Alibeg.

In time trade turned the other way, deserting the Vishegrad road, and foreigners were not seen there often. The police force was reduced and many left; Alibeg was the only member of the force who did not abandon Vishegrad; he stayed on and became the mayor, or kaymekam. With his father he went to war twice, to Vlashka and to Serbia, but on both occasions he came back to his position in Vishegrad.

He had two homes, the most beautiful in town. Both were on the bank of the Drina, and between them there stood a large garden. The Kaymekam had been married several times, but all of his wives were dead. He was known for his weakness for women. With the years he drank increasingly, but always with moderation and taste. Despite his age and the irregular life he had led, he still had a slender figure. The sharp and restless features of his youth had, by this time, mellowed into a calm, smiling expression. Between his gray mustache and his big beard, youthfully reddish lips were clearly delineated. He spoke without gestures, but with warmth in his voice and frankness in his eyes. He had a passion for hot springs, and whenever he heard report of a new one, he would go to look it over, no matter how far away it might be. He would frequently have a fountain or a spa constructed there at his own expense.

In the *kasaba,* which had dwindled both in population and in commerce, the Kaymekam's duties had for a long time been few. With the distinction of a man of noble birth, he was slowly growing old and was living for his own pleasure and for the pleasure of others. He visited his estate at Plevlye, or went calling on his friends, the begs of Rujani and Glasinats.

The Kaymekam had always felt uneasy about the Dobrun priest, who was as straight and stiff as a plank. When the priest called on the Kaymekam, Alibeg received him coldly, but listened to his complaints about Anika, and promised to investigate the matter. He had also heard about the daughter of the late Krnoyelats, and had already received many complaints about her. He promised the priest that Yaksha would be sent to Dobrun and the woman brought under control.

Overcome with shame, the priest spent two days at Vishegrad, staying at the home of a friend, a frightened, half-blind priest, named Yosa. But when he saw that his son was not going to return with him and that the Kaymekam was not going to help him, he mounted his gentle black horse, and, with a soul full of bitterness, returned to Dobrun.

As soon as the priest had left, the Kaymekam called in the chief of the Vishegrad police, a certain Hedo Salko, and ordered him to call on this Christian woman, to threaten her with prison if she did not control herself, and to send Yaksha back to Dobrun forthwith.

Hedo carried out the order. He mounted his horse as on an important and solemn occasion, rode up the Meydan, and strutted back and forth in front of Anika's yard, yelling sharply to Yelenka, who was busy in the garden. The disorder around their house would not be tolerated any longer, he said, and furthermore, if that miserable son of the Dobrun priest did not go home immediately, he, Hedo Salko, would have a word or two to say to him. Yelenka ran to the house and reported it all to Anika, who instantly appeared at the door, but Hedo, anticipating this, had already trotted off on his high horse.

As lethargic as a court of law and as punctual as its worldly justice, Hedo had for thirty years carried out his duty in this manner. His face was entirely unique, full of deep and unusual wrinkles which had developed in unexpected directions, covering his forehead and nose and chin, swallowing up his thin mustache, and descending like streams of water down his scorched neck. From this labyrinth of lines protruded two round eyes without lashes, giving him the expression of an old horse. Thirty years as a policeman in the *kasaba* had shaped him in this way.

The Kaymekam was a man who disliked unpleasant things, even in the neighboring *kadiluk,* the man to whom Hedo never dared report a single problem that had not already been satisfactorily resolved. Policemen came and went and were either too easily bribed or too scrupulously zealous. So during the past twenty-five years everything had landed on poor Hedo's head, from crop damage, drunkenness, and the neighbors' rows to the most horrible murders and the biggest robberies. He had distinguished himself as a young policeman, and so became the chief. But soon thereafter he realized that riots, murders, and misfortunes occur as some natural and inevitable evil, and that his, Hedo's, hands and eyes were too weak to cope with them all, and resolve them, punish offenders according to merit. Instead of gradually acquiring a sense of authority and power in his position, he had acquired a superstitious awe of crime, and indeed almost respect for a person who had thought up and then carried out an evil deed. He automatically appeared at every place prescribed by his duty, not to clash with the violator, but to chase him out of his district and into someone else's. In constant touch with human evil and human suffering, he had gained over the years a most peculiar experience, to which he unconsciously adjusted all his actions. On the basis of this experience he had arrived at two seemingly opposed truths, but both equally valid. First, that evil, misfortune, and unrest are constant and eternal and that nothing concerning them can be changed. Second, that every single problem will somehow be resolved and settled, for nothing in this world is lasting or eternal: the neighbors will make peace, the murderer will either surrender himself or else flee into another district where there are other policemen, with their chiefs; stolen objects will be recovered sooner or later, for people are not only thieves but also blabbermouths and informers; drunkards will sober up and therefore one should not tangle with them while they are drunk and know not what they do.

These two maxims guided Hedo in all of his official business. But when a woman was involved in some dispute or crime, this passivity of his turned into complete numbness. In these moments he resembled a man on whose neck a wasp has descended; he stiffens and lets it walk up and down, while he himself does what is most wise: waits for it to fly away by itself. As soon as Hedo Salko came across a woman in the course of an investigation, he would go no further, unless absolutely necessary. Of course this was not done deliberately. Experience had taught him this lesson and instinct had led him to it: to get involved in a dispute in which women are mixed up meant putting one's finger between a door and the door frame.

When Yaksha arrived that evening, Anika would not allow him into her room, in spite of all his entreaties and arguments. She had simply decided not to receive him, and did not wish even to discuss it. To all of his ardent words, she replied scornfully:

"Why don't you go back to Dobrun? Your father wants you."

And Yaksha answered:

"I have no father. You know that."

"What do I know?" she inquired softly.

"You know well what I have said to you every night and I know all that you have said to me."

He recalled the caresses and confused words; the dawn approaching and her palms covering his eyes.

It was ridiculous and sad to see that huge man recounting like a woman the details of the past nights. But it was obvious that the words had intoxicated him as love itself had, and that he did not know what he was doing or saying. Anika listened to him patiently, without a word, without compassion, but also without derision. He knew he had to leave, but wanted to know when he might see her again. She replied, smiling:

"Well, perhaps at the Dobrun fair, on the day of Our Lady."

From then on Yaksha stayed at Zariye's inn. His pride would not allow him to loiter in front of Anika's door. He treated people to drinks and drank himself, sitting motionless, his fists on the table, his handsome head tilted back resting against the wall, his face turned upward to the grimy ceiling as though reading something on it. No one dared mention Anika to him, although they all knew why he had taken to drinking.

Thus he sat for hours, looking at the ceiling, and recalling not so much her words as her silences. He was full of that silence of hers and felt it in his intestines. Even without closing his eyes he saw her sitting on the low *minderluk*, a white scarf firmly tied around her head covering not only her hair but her forehead down to her eyes. Her hands are in her lap; she firmly presses one palm against the other, as though telling a fortune. Her face is large and white, her cheekbones prominent, her eyes, which have become deep in color, are surrounded by a smile which illuminates them. Her silence shortens his breath and clouds his sight. If he could once more sit next to her, he would take that head in both his hands, twist it violently, bend it down to the bed, to the floor, to the grass. But then he recalled her cold scorn, which had made him suffer so much, not because he could not destroy it, but because there was no use destroying it. And he was startled, as if he had hit a wall; his large fists on the table trembled.

While Yaksha was thus drinking at Zariye's inn, there were new disorders around Anika's house, of which Hedo Salko pretended he knew nothing. Since she did not wish to receive guests, drunken men rushed at her gate while others, hoping thereby to win her fancy, ejected the drunken men from her door.

Knowing Hedo's weaknesses, the Kaymekam finally decided that he would have to go to Anika's house himself to see what was causing the trouble. One afternoon he paid her a visit, accompanied by a gendarme who soon returned alone. The Kaymekam stayed until nightfall. And the next day he came again.

And it could not be otherwise. The Kaymekam, who had seen many women in his lifetime and had not been without a wide choice, felt that here he had found something extraordinary—a woman of such movements and such looks as had not been seen since the *kasaba* had first entrenched itself in Vishegrad, or, indeed, since men and women have known each other and borne children together. This body was not born or nurtured in connection with anything surrounding it; it simply happened.

The Kaymekam paused in wonderment before so much beauty, as if he had come upon something familiar and long

lost—the rich whiteness of her skin, which so completely covered her veins, and from which the deep red of her lips was
separated only by a sharp, abrupt line; that same rich whiteness which turned so gradually into a hardly perceptible pink
around her nails and under her ears. This whole, large, harmonious body, solemn in its tranquillity, slow in its movement, seemingly preoccupied only with itself, feeling no desire or need to resemble others—it was like a rich self-sufficient
empire, with nothing to conceal and no need to display its
wealth, living in silence and despising others for their need
to talk and explain themselves.

The Kaymekam took all this in with the eyes of a man of
mature years who believes that he knows the full value of life
and at the same time recognizes that this life is slipping away
from him. What woman would have dared put off this man,
this Turk, if not Anika herself? But Anika chose not to do so.

The following day, after the Kaymekam's second visit,
Anika asked to see Tane the silversmith, who was still in her
yard after these many months.

"Can you write?"

"Yes, I can," replied Tane, and to demonstrate it he spread
out the fingers of his right hand, his eyes moist with pleasure.

Tane brought from the shop his ink, pen, and paper. Now
he sat on the *minderluk*, Anika next to him.

"Can you write down everything you are told?"

"Well, yes, I think so."

The fury that lives in every idle woman dictated to Anika,
and she, through Tane, to the pen. Tane began to write, his
whole body leaning to one side, slowly stringing one letter
next to the other, and his wrinkled cheek constantly being
thrust out, lifting up and down as he followed the movements
of the pen with his tongue. Anika dictated:

"You are the priest of Dobrun and I the whore of Vishegrad. Our parishes are divided, and it would be better for you to leave alone that which does not belong to you."

Tane, who was already hesitant about putting down certain words, stopped writing altogether at this point, and gave Anika a ridiculously worried look, as though he wanted to be told that it was all a joke and that she was not seriously thinking about sending this letter to the priest of Dobrun. Without looking at him, however, Anika caught him up sharply:

"Write!"

And he went on writing with the same ridiculously worried look on his face.

"Before I was even born, you were jumping the fence at Nedelkovitsa's, while her husband, Nedelko, thinking it was a badger in the cornfield, almost killed you. And today your priestly robes are still being mended in the homes of friendly widows. And I, for my part, have never inquired after your health, or asked about your doings. And yet you felt called upon to send to me the Kaymekam and his police. It would have been better for you to have touched a snake under a rock. Well, priest, I want you to know that the Kaymekam has come to me twice since then, and that I have ungirdled his sword as though he were a child, and, old as he is, he held a basin and a towel for me; perhaps you would like to know these things. And since you are worried about your handsome son, there he is at Zariye's inn; shaven like a bridegroom, it is true, and dead drunk, but that doesn't matter; take him home by all means; he will sober up, his beard will grow, and, as far as I am concerned, he can even become a bishop."

She paused. Tane recovered his breath. He could just barely manage to follow her, although he had left out many letters and whole syllables too.

Anika's letter to the Dobrun priest was known in the *kasaba* the very next day. But after the Kaymekam's first visit, the town could no longer be surprised. It was even said that upon learning the latest news, the Dobrun priest delivered vespers wearing his robes inside out, the candles burning upside down.

It was believed in the *kasaba* that no human act could alter this situation; they must await God's hand. Even so, Anika managed to turn the *kasaba* upside down once more.

On the day of Our Lady, a great fair was held at the Dobrun church, to which peasants come in large numbers, even from the most remote villages.

Anika, too, had decided to go to the fair; she left for Dobrun at noon of the day before, riding with Yelenka on quiet well-fed horses, a servant following behind them. They rode through the side alleys, but even so the news that Anika was on her way spread quickly through the *kasaba*. Men moved about and twisted their necks to catch a glimpse of her as she set off on the steep road below Strazhishte. Apprentices and novices ingeniously conceived of jobs to do in the attic, climbed up and looked through the attic window to see Anika disappear behind the hill.

Following Anika on a lame horse, which, in his hurry, he had hired from a gypsy, was Tane the silversmith. Paler than usual, with a long face, he followed Anika, riding right through the heart of the *charshiya* without shame or embarrassment. He paid no heed to the laughter and mockery which greeted him; perhaps he did not even hear their cries. But after he had disappeared behind the hill, an uncomfortable silence came over the town. The men had withdrawn into their shops and were trying to busy themselves with whatever was at hand. And many of those who only a few minutes earlier had laughed at Tane were now devising some pretext by which they might unnoticed follow Anika. Some decided to go to the villages to buy hides, others to Dobrun on urgent business, and still others set off for the market at Priboy. And when night fell, young men stole away, taking short cuts in the same direction in which the older men had already gone. Many of them were still boys and had no hope for themselves, but it pleased them to lose a night because of her and to tumble among the crags along the Rzav.

Tane caught up with Anika and her escort at Chelik's bridge. Yelenka scolded him, but Tane only grinned and gazed at Anika as though expecting her to say something.

"What have I done to hurt you?" asked Tane.

Yelenka was furious. She halted her horse.

"This is what you have done to me. You are sitting on top of my head. We've had enough of you at Vishegrad. Why do you have to follow us? Go home and rock the cradle for your wife!"

While arguing, they were both watching Anika, but she was riding ahead, not looking back or indicating in any way that she was listening to them. Yelenka angrily spurred her horse, and caught up with Anika. And Tane, with his head lowered and his reins limp, rode in step with them.

So they rode for about a hundred paces, until Anika stopped her horse and turned abruptly. Tane found himself face to face with her, their horses bracing one another. Her face was glowing from the heat, framed with a thin white kerchief whose ends fell over her shoulders. She was smiling gently, childlike. Tane felt the skin on his face tighten. His teeth and his pale gums appeared, his sad gray eyes became moist.

"Tane, I bought some lemons at Mejuselats', but forgot them by the door. Go back to Vishegrad, I beg of you, and get them for me. You will catch up with us before we get to Dobrun."

Grinning with happiness, Tane barely understood what she had asked him to do.

"Lemons . . . at Mejuselats' . . . I am going, I am gone!" He turned round instantly and sadly rode toward Vishegrad, vainly spurring the gypsy nag, who was impervious to blows. Once or twice he turned back to see Anika's long white scarf as she and Yelenka disappeared toward Dobrun.

As soon as Tane had left, Yelenka burst into laughter, she was so amused by Anika's cunning. But Anika only rode on, smiling, not saying anything. The servant had gone ahead of them and was waiting in the shade.

The next day the Dobrun fair opened and soon was in full swing. It was said that Anika had arrived, but no one had seen her during the morning service or around the church in the afternoon. In the boisterous and excited crowd Tane the silversmith could be seen, roaming about, looking sadly right and left. Drunken peasants pushed him and stepped on his toes, but he continued walking all morning, carrying the bagful of lemons which he had bought yesterday, out of his own pocket, when he realized that Anika had not forgotten anything at the store. Toward nightfall, Anika appeared with Yelenka. They walked to the middle of the churchyard, entered a large tent set on an elevated platform, and seated themselves.

As soon as he had heard of Anika's arrival, the priest, beside himself with anger, announced that he would approach her personally, and order her to leave. But the church elders stopped him and said that they themselves would speak to her.

A huge crowd of men, however, had already gathered around Anika. When the elders appeared, they were greeted first with laughter, and then with abuse. Anika acted as though she neither saw nor heard this tumult. The church emissaries tried to get to her so that they might throw her out by force, but a wall of drunken young peasants instantly formed between them and the two women. The elders were squeezed back against the fence in front of the priest's house, and just barely escaped through the door.

It was almost dark when the elders and the priest himself came down the stairs. But the mob was so large that the door was blocked, and they could not make their way out of the house.

When matters are most confusing, people least know what they want. They rushed from Anika's tent to the door of the parish house and back again. In truth, the actual rushing was confined to several drunken young men, while the rest of the mob only swayed with them. The men from Liyesko, who find a cause for a scuffle at every church feast, threatened and shouted more than anybody. Happy this year to have found so noble a target for their fury, they shouted with double strength:

"No, we won't let you!"

"No, we won't."

The Limich brothers, the best known among the Liyeshtani, loosened their belts, gnashed their teeth, brandished their knives, and needlessly assured one another:

"Brother, I am with you. . . ."

Night had fallen completely. A little earlier Yaksha had arrived from Vishegrad; he had struggled with himself all day, and when he could stand it no longer, he started for Dobrun. Everyone gathered around the illuminated tents or around the fires burning on the plain. Those who were very drunk disappeared into the fields, vomited, groaned, and talked to themselves along the fences in the dark. By the door of the parish house, there was a constant din, of which nothing could be understood. The priest stood there, black and pale in the light of a torch that someone held behind him in the corridor. He rose to speak, tried to advance, but was held back by the church elders, and the noise was such that he could not hear himself. There was no trace of fear or confusion on his face, but only wrath and wonderment. For a long time he tried to speak and to approach the drunkards. Attempting to stand on his toes and to break free of the crowd, the priest suddenly stopped in his tracks, his glance falling on the middle tent, the most brilliantly lit of them all. In the red glow he saw Anika's upright and proud figure, with Yelenka on one side and Yaksha, who had just entered, on the other, bent toward Anika with his arms outstretched, with a gesture full of tenderness and devotion, a gesture both shameful and inexplicable in the eyes of his father.

The priest pushed aside the people standing near him, and rushed up the half-dark stairs into his room. His wife, who was trembling on the porch and striking her forehead, weeping with hopeless shame and twofold sorrow, rushed up behind the priest, followed by several of her women friends. Some relatives and the elders joined them in the room, while others tried to stop the mob from breaking into the house and up the stairs. In the dark room they found the priest removing a long rifle from its place on the wall. They caught up with him by a window from which, in the middle of the swaying mob, Anika's fiery tent could be seen. Yaksha was there, still bent, and Anika sat in the middle like a finished portrait. The elders clasped the priest around the waist, and his wife reached for the rifle, but he held onto it with great determination. As they wrestled with him they tried to calm him down:

"Father, Father! We plead with you!"

With horror in her voice his wife whimpered hoarsely and quietly.

"I implore you, for our sake, for God's sake!"

Finally they managed to drag him back into the dark room,

from where the yard outside could not be seen. At last he let go of the rifle which he had held in his raised arm. His wife fainted. While the women busied themselves with her, the men took the priest into another room on the other side of the house.

Outside the din had subsided and the mob was dispersing. Drunkards quickly forgot the priest, and, finding a new cause for an outburst, were fighting among themselves or with their relatives. The relatives, for their part, were loading the drunkards on horses like goods, or leading them away between them down the road. Only a few remained in front of the tent, blinking and staring at Anika, sweat reflected on their foreheads.

Anika, too, was getting ready to go. She refused Yaksha's offer to escort them to Vishegrad. In his confusion and helplessness he was bitterly and repeatedly asking her:

"And the Kaymekam comes to you all the time?"

Anika listened and replied absent-mindedly, as if she were thinking of something else:

"Every evening, Yaksha. How come you haven't seen him? Or perhaps the Kaymekam stays out of your way?"

Yaksha winced at this insult. She continued softly, in a quiet voice:

"Or perhaps you stay out of his way?"

As though not thinking about what she was saying, she added:

"He will come to me tomorrow, too, right after supper."

By that time hardly anyone was left in the churchyard: innkeepers and candy and food vendors were putting their goods and utensils into the cases on which they had been displayed. The fires were going out, sprinkled with water or simply abandoned. In the dark the sighs and moans of drunks were still heard. And now even those sounds were receding. Only a few of them lay in a nearby ditch as though struck down in battle.

In the priest's house lights flickered in the windows as torches and candles were moved from one room to another; women were whispering to each other, serving coffee and rakiya to the men. The priest had regained control over himself and was talking with the men, but the talk was constrained, as though it were after a funeral. Finally, the remaining visitors rose and took leave of the priest, who was doing his best to appear self-possessed and calm. Two women stayed with his wife for the night.

After they had gone, the priest remained in his room for a while, and then, getting up, walked across the house to the window facing the churchyard and the Tasichi home. Hearing his footsteps the women were full of foreboding. But not a sound was heard from him any more. They assumed that he had decided to take a nap in the large room, which was cooler and better ventilated than his own.

The priest locked the door, lit a candle, and seated himself before it. The candlelight illuminated his chest, his beard, his wide gray face, with eyes like dark holes. Outside, the dogs barked. The churchyard was in darkness; on the other side of the brook, by the Tasichi house, a few torches were still burning. With his hands in his lap the priest sat as though watching over a dead body.

His rage had subsided, his thoughts had been put in order, but the pain had grown. He could not bear the present state of things, so he sought support in past memories, in the time *before this.* He had been a priest at Dobrun for almost thirty years. Living in the church and with the people, he had seen and could still remember a great deal of evil, but he could not have anticipated this—that he would live to witness, in his own blood and on his own threshold, this depravity, coming invisibly and unexpectedly, tearing into parents' hearts, spit-

ting in their faces, a malignancy that can in no way be pre-
vented or driven away, neither through outright struggle nor
through death itself.

Suddenly a new and painful feeling of boundless pity broke
through the complete vacuum that was forming within him.
He felt pity for man's brood, for the air they breathe, for the
bread they must eat. His pity went to that big crazy child
Yaksha—for the humiliation and the disgrace into which he
had fallen. Sitting on a trunk, cowering like an orphan, with
his face in the palms of his hands, he started to cry for the
first time in his life, loudly and without restraint. Powerless
and disarmed before so much evil, shame, and injustice, he was
choking through his clenched teeth, trying in vain to overcome and stop his tears. It seemed that those tears had brought
everything to life and shaken everything inside of him. In convulsions, his head dropped to his knees. But suddenly he grew
greatly disturbed and rose unexpectedly; and with all his mind
and all his soul he cursed the harlot, this horrible creature
without shame or reason.

· III ·

Anika returned to Vishegrad that night, in the moonlight.
Yaksha followed immediately after her. The next evening,
while the Kaymekam was visiting Anika, someone took a
shot at him from behind a fence overgrown with ivy. Alibeg's
right arm was slightly wounded; the same evening Yaksha
vanished from the *kasaba*.

Anika sent her gypsy to Alibeg's home to inquire how he
was faring, but the servants chased the gypsy away with

sticks. Anika did not worry about it too much. She knew that the Kaymekam would come to her as soon as he had recovered, and sooner if she asked him. Her visit to Dobrun had convinced her that she could do anything she pleased. The *kasaba* was equally convinced.

It was September. Yaksha had fled to the forest above Banpolye, and every night his fires could be seen from the town. He would not return to Dobrun and he could not return to Vishegrad. Hedo Salko was sent out to capture him, but got nowhere. Soon they stopped pursuing him altogether; and Yaksha's fires continued to burn above Banpolye, half an hour's distance from the town. Everyone in Vishegrad knew they were Yaksha's fires, and Anika herself sometimes came out into the yard to watch the first flames, which always appeared at about the same time as the first stars, growing bigger and redder, conquering the darkness of the hills and the heavens above.

While Yaksha was hiding in the woods, the Dobrun priest lay in bed at home, pale and still, like a dead man. His weeping wife sat next to him day and night. She begged him to say something, anything, to give out orders, but he went on biting his lips, drowning in his white beard and mustache, his look faded, rigid, and lost.

The Kaymekam spent the evenings in his garden on the Drina, drinking with friends. He would order his police to go out and seize Yaksha, only to forget the whole matter the next moment. His wound healed quickly. From Sarajevo came two guests, two well-fed Turks.

During the day the three of them sat gambling in the Kaymekam's garden by the river. They ordered soldiers to set yellow pumpkins afloat on the river, which they used as targets for shooting contests. As soon as it grew dark, gypsy musicians began to play. The guests had brought with them firecrackers, purchased in Austria, which were fired at night. These new and unheard-of games excited the whole town. Children would not go to sleep, but waited until the firecrackers had been set off from the garden. The townspeople watched with misgiving and wonderment as the red and green sparks scattered under the summer sky, broke and fell to the ground like a brilliant rainfall, leaving the land in a darkness more dense than before. And all the while Yaksha's fire burned in the mountains.

Anika did nothing. She no longer received anyone. Toward the evening she locked the garden gate and ordered Yelenka to sing for her. Yelenka had a sharp, high-pitched voice that carried through the whole *kasaba* from hill to hill. Anika sat next to her and listened expressionless and without a word. It was said that although she had humiliated the priest on his own threshold and subordinated the whole town to her will, Anika was still neither calm nor pleased. The only word they had of her came from a drunken Turk who was camping in front of her house and would not leave, and whose words were repeated in the *kasaba* with awe and fear.

This Turk was a rich and wild fellow from Rudo. When sober he might be found at the han and around town; but as soon as he got drunk—and that was not seldom—he went up to the Meydan, straight to Anika's gate. From day to day he grew increasingly mean and surly. He assaulted Yelenka and Saveta and the men who came and waited as he did. He yelled underneath Anika's window, threatened, and thrust his big knife into the gate. One evening he again brandished his knife in the yard, shouting at the top of his voice that he would kill someone that evening. Anika herself appeared, dressed lightly in white stockings and without slippers, and approached the Turk.

"What is it? Why are you screaming? What do you want?"

116

she asked in her low husky voice. Her face was still, except for her arched brows. "Whom will you kill? Go ahead, kill! You think anyone is afraid of your knife, you peasant fool! Go ahead, kill!"

The Turk's eyes were stock-still; he was chewing and swallowing so that his long reddish mustache and his sharp, unshaven Adam's apple were quivering. He forgot that he had a knife in his hand, that he had ever said anything, and stood there as though waiting for her to kill him. Anika pushed him out of the yard and slammed the gate behind him.

It was said that on her way back through the house—as she was passing Yelenka, Tane, and a young man—and still cursing the drunken Turk, she had muttered loudly to herself:

"Whoever would kill me would do me a great favor."

In this scene of evil and confusion there were two griefs of which no one in the *kasaba* knew anything. Two men were tormented, suffering each by himself and in his own way, secretly and in silence: a torment shared with everyone, but which to them had a special depth and meaning. One was Lale, Anika's brother, and the other Mihailo.

Lale had left home when Anika's behavior first became notorious. Nor was he seen any longer in the *charshiya*. He lived and slept in his bakery shop. When someone accidentally mentioned his sister, his bright boyish face would cloud over and his eyes would fix themselves rigidly on one object. But almost instantly, he would shake his fair head, covered with flour, and his usual feeble-minded smile would return to his face. Humming quietly to himself, he went on punching quickly and automatically the monotonous patterns on the bread loaves, as his father had taught him to do in his childhood.

That was Lale, Anika's brother. What was on his mind, or

how much this feeble-minded youth suffered in that half-dark room behind the big stove, no one knew.

Mihailo lived in Master Nikola's house, which was a little way off the *charshiya,* not far from the Krnoyelats bakery. Since Anika had taken to this way of life, Mihailo had gone on trips as often as he could, but while in town he could not help overhearing the talk about Anika, and he knew everything that had happened.

Master Petar Filipovats, who had chased his own son away from home, and who was no longer on speaking terms with either his wife or his daughters, was exceptionally fond of Mihailo. They frequently got together early in the morning, in the shade of Master Petar's shop. Most of the *charshiya* shops were still closed. It was peaceful. Gloomy and bloated, Master Petar spoke in his hoarse voice:

"See, you are a young man, but I tell you that the sayings of old people still hold true. In every woman there is a devil that must be killed, either by hard work or through childbearing. A woman who escapes both should be done away with."

And as though they had never discussed it, Master Petar's voice would rise, and he would address Mihailo with one and the same complaint.

"Mihailo, brother, a thing such as this has never happened in our town."

Mihailo would remind him of Tiyana, or Saveta, who had been known for evil long before Anika, but Master Petar would interrupt him:

"By comparison to this one, Tiyana was a saint. If Saveta were the only problem, the town would sleep peacefully. There has always been some gypsy or slut, and her place was known: with soldiers in the ditches. No one looked at them or paid any attention to them. But this! Don't you see what's going on? She has shamed the church, won over the authorities, and will finish us all off. And no one can do anything with her."

"No one?"

"No one, by God. In our *kasaba* she is today both the pasha and the bishop. We should all roast in hell because not one of us has the courage to kill her. Those who sit in an ambush along the road have done less evil than she has."

Once more Master Petar enumerated her evils and wicked deeds, referring briefly to his own son's misfortune, at which point he would only wave his hand and silently swallow his bitterness. Mihailo tried to comfort him:

"A day will come when there will be an end to her too."

"No, there is no end to such a woman. She will carry on for as long as she likes. You don't know us, or this *kasaba*. We can resist every evil, but not *this*. She is riding us and no one can shake her off."

With this phrase Master Petar ended all of these talks to which Mihailo listened thoughtfully.

If this embittered old man had known the anguish these talks caused Mihailo he would doubtless have sought another companion, or would have mulled over his misfortune alone.

Mihailo sometimes wondered where he found the strength to move among these people, to work and to talk with them, without losing his control. Watching Anika all this time, his short-lived and quickly betrayed hope of redemption turned once more against him. Disgusted with himself, he wondered how he could have believed, even for a moment, that what had happened at the han could ever be erased and forgotten.

Years ago, in Sarajevo, he had seen a Serb stab a Moslem in the street. The stricken man never looked back to see the murderer whom others were chasing, but started slowly and solemnly for the first open door. He walked as though counting his steps, without looking at anyone; he was pressing his wound with both his hands, clearly feeling that he would live only as long as the knife remained in the wound.

Mihailo saw Krsto's murder as his own death, inevitable and imminent, and understood that it had not been redeemed even with eight years of suffering. He, Mihailo, had been mortally wounded that night. These eight years have been like the few steps the Moslem took to the first door, his eyes downcast, both hands on his wound.

Mihailo took pity on himself.

"The time has come to release the knife from the wound. It is no use deluding oneself."

He could no longer recall when it was that he first lost his ability to distinguish between Anika and Krstinitsa; in his mind, the two women had for a long time been one and the same person. Indeed, any woman he desired or possessed became one woman: tall, buxom Krstinitsa, with her reddish hair, powerful arms, and blazing eyes.

On a hill above him, within calling distance, lived a woman who, more than any other, reminded him of Krstinitsa; and, like Krstinitsa, she had raised his hopes and then, after a brief and torturous game, had revealed herself for what she was, confirming all his forebodings.

Brought up by a wise and honest father, sensitive by nature and yet hard inside, Mihailo was capable of great suffering; yet he knew how to conceal these feelings. But his torment had now grown to such proportions that concealment had become almost impossible. Shame hovered in sight like an apparition, more painful and more horrible than death itself. And the torment penetrated even the most trifling details of everyday life.

With childlike persistence, he returned to certain details again and again. For instance, he was convinced that he would have felt better had he taken the knife from Krstinitsa's hands when she had offered it to him. But having left the knife at the han, it was as if it were pawned to her, forming a link between him and the horror from which he had fled that night. And whenever he heard the word "knife" mentioned, accidentally and in no relation to him, he would think to himself: "She still has my knife."

This incomprehensible game of conscience slowly conquered Mihailo's whole existence.

In his frequent settling of accounts with himself, there was one horror he did not think possible: dreaming the same dream repeatedly, always in the full awareness of what had happened in the previous one. He no longer remembered his first dream of this nature, but sensed that each repetition added something to reality, some detail, some trifle to an increasingly sharp image. The image slowly condensed, separated itself from his dream world, approached reality, and infiltrated it imperceptibly.

This was his dream: the morning is bright. He feels its freshness and coolness on his face, in his mouth, on his whole body. He walks upright and solemn under the impact of a certain decision which is so immense that he cannot grasp it, but only feels its great weight. It seems that the alleys and squares are emptying before him; only the weight of his decision is pushing him ahead. Thus he passes by Krnoyelats' bakery, from which Lale's cheerful singing can be heard. He climbs up the Meydan. Anika's yard is full of bright, fresh flowers. The door of the house is open, inviting one to enter.

What desperate effort Mihailo made, both in reality and in the dream, not to cross this door, not to pass that threshold! For years he had made work for himself and traveled, even when he did not have to, simply to stay away from this yard. He had been successful in this for a long time, but now he felt that he was no longer in control. He would forget business arrangements, arrive late for appointments. Realizing that he was becoming absent-minded and negligent, he was frightened, as though he had discovered that he had a disease.

There was perhaps another possibility: to leave everything before a disaster occurred, to flee into the world, a man without honor, a criminal. If his problem had been real, his enemies visible, he would have done so. But as things stood, where would he flee? The object of his fear would await him on every road, in every town.

He even considered sending a letter to Anika, threatening her, begging her to go away, for her own sake, for the *kasaba's* sake, for his sake. But he instantly understood the futility of such a communication.

He frequently thought of Lale. He had always been attached to this handsome, simple-minded youth. Between him and Anika's brother there had always been a certain attraction, a mixture of affection, distrust, and brusqueness. After his talks with Master Petar he frequently thought of Lale. It seemed to him that, as Anika's brother, Lale saw it all and felt it all, and that perhaps he should be the one to disarm and defeat her. Passing by the bakery early one morning, Mihailo called on him. He found Lale singing loudly and punching the full, white loaves with a big, black knife. They chatted, as much as one could chat with Lale. Mihailo would bring Anika into the conversation, but he got nowhere. Lale continued smiling like a happy idiot, talking about the flour, the water, and the bread.

Thus Mihailo lost all hope of involving Anika's brother in his torment. Everyone was slipping away, leaving him alone with Anika. Everything was driving him forward and only occasionally could he step back to measure the distance he had traveled along the road down which he was sliding imperceptibly.

It was a beautiful Vishegrad autumn. Mihailo sensed that he would soon be on his way; this, too, had come imperceptibly. He woke up one morning full of thoughts of departure. While washing his face a little later at the fountain in the yard, he suddenly uttered the word "farewell" into a handful of cold, cheerful water, and immediately spilled the water, and his thought went with it.

Mihailo was taking leave of everything around him. One day he went up to Anika's gypsy, whom he saw often in the *charshiya,* and said to her in a natural tone of voice:

"Ask Anika whether I may come to see her tomorrow morning; I can only come when no one else is there. I have something to tell her."

The gypsy vanished. Mihailo shuddered a little and looked around as if seeking help or advice. But for the rest of the day he was composed. He worked carefully on his accounts and cleaned up around the house. Just before sunset, he started toward Strazhishte, the hill on which he had so many times welcomed the evening with his friends.

He climbed slowly, and sat down in the clearing above the Turkish cemetery, laid on the ground next to him a flask of rakiya and some food. He slowly struck a piece of steel against the flint and delicately held the burning cigarette between the fingers of his left hand. He could not take his eyes from the smoke which rose in front of him, blocking his view, whirling around and disappearing slowly into the still air. There was still a faint gleam of sunlight among the fir trees. Below him the smoke lifted slowly from among the black and the red roofs of the white Vishegrad houses. One flooded arm of the river Rzav reflected the skies and the willows along its bank.

Mihailo also saw many things that were not visible from this spot: the shop doors, the house gates with the large polished stones outside on which the children played, the men, their glances and their greetings.

He drank a cup of rakiya, but forgot about the food. The smoke was turning purple, and rings hovered in the air a long time and slowly grew thinner. In the twilight all things seem to retain their shape longer. And Mihailo inhaled the smoke and the air, the Vishegrad air, looked at the houses, the sharp peaks of the mountains and the glades, to all of which he had been linked for many years now. As he was thinking, the peaks disappeared and were enveloped in the dark blue glow which precedes the night.

It was now six years since he had come to live among these hills and with these people. Here he had once again found his place among men. Here he had extended his roots, here his life resumed. How he hated to change his shape and break his rhythm once again.

He took a few puffs on a cigarette, and the smoke hovered over the town, where fires were being started in the homes. He continued to draw on his cigarette, and in his chest he felt a humming caused by the rakiya. At the horizon, near where the sun had set, the clouds were a burning red, illuminating a glade on the top of Yanyats mountain, a glade that Mihailo had never seen before. At that point, as though at a given signal, he arose and descended into town with the dark.

He went straight home. He pressed on the yard gate and felt its wooden padlock—that same worn gate that he had been pressing for years and whose peculiarities and faults he knew so well. The door to the house was half open and a fire was burning inside. Crossing the yard, he suddenly started, as though he had tripped over something. Standing by the barn was Anika's one-eyed gypsy. Embarrassed by his own bewilderment, he went over to see what she wanted. She spoke first, almost in a whisper:

"Anika wants you to come to her house tomorrow morning, as early as you can." Then she walked off, softly, almost inaudibly.

That night he put all his papers in order for his partner, Master Nikola. It was dawn by the time he had completed his preparations. Mihailo had not slept, overcome by a quiet ecstasy which had shortened the night and eradicated every reality.

Surrounded by steep, tall mountains, the sun arrives late in Vishegrad. But long before the sunrise the *kasaba* is reached by an indirect light, which seems to fall from the very center of the skies. It was in this quiet light that Mihailo crossed the yard, threw a bag over his shoulder, as he often did when going on a journey, and set out for the Meydan.

The streets were deserted and looked wider and brighter. He passed Lale's bakery, but heard no singing from it, which was unusual at this time of day. In fact, the bakery was closed; it looked lonely and dark, like an old tomb. But everything else in town seemed to be in its place.

The trail up the Meydan was deserted. The skies looked like a burning field from which the sun would soon rise. Under the eaves the doves were cooing. The doors of many houses were open and black, as if the inhabitants wanted the darkness to leave by the door.

Anika's gate, too, was wide open. High up in the steep garden above the house Yelenka was hidden in the greenery, picking string beans and singing like a cricket.

As soon as Mihailo entered the house, his eyes fell on the fireplace. Among the ashes was lying a black baker's knife, bloodstained up to the handle. It was the same knife he had so often seen in Lale's hands while talking to him at the bakery.

Astonished, confused, as if it were one strange dream within another, Mihailo walked slowly to the door of Anika's room, opened it without hesitation, and stood there. It was a small, neat room, covered with rugs. Two cushions from the *minderluk* were out of place. Anika's body lay on the floor. She was dressed; her vest and shirt were pierced between the breasts, and she looked as though she had died quietly, without the tortures of death. She looked even bigger than usual, stretched out on the floor, her back on the mattress and her head on the pillows against the wall. There was a flower in her hair. No blood was to be seen anywhere.

Cold with fear, Mihailo raised his hand to cross himself, but paused and with the same raised hand shut the door to Anika's room. As he was leaving, he looked once again at the bloodstained knife in the ashes, which lay there in the stillness as things do that have been dead for centuries. He turned around and, with a deep shudder, picked up the knife, wiped it off first in the ashes and then against the wooden frame of the hearth, and tucked it under his belt, next to the big knife he himself had taken with him that morning.

Outside, the sun was rising and Yelenka was singing high up in the garden. The fountain was bubbling loudly. The crazy Nazif had already seated himself for the day on a low bench beneath the window, arranging heaps of sugar around him, mumbling cheerfully. He did not even look up at Mihailo as he passed him, walking fast toward the brook over which the shadows of the morning still hovered.

Anika's death changed Vishegrad, as it had to. The speed with which everything was restored to the old rhythm was indeed almost hard to believe. No one was curious to know where the woman had come from, why she had lived, and what she had wanted. She was harmful and dangerous, and now she was dead, buried, and forgotten. The *kasaba*, which had been momentarily deranged, could again sleep peacefully, walk freely, and breathe regularly. If a similar blight should occur—and it will at some point—the *kasaba* will again resist it, succumb to it, struggle against it, break it, bury it, and forget it.

Hedo Salko conducted an inquiry into the murder. Yelenka, Saveta, and the gypsy were questioned and beaten, needlessly of course, since they were all telling the truth anyway.

As it turned out, Anika had wanted to be left alone that morning. She had given the house a thorough cleaning, and had barred everyone from it; she sent both the gypsy and Saveta to Vuchine to call on a certain woman (a trip of several hours) and ordered Yelenka up into the garden to pick string beans, telling her not to return until she was called.

The gypsy revealed that on the same evening that she had delivered Anika's invitation to Mihailo, she had called on Lale and given him the same message:

"Anika wants you to come for sure, tomorrow morning, as early as you can."

Lale had given her no reply.

Why had Anika asked her brother, whom she had not seen in such a long time, to visit her on the very morning for which she had asked Mihailo? Was this an accident, or had she been preparing a trap and a surprise? And which one of the two killed Anika? The gypsy could explain nothing, and neither could Yelenka or Saveta, for Anika talked rarely to them, and certainly never revealed her plans.

Yelenka could only report that from the hill she had kept a close eye on those who came and went, and that she had

127

seen Lale enter first and that sometime later she saw him run out of the house. This did not surprise her, for she knew that Lale was a little mad. But then Mihailo entered; he stayed inside even more briefly and left the house with a firm stride. Although she was very curious to find out what had brought Lale, with whom Anika was feuding, and what business she could have had with Mihailo, of whom she had seen nothing of late, Yelenka did not have the courage to leave the garden until she was called. But she ran down when she heard the wailing of an old woman who had come across Anika's body accidentally while offering cloth for sale from house to house.

Peasants said they had seen Lale above Dobrun, on the road to Uzhitse, while it was generally known that Mihailo had left in the opposite direction, along the Sarajevo road. The knife with which Anika had been killed was never found.

Everything was unclear, confused, and seemingly beyond explanation. Hedo Salko welcomed the confusion, because it meant that he could bring to an end an inquiry that could reveal nothing, corroborate nothing, and that, if the truth be known, no one was in need of, and no one had asked for.

The Kaymekam spent two or three weeks at Plevlye with his relatives, and later returned to Vishegrad and went on living as he had always done, for his own pleasure and for the pleasure of others. It is true that, sitting in his garden, smoking his narghile and gazing down at the fast river Drina, he sometimes thought of the Christian woman from the Meydan. "Miraculous! That nothing should be left of so much beauty!" This was, at any rate, the theme of his meditation. But he did not believe that there was anyone in the *kasaba* with whom it would be worth discussing these things.

And the rest of the town was rapidly recovering and taking on its customary appearance. The women were more cheerful, the men more tranquil.

Master Petar Filipovats' son made peace with his father. He held his head lower, suddenly grew heavier, sprouted a thin, long mustache, bent his legs at the knees, and so tottered around the town. After Christmas they will marry him off.

Master Petar was the only one among the men of the *kasaba* who sat ill-tempered and grim in his shop, just as before. He felt deep sorrow for Mihailo, an odd young man who must have kept hidden some great torment. And when the *charshiya* men said how lucky it was that the *kasaba* was rid of Anika, he only waved his hand:

"That one will poison us even in her death, and it will last for a hundred years. Mark my word, her poison will be in us for a hundred years."

But he was the only one who spoke in this manner.

Even at the home of the Dobrun priest things took a turn for the better. After Anika's death, Yaksha had started to cross into Serbia, but on his way he learned that his father was on his deathbed. Suddenly he changed his mind. Arriving in Dobrun at night, he went straight into his father's room, kissed his hand, and was given forgiveness and the blessing. His father sent him immediately to Trnavtsi, where he was to wait until the storm had blown over. Shortly afterward the priest was well enough to ride into Vishegrad. There he found out that the Kaymekam had no intention of persecuting Yaksha. Hedo, for his part, pretended he did not know who had taken a shot at the Kaymekam. Everything was forgotten as if by secret agreement, and everything was settling itself as though by a miracle.

Yaksha was married the following summer, and his father lived to see him ordained and installed as his successor in the Dobrun parish.

Lale's bakery and Krnoyelats' house have been taken over by the municipality and are rented out. Other people live and work there now. Few even remember the children of Anja Vidinka. And Mihailo, too, is being forgotten. Only his former master and partner, Nikola Subotich, thinks of him. Having lost Mihailo, he found it necessary to settle permanently in Vishegrad, for there was no one to replace him in his shop. He travels less and gambles less. It seems that illness was gnawing at him anyway. Now he chats with Master Petar Filipovats, who comes often to see him in the early evening, after the heat has subsided. In a large handsome yard, they spread out a rush mat along the boxwood plants above the fountain. Drinking rakiya, they often talk of Mihailo.

"The man fell as though into muddy waters," says Master Nikola in his deep, hoarse voice, "and if he were my own son, it seems to me, I could not feel more sorrow."

And he blesses a hundred times the salt and the bread which he and Mihailo had eaten together. An immovable spark glitters in a corner of his eye, a tear that has never rolled down, but has sparkled every time the talk moves on to Mihailo, as though it were always the same tear.

· Zeko ·

SEVERAL YEARS AFTER THE FIRST WORLD WAR AN APARTMENT house was put up on one of those steep streets that connect Sarajevska with Kneza Milosha Boulevard. It was a handsome five-story structure which, with its high mansard roof, appeared to be a six-story building in the eyes of envious neighbors. While its facilities would not have completely justified the term "modern," it had been built well and kept well, white and neat as it was from its foundations to its roof. By its very appearance it turned away tenants with lots of children and modest incomes.

The owner of the house . . . Or perhaps not, it would be very difficult to tell who the real owner of the house was, for it is a complex legal question, further complicated by other questions, such as morals, marriage, youthful illusions, and the belated remorse of prewar Belgrade life. We are not going to clear up this difficulty here. The undisputed ruler of this house was Madame Margarita Katanich, generally known as Cobra. She let the flats, collected rents, negotiated disputes with the tenants, paid taxes, and answered to the authorities. She was for all intents and purposes the superintendent of the building as well, for that beardless *hausmeister* from the basement, who came from Bachka, and who looked like a chicken which just missed having its throat cut, was only a hireling in the hands of Madame Margarita. As a matter of fact, everything else was also in those powerful hands.

Madame Margarita lived with her husband and son on the ground floor of the building, in a large six-room flat. But before we go on about the husband and the son, a little more at least should be known about Madame Margarita. She was a woman who was approaching her fifties, weighed one hundred and ninety-eight pounds, was shortish, completely gray, with a high imperial hair style which was not neat, even on Christmas Day. She was full of a curious and aggressive energy which made her whole body twitch and hop. This was the essence of her personality. It is true, she had a pair of elephant-like legs that moved with difficulty, but from her legs upward, her person became increasingly lively and active. This bustle reached its peak in her pale, fattened face, on which, like a dark wavy line, sat her large mouth with its thirty-two false teeth and one hundred and twenty words per minute. And finally, she had two big round eyes, with black pupils spreading slightly into the whites; greedy, mistrustful, deadly eyes in which was concentrated all her strength and attention, generated by this large body for purposes of defense and attack.

Overweight, ailing with a half-dozen real and imaginary illnesses, Madame Margarita was nevertheless in all places at all times of the day. In her spacious flat, with its circularly placed rooms, she moved like an enormous spider, casting glances alternately at the street, the garden, and the main corridor. In this way she saw everything, questioned everyone, ordered everyone around. But all this was not enough. Her will to command, restrain, tame, and crush was so relentless that a regiment of soldiers would have proven insignificant in the face of such energy. And since fate had given her only a small circle over which to exercise her power, those who were in that circle—her husband and son, and the tenants of the building—had to endure all the stress produced by her energy and her furious will to command.

Life gave this woman a husband totally different from herself, a quiet, smallish man, about whom everything was tame and polished—his movements, his clothing, his speech, and his look. To be precise, he was given to her by a friend of her father's, a manufacturer, in whose house she had lived for three years before the war, which meant, in the vocabulary of her generation, before 1914. In his confused will, the manufacturer had left her, in addition to other things, this hand-

134

some house for "pleasure and enjoyment." It was to this powerful, steel-like body of the young woman Margarita, and that strange face of hers with eyes that never smiled, that this tame little man, who was to become her husband, was drawn.

Although born in Panchevo, he was in fact a Belgradian; he was only two years old when his father, a modest music teacher, moved the family to Belgrade and settled there permanently. His mother died early, and he was brought up and educated by his father, who was reserved and taciturn to the point of dumbness.

Margarita's husband was a calligrapher by profession, employed in the Office of Royal Orders. He also worked on documents for other institutes and private organizations, for such handwriting and such mastery could not be found in all of Belgrade. Although he had a good masculine name, Isidor, his wife nicknamed him Zeko (that is, Bunny), and it was by this name that he was known among both his family and his friends. Even his own son called him Zeko, rather than "Dad," and had done so since he had learned to talk. And everyone, everywhere and forever, called him: Zeko, Zekane, Zechko!

This sedate, always clean-shaven man—moist-eyed, carefully and neatly dressed at all times, full of kindness and goodness—had been pulling this dragon of a wife along for some twenty years (like pulling a galley along the dry sand, said a Bosnian, their tenant). For the irresistible and unhealthy passion of his youth—to possess this pale, athletic manufacturer's stepdaughter—he was paying with a servitude to which, even today, he could see no end.

This couple had only one child, a son, who was born in 1915, in the first months of their marriage, under the difficult conditions of war. Now a tall, strong fellow in his early twenties, he had fair, curly hair, and was a well-known athlete, local tennis champion, member of numerous athletic councils and committees, a spoiled coxcomb and idler, with his mother's arrogance, but with some sort of animal indifference toward everything, and with good looks which he inherited from God knows whom. His name was Mihailo. His mother called him Michel, his friends nicknamed him Tigar (that is, Tiger), and it was by this name that he was known to Belgrade society and to the sports public. And indeed, his eyes, with their yellowish overtones, matched the nickname; not unlike his mother, who before she had gained so much weight resembled, in her eyes and in her occasional unexpectedly swift movements, a great tropical snake.

This handsome and egocentric fellow, with no specific occupation or function in society, no moral values, and not a single trace of "human sensibility," as his father would put it, was the only living person who could resist the will of Madame Margarita, squeeze the last savings out of her. She would scream at him, too, and scorn him, and explode at him because of his wild spending habits and constant idling, but she could refuse him nothing. In the end she forgave him everything.

And, anyway, whatever went on in this house went on between the mother and the son. They simply bypassed the father, overruled him in all matters. On the verge of saying something, Zeko would refrain, for even to him his thoughts seemed somehow useless, stupid, insignificant. His salary, which he gave to the household almost in full, was not, however, insignificant, but this did not enhance his esteem. And whenever he was forced to ask Margarita for some of his own money, he did so with embarrassment, fearing that she might refuse him.

That was how this family, composed of Zeko, Cobra, and Tigar, appeared in the eyes of the tenants of the six-story building. They called them the "menagerie," and every new tenant accepted this term along with the keys to the flat and Margarita's numerous and relentless conditions. But in no family is life either as complex or as simple as neighbors see it or like to describe it. Under somewhat altered circumstances both the people and the relationships among them appear in a different light, often quite contrary to the light in which we are accustomed to seeing them.

Like many people who pass us in the street, Isidor Katanich was better and unhappier than his appearance would suggest. Yes, unhappier, even though his appearance was, as we have said, quite unhappy. As a matter of fact, he was one of those people whose life, the faster it approached its end, the less it resembled its beginning.

He had been a gifted child with intelligent eyes and full lips, endowed with a good memory and an alto singing voice which his teacher liked to describe as "divine." In high school he was one of those rare boys liked by both his friends and his teachers. He contributed to the student literary group both verse and prose, which were serious and promising, and at the same time played the piano well and was even more skilled at drawing. In fact, it was in painting that his greatest talent lay. However, this was the year 1908, the year of Austrian annexation of Bosnia and Herzegovina and of troubles that never slackened, unsettling all of Belgrade, particularly the life of the students. It broke into the life of this gifted boy at the crucial time when all these many talents might have been refined and resolved. He followed the majority of the young men of the day who preferred boisterous conversations and idle walks to activity and thought, and who could somehow never say enough or express themselves clearly. But he did matriculate, and it was then that he began to feel an inner emptiness, which was in strange and painful contrast to the bustling, rich life around him. It seemed to him as though all those talents,

137

for painting, poetry, and music, got tangled inside of him like water sinews in the earth, and, thus mixed, they all vanished later, through an invisible crack. His pencil and India-ink drawings were recognized not only among his school friends, who praised him in the student paper as a "young lithographer with a light touch and a fine line," but in professional circles as well. But as days went by, this "fine line" became less clear and less intelligible to him, and he became convinced that they were all mistaken in praising his drawings, as his onetime music teacher had been mistaken in praising his musical talents. And when the question of further studies came up, his father, disillusioned and mistrustful of everything connected with the arts, did not have much trouble in breaking him and forcing him to study law. The young man did everything as though in a dream, as though it had nothing to do with his own destiny and his own life. With no faith in himself and no understanding of the world around him, he enrolled in law school, simply and irresponsibly, as though joining the Foreign Legion.

He had hardly begun his studies when, in the autumn of 1912, the First Balkan War broke out. Suddenly Isidor Katanich's inner emptiness vanished. He went to war. There he was again inspired by a universal enthusiasm, and carried away by a belief in the justice of the cause for which they were fighting. His youth and his enthusiasm could not, however, conceal the ugly details of the war, which induced him to think and question. He saw little action, for he was sick much of the time with typhus. He returned to Belgrade thin and completely bald. He stayed at home while his hair slowly grew back; at first it was thin and soft, as on a newborn child. With each day of recovery, he felt a certain joy of life, a solemn and modest feeling of gratitude for all that was, for even the most insignificant trifles in the life that lay before him.

This mood persisted a long time and forestalled a more serious consideration of wars and victories. It was while he was in this frame of mind that he met Margarita. And from that time on, everything he did and everything he thought was related to her. Love seized him like an illness and in it lay all the passion that he had been unable to express in poetry, music, and painting.

In the autumn of 1913 he entered the Office of Royal Orders, intending to take his final law examinations at the University the following year. His job was, in fact, calligraphy; he lettered names in the blank spaces on charters that accompanied medals. He drew letters that were as thin as cobwebs, and initials finely colored, to the delight of both colonels and court adjutants.

"You can hardly see this man, but he's there, he's there. . . ."

Officers said this, pausing briefly on their way through the room, robust as they were, fresh from the war, whip in hand, new medals on their chests, secure in their movements, smiling above the red collars of their unbuttoned overcoats.

And Zeko went on drawing and writing out the scrolls on the charters as if playing a game, dreamily following the delicate lines of his pen and never for a moment believing that this could become the sole occupation of any man or the source of an income. Even so, it had become just that in his case.

In April, Margarita finally accepted him, after hesitating for a long time. The gray-haired manufacturer gave her a decent dowry and a fatherly blessing, but Isidor Katanich did not care much for either. He kissed the manufacturer's hand, but then, in those days, he would have kissed the whole world in the same way.

Then that type of situation arose of which people speak little, but from which they suffer most. At the very beginning, their marriage revealed itself for what it really was: a horrible illusion on the one hand, and a horrible deceit on the other.

But something else happened, to which Zeko had never given a thought: the War of 1914.

With his generation he was once again mobilized.

During the three years of exile, Zeko passed through Taranto, Corfu, and Toulon, a tiny, unheeded man in stormy and weird times. He tried hard to get in touch with his wife in Belgrade, but it was in vain. His father wrote to him only once, but, strangely enough, mentioned neither Zeko's wife nor their child. When he sought an explanation, he received no reply, but instead a letter came from his father's neighbors, whom his family did not know well, informing him that the old Katanich had died, alone and taciturn, as he had lived. It was not until the summer of 1918 that Zeko heard from his wife and gathered from several tearful and unintelligible words that "the son Mihailo sends kisses and hugs to his daddy."

Upon his return to Belgrade in January of 1919, Zeko found a wreck of the onetime Margarita, and with her a strong, fair-haired, four-year-old boy. Even at a time such as this, when so many extraordinary and unbelievable things take place, Zeko found this change too painful to accept. It was not merely a matter of aging and physical change, but she looked disjointed and loose, and had acquired sharp and swift movements and some sort of a dangerous and boisterous verbosity.

This was the woman he found instead of the girl Margarita, and with her he found Margarita's story, one of those occupation tales in which sad truths and poor lies are inextricably mixed. Having been husbandless, Margarita had had a hard time. To her horror she had realized that she was pregnant. At the time, the old manufacturer had been temporarily interned by the Austrians. Alone in deserted Belgrade, she went across the Sava to Zemun to stay with a cousin, and there gave birth to a child who, she thought, would grow up fatherless, for she had not heard from her husband for a long time. Not long afterward, the manufacturer was fortunately released, and thanks to him she remained alive, together with the child. Almost a year later she moved back to Belgrade and finally managed to get news from her husband.

All this was related by Margarita, along with a number of secondary stories and various plans as to how they were going to live now that the war was over.

It was also true that other news of Margarita's war years had reached Zeko. His Panchevo cousins, two women of advanced years, presented Margarita's wartime story in a somewhat different light. According to them, her behavior during the occupation "was not such as would become the reputation of our family." They dropped hints about an Austrian supply officer in Zemun, and questioned the exact paternity of the child who had been baptized only in June of 1915, and was subsequently entered in the book of births for January of the same year. Had old Katanich been alive, he might possibly have provided more reliable information, but then, he never said much.

Margarita reacted fiercely to the Panchevo stories, but without embarrassment, as though enjoying the struggle. She claimed that she was a genuine martyr, that the child was born in the month of January, which she could prove in black and white, but that for months she had hovered between life and death, and that at the time no one knew what was going on anyway, and therefore the child had been baptized only in June. Most frequently she defended herself by making similar or worse charges against the Panchevo spinsters.

141

And Zeko stood between these violent opposing waves which crashed against him, taking away that little bit of breath and clear vision still left him. And there were many other waves beating at him, and from different sides and from different sources. Everything around him was changed, turbulent, shattered, all of it confusing to a man who had come back already confused by the great world; refugee life had diminished and muddled the horizons before him and deprived him of the capacity to judge.

Had Zeko possessed more pride and determination, he could have reached the truth and found confirmation from other sources for the charges of the Panchevo cousins. But this was a time of fatigue and of the acceptance of half-truths, a time in which the passion for truth, which is the best expression of life energy in a man and a special form of self-respect, frequently fades in men of Zeko's stock.

At first it seemed to him inconceivable that this woman was his wife and this place his home, that he was to settle here, eat and drink here, and live here for the rest of his life. However, that was exactly what happened. The old manufacturer provided some relief. He seemed to have emerged from the war unchanged: calm, impassive, and as if smiling compassionately from his business and financial heights.

But Zeko was even closer to Margarita's sister, Maria. Before the war, Maria had been a timid little girl; now she seemed to have developed considerably, not so much physically, but in her behavior and manner. She was a cheerful young woman with dark, lustrous eyes in her pallid face, above which stood out a shock of black hair, always shiny with moisture. Quiet and smiling, full of good will and some youthful energy, she was different from her sister in every way. She lived with them during the first year after the war, a most trying and most critical year, and thanks to the warm friendship with this girl, Zeko found something resembling happiness in family life.

Shortly after he arrived, Zeko returned to his old job at the Office of Royal Orders. Everything there was bigger now, the pay, the title, the job. Everything was growing and expanding, just as Belgrade itself was growing and expanding, in leaps and bounds, violently and without order.

Two years later, the old manufacturer died and, among other things, left to Margarita, for use during her lifetime, the five-story apartment house, which was then under construction. One of the engineers on the job took a fancy to Maria, and immediately asked her to marry him.

He was a simple, modest fellow from Bachka, good-natured to the point of weakness, a giant of a man, only "two centimeters short of two meters," but who made up for these two centimeters by the width of his shoulders, the force of his stride, and the rough magnitude of his broad worker's hands. Not exceptionally able, he had a limited interest in the world. His name was Yovan Doroshki; they all called him Dorosh.

With genuine sorrow, and at the same time with gladness, Zeko saw Maria off when she moved with her husband to Shabats, leaving him alone, caught between Margarita and the boy, whose paternity was still unclear to him.

Having freed herself of the unpleasant aftertaste of the war, having acquired by inheritance a large building which brought in a good income, and having increased her capital by skillful manipulations and by good connections, Margarita began spreading and gaining weight, as well as more courage and aggressiveness, until she assumed her final shape and developed into the woman known to the whole building and the neighborhood as Cobra.

And at her side her boy was growing and developing, evincing strange coldness and indifference to the whole world, including his parents, friends, and learning. He grew into a football player, then into a tennis champion, and finally into a perfect example of a contemporary Belgrade *bon vivant*.

In the course of these twenty years, Belgrade developed into a large and extraordinary city, and in Zeko's house, a "menagerie" was created, while he himself assumed that strange attitude toward the family and society which we mentioned earlier.

Commenting on life of those years is no easy matter, particularly when talking about a fellow like Zeko, who contributed so little to life and received so little from it. There were many such people in Belgrade in those days, unaware of the uselessness of a life lacking in order and dignity. Most of them never experienced a crisis or a breakdown; but Isidor Katanich did.

Submissive by nature, Zeko would have tolerated this state of affairs for who knows how long. But as the years went by, Margarita's ability to control both herself and her son's bad impulses dwindled considerably. Zeko had many ideas, came up with all sorts of unfeasible solutions and impossible ways out. He thought of abandoning everything, of living alone somewhere on the outskirts of the city, of running away into the world, of provoking a scandal and breaking up the marriage. He toyed with such ideas, and then disposed of them, wondering all along what made such a family possible, in which neither the mother nor the son showed a single decent human characteristic. At any rate, not on the side that was turned to him.

His position in the office was not much better. For Zeko was one of those people whose status at home determines their place outside of it. While exploiting his professional skills, they ignored him as a man. "No one heeds this Mr. Zeko, but no one," the old attendant at the Office of Royal Orders would say with wonderment and pity. And when we in this city say that someone is not heeded, it frequently means that he is trampled on by everybody.

The situation was the same outside of his office. Humiliated and isolated in his own home, he searched for something, anyone, anything to which he could attach himself. He went to the coffeehouses, where his colleagues met regularly at special tables. But he did not belong there either; he was tormented by the realization that they never addressed him, either in jest or in seriousness, that he himself had nothing to say, and what he did say fell without an echo. In his loneliness, he recalled the time when he used to paint; even his verses came to mind, everything, including his "divine alto," but this world of art had been closed to him for a long while; he was rejected by it as he had been rejected by everything else.

The only thing left to him of his youth was his reading habit. But even his reading had been, for a long time now, confused and accidental. Like many people who read books primarily in search of comfort and oblivion, he grew selective, and only with difficulty found literature that could remove him from his real life.

Thus, even this last door appeared to be closing in his face.

· I ·

Sometime around the year 1930, Zeko's miserable position reached its lowest ebb. Margarita was then at the peak of her power. Her son, the strong, long-legged Tigar, had shown the first signs of a premature manhood and his growing arrogance made an already painful life even more difficult. At that time Zeko weighed only one hundred and ten pounds. His eyes filled with tears during every conversation, his hands trembled. His nervousness was reflected in his calligraphy, too. He ran away from society and was afraid of work. Margarita and Tigar were simply squeezing him out of life. Zeko thought of suicide.

This black thought, which was infecting the prosperous Belgrade of the thirties, became Zeko's constant companion and his only solace. Whatever was healthy and sensible in him opposed the very idea of suicide and decidedly condemned it, but his weakness and deep depression were stronger and he felt firmly drawn to it. The sense of order and human dignity, which was indestructible within this man, compelled him to search for a decent way of carrying out his plan for a voluntary departure from this world. Without a scandal and ugly ostentation, he thought to himself in his derangement.

Engrossed in his preoccupation with the end of life, he roamed the railway tracks along the bank of the river Sava, searching for the most suitable and the least ostentatious way of dying. He found not death but the river, and the strange life on it.

One day in May, walking along that disorderly bank, dotted with irregularly scattered houses, shacks, barges, and towboats, persecuted by the most gloomy thoughts, he found an old acquaintance sitting on a worn, overturned pontoon. His name was Mika Jorjevich, by rank army captain, first class, retired. Zeko had known him in the war of 1912 as a young second lieutenant, and then had met him again at Toulon in 1915. He had seen him once or twice since the end of the war, but knew only that he had left the army for some unknown reason. Now he found him shirtless and sunburned, fishing in the Sava. He sat down next to him and they started talking.

Captain Mika was a short, robust fellow with a round head, always clean-shaven, and with dark eyes which had a peculiar luster to them. As an active army captain, first class, and a sixty-per-cent invalid, he had been put on the retired list almost immediately after the war. Now he lived in a small room, somewhere in Senyak.

"To be exact, my dear fellow, I live on the Sava, with this water and these people."

Zeko, who had, until then, been engrossed in his own thoughts and had noticed nothing, looked around a little more carefully. And, indeed, the bank was bustling with people—bathers, workers, fishermen, loafers, men of uncertain calling and origin.

Zeko came by again the next day and found Captain Mika in the same benevolent mood, rooted to the same spot like a statue.

"I live like a pasha, brother," Captain Mika was saying to him, pronouncing the word "pasha" mockingly and making a grand gesture with his hand. "No one bothers me. No matter what the weather, you will find me here on the Sava, fishing, which brings no harm to the fish nor any profit to me, and so it goes. But one gets mixed up with these people, the water-front people. I know every barge, every beach, every raft, every shack and café, along this bank. In one place I have my lunch, in another I play a game of cards, in still another I take a nap. In the evening, we have some fish and with it a little wine. I wouldn't have it any other way. Every year I spend seven or eight months like this. When the autumn comes, I go to my village for a while. Good life there, too. In the spring I come back to Belgrade and lie down on this Sava, and so it goes until the autumn."

Thus Captain Mika talked, somehow too loudly and with too many details, overly stressing his carefree life and his idleness, but Zeko did not notice this, so pleased was he to have found a man who was willing to talk to him kindly and who spoke of life so cheerfully. He was not clear as to what sort of a life it was, nor what was so compelling about the Sava. But so far as he could gather, he was confronted by a healthy and seemingly contented man. He thought instantly of his own life and of the idea that had brought him here. And Captain Mika, as though sensing it, took him by the shoulders and shook him.

"And you, brother, you have lost much too much weight. True, you've never been husky, but you've shrunk in half since I last saw you," Captain Mika said to him in a loud voice. (It was as though he could not speak other than in a loud voice.)

Zeko felt his throat tightening, his eyes filling with tears, and for the first time had an urge to talk freely about his life, but his inborn shyness was stronger and he only mumbled a few words:

"You know how it is . . . work . . . worries. Each one of us . . ."

"Don't give me that, brother, that talk about 'each one of us', as if you were one of *them;* let them go where they have a mind to, and you get some kind of a stick with several fish-hooks, and take off that stiff collar and all those rags, and sit here next to me—or, rather, not next to me, but a little farther up, because you will chase all my fish like other fools. Sit here, I tell you, and you'll see what this sun and this water will do for you within a week. A different man! And what a man, too! A wise man today lives only on the Sava; listen to what I say! And that, there . . ." and here he pointed to that curious gray, pale-greenish heap of houses that rose one above

148

the other to form the center of Belgrade, but said nothing and only spat in the water.

Zeko returned to the river, not so much out of obedience to Captain Mika, who always seemed to him a bit odd, but because everything inside of him was irresistibly drawn to the river. For as he sat on the raft next to Mika that day he could no longer separate himself from this strange passion—the Sava.

Needless to say, Margarita attacked him.

"What's the matter with you? You must be quite mad to associate with fishermen in your old age," hissed Margarita, who hated everyone's pleasures. "Where did you ever hear of respectable men going down to the Sava among those gamblers and hooligans."

How could she always find an ugly side to everything and cover everyone with abuse? Where does she get it? thought Zeko. But he had puzzled over this thought for years and could never come up with an answer. There was quarreling about buying the fishing equipment and the clothing in which he would go to the Sava. She felt instinctively that Zeko had found some sort of pleasure of his own which she could not spoil or alter, and that he was getting out from under her control. That made her furious. There was a great deal of railing and slapping of the fat hips, a lot of ugly words, but Zeko was, surprisingly enough, unyielding and patient, hanging on to his pleasure, like a man who is prepared to endure everything for his great and only decision.

Even so, Zeko might ultimately have given way if she had not suddenly and inexplicably given way herself. She went on abusing both him and the Sava, but her resistance was no longer serious. It became obvious that she had discovered some advantage in this arrangement, although no one knew what it was. For Margarita was the type of woman who will rail and thunder, turn heaven and earth to eliminate something that is opposed to her will and interests, but who will remain silent and not display the least sign of pleasure when a situation has evolved to her advantage.

The main thing was that Zeko had become a man from the Sava. He received his first lessons in the art of fishing from Captain Mika. They were very meager lessons. An eccentric in all things, the Captain introduced the subject to his student with a speech which, more often than not, touched on everything but the matter at hand:

"I am not a pedagogue, and you'll never learn how to fish. As though the fish were important! Sit here, look at the water, and 'think your thoughts.'" (He said this in Russian, for he liked to use mutilated remnants of the Russian he had been taught some time ago at the Military Academy.) "And when you've had enough, jump into the water, freshen up, and then you can start again."

Embarrassed, Zeko admitted that he did not know how to swim.

"Eh," said Captain Mika gently, without lifting his eyes from the fishing rod, "you are some fellow! You've finished schools and learned all sorts of trifles, but you don't know how to swim. That's your learning for you! The main things you haven't learned. And now if someone threw you into the water, you would sink like a crowbar, together with your intelligence and learning."

But that did not matter. Zeko was there on the Sava, sunburned, more secure in his speech and his movements, and free of the horrible thought that had brought him to the water front some time ago.

It is true the situation at home was no better. But this burden was easier to bear now, for between April and November there was the other world on the Sava.

During the first summer on the Sava, Zeko made a number of friends, but it would be some time before he could really penetrate this distinct and strange world. At first he went everywhere accompanied by Captain Mika.

"Captain Mika has an adjutant," the men by the Sava were saying.

Many in Belgrade hardly suspected the existence of this river-front community, which stretched all the way from the railway bridge to Chukaritsa. On this steep, swampy, often scorched embankment, alternately bare and overgrown, a whole nation is born, exists, and dies on water.

This community, which swarms over the Sava bank during its season of six to seven months, was divided into two groups. The larger group was composed of citizens of Belgrade—bathers, fishermen, rowers; they came here for sport, for women, for recreation, or simply in order to shed their clothes, and, in so doing, shed whatever was most oppressive in their city lives. The other group was comprised of the permanent or seasonal inhabitants: fishermen, boatmen, small tradesmen—mostly blacksmiths, carpenters, cart drivers—people who leased the rafts and bathhouses and managed the small cafés along the river, cafés haphazardly put together, patched and glued, leaning to one side. And added to this were loafers of various occupations and idlers with none.

A strange collection—these people. There were workers among them and regular "family" men, and modest and quiet bachelors, and there were professional smugglers and gamblers, singers, gigolos, and spongers; and there were those who drank nothing and those you never saw sober; there were brawlers and bullies, and others as sweet-natured as sheep. But they all had one common trait: the city had expelled them all, by a curious and inconspicuous process of selection, here to the Sava bank. Each one had an unfinished account to

151

settle with life. As a group they were somehow more genial and more interesting and possibly better and more innocent than similar people at the other end of Belgrade. This was perhaps because they lived on the water, which washes away all things, and because they lived under the pure light of the sun, as in a tropical region. They came to life only during the "season." (Even the most illiterate along the Sava were acquainted with this word of foreign origin.) During the winter this section of the city disappeared from the maps of the capital, and most of the people scattered or crept back into their little houses.

Even work was different on the Sava, in impact, shape, and duration. And so was vice. For here everything took place under the sun of the season, on the tremulous and soft surface of the running water, on the fickle sand and under the lively willow thickets of the river islands; everything happened in the open.

When Zeko compared the Sava people to Margarita and her friends, the comparison invariably favored the river. His wife sometimes sneered at his association with "vagabonds and drunkards," but Zeko would not respond; he thought of his acquaintances, who would, it was true, clear their throats into the water and laugh at one another and forget to pay their debts and curse often and in a big way, but who, on the other hand, did not have such fierce movements, or such base and ignoble thoughts. True, they, too, could be mean and vicious, depending on how life guided and treated them, but they also had unexpected fits of kindness and generosity without design or calculation.

Year after year Zeko went to the Sava, at first with Captain Mika, and later alone, and he got to know these people and their way of life. It was not a constant, tight society, but fluid and restless like the river. Each year there were new arrivals, each year some disappeared to wherever people disappear, into the world in search of work, to the cemetery, or to jail. They spoke kindly of those who were no longer with them, and viewed the new ones with distrust, at least during the first season.

Apart from several modern beaches at Shest Topola, where thousands thronged on hot summer days, the center of this part of the river bank was a bathhouse with no name, made of boards painted green; nearby, protruding into the river, there was a low, slightly tilted little café overgrown with ivy and shaded by an enormous acacia tree. This was Captain Mika's "headquarters" and the starting point for Zeko's movements along the bank.

Its manager was Stanko Neshich, a husky, tall man with thin legs and a large belly, hairy chest, and strong arms, a solid head with an unshaven face and cheerful, impudent eyes. Everyone called him Master Stanko, although no one knew why. His wife and daughter alternated at the cashier's desk, a servant looked after the cabins, and he himself wandered about the river bank, allegedly at work. During the season Master Stanko was always dressed in the same way. His outfit consisted of rather wide, long black bathing trunks, which looked like bloomers, and a rimless straw hat that resembled a fez. Add to this a permanent cigarette. That was all. Thus equipped, he would pass among the rafts, houses, little cafés, and other bathing places along the bank, approach groups of bathers lunching under the trees, holler and bargain with fishermen who passed by in their boats.

He was the unelected and unofficial but generally recognized head of this small municipality by the river; as such he was the arbiter of disputes and counselor to all.

Stanko's business consisted of buying old objects—boats, motors, refrigerators, stoves, wardrobes, and various other wood and steel items—which he would repair and resell. His bookkeeping was in his head, his arithmetic infallible. He never made a mistake in anything. And yet he never had any money. Were it not for that good wife of his, who, by arguing and cheating, managed to put aside a few pennies, they would not even have had that little wooden shack by the Sava. When he was in a good mood, Stanko explained this situation in the following manner:

"You all know Pero Stevchich, the millionaire? Well, he and I were expelled together from the first year of high school, and we started working together. Today he is one of the foremost contractors in Belgrade. He owns three houses. One on Grobljanska Street, six stories high. They wonder, how come? Fine. First of all, he cheats in a big way, and I pilfer in a small way. Second of all—it's no use trying to conceal it—I like to drink and to have a good time; and so: he puts up a brick and I put away a glass of beer; he a brick and I a beer; also I like wine and everything else. So it goes, day in, day out, and there you are! God helps us both, me in spending, him in saving. And yet they call me master, and they call him, if you'll forgive the expression, a stingy bastard. That's the world for you."

Stanko had a philosophy of his own, although he was not given to philosophizing. Next to the entrance of his bathhouse, there was a plaque with the following inscription:

THIS TOO WILL PASS

At first, the words had been inscribed on an ordinary piece of cardboard, but between the bathers and the weather the cardboard began falling apart, and he had a new plaque made of white enamel with black lettering. New guests would frequently ask him what the inscription meant. More often than not, Master Stanko would not reply at all but only survey the guest with his brown eyes which were devilishly small and slanting when he laughed, but became large and round when he was surprised or displeased. If not replying was rude, his replies were even ruder. One day, a thin reddish man kept asking him in a thick Czech accent what this curious inscription meant and what "purpose it served."

"To remind people that all things are transitory," said Master Stanko peevishly.

"Every intelligent man knows that."

"Every intelligent man knows it, but this is for the fools who keep asking questions."

Stanko's immediate neighbor was Naum, a café owner, a stout, ruddy Macedonian, immersed in his work and not much for talk. He had a little shack made of different-colored boards, and in front of it there grew velvety flowers and ivy. Some dozen tables were thrust in front of the café, covered with tablecloths which were immaculately white every Sunday morning. Naum was here during the season, earning a nice income, while his wife and family, whom he did not "mix with this," were in the city. Although sparing of words, he liked to boast on occasion that he had a son who was a lawyer, and a daughter who was in high school.

Another neighbor of Stanko's and a permanent resident of the river bank was Milan Stragarats, a tall, gray-haired man, with long mustaches and a sharp profile. He also spoke little, and moved with difficulty, for a long time ago (no one knew when or how) he lost his right leg and now had an artificial limb. He lived in a half-demolished little house with his tall, redheaded wife. He had been an employee of the River Transit Authority, a fisherman, a boatman, and a jack-of-all trades. Now he was making nets, repairing tools, right in front of the house, under a walnut tree much bigger than the house itself. It was said, with no evidence to support it, that

155

Milan had been an informer for the police and that it was probably in this connection that he lost his leg. He was now receiving some sort of a pension in compensation. This was not said openly, but after several rakiyas with a water-front worker or a fisherman, they would tell you:

"And Milan . . . everyone knows his game. . . ."

And if you asked exactly what it was, they would reply:

"I didn't say anything."

And with a gesture of the hand they would point somewhere in the distance, where things were neither "nice" nor "good" and of which it was not advisable to talk.

Milan was an ill-tempered, gloomy man who growled rather than talked. Although he moved with difficulty and was quiet in demeanor, everyone was afraid of him, everyone avoided conflict with him, even if, in so doing, they lost a few pennies; everyone tried to please him, including Stanko, who spoke with him somewhat more softly and carefully than with others.

It is difficult to tell precisely how this bully exercised his powers, but he behaved so calmly and at the same time so imperiously, and imposed himself so firmly, that everyone accepted his insolent attitude as inevitable. To avoid his wrath they tried not to displease him even at the price of minor surrenders, although such behavior did not earn them his gratitude, nor did this temper his contempt, which was fixed and universal.

There are such people in our midst. Not only in police headquarters, but also among small-town shopkeepers, government ministers, and in newspaper editorial offices and schools. Who has not known such men in our country, bullies and parasites, with sullen and dignified façades concealing nothing? And who is there whose pride and interests have not suffered at the hands of such people? Who is there who does

156

not carry in his soul the sting of their presumptions? Sometimes their territory is a region of the country, sometimes a regiment of soldiers or a classroom of students, sometimes only a single victim, or, in the case of this Milan, several hundred square yards of poor-man's land by the river.

It was from Milan that Zeko learned one day a few details about Captain Mika.

It was toward the evening of a hot, muggy day. Milan was sitting, as usual, on the grass under his walnut tree, and a few of the Sava people stood around him in a circle. They were drinking some Valyevo rakiya that someone had brought along for "sampling." Zeko arrived unnoticed and stood outside of the circle.

Milan emptied his tumbler, pressed his lips so that his white mustaches sprang into the air, and, obviously elaborating on some previous argument, he said sharply, not looking at the person whom he was addressing:

"What? Who? You mean Mika? He is a clown who has tried to appear half-witted all his life. He is a Communist, or, at any rate, one of their men. He was discharged from the army in 1921; they found Communist leaflets which had been typed on a machine from his office. There are no two ways about it. He was supposed to have gone to jail, but there you are, somehow or other . . . And later he received a pension. Now he lays low, and acts as though nothing had ever happened, but I wouldn't trust him."

And Milan Stragarats spit to one side.

Imperceptibly, Zeko removed himself from the gathering. He was overcome by a fear that forever lingers in the minds of city dwellers, the fear of words as such, the fear of the wonders that lie within them, the fear that precedes thought and prevents an examination of the real meaning and the true content of words.

157

From that time on he observed Captain Mika with greater care, with a feeling in which curiosity was mingled with warmth, respect with fear. What was the nature of his buffoonery? What was the substance of it all? Is this only a mask? If so, where is his face and what is he like?

One time he had a painful dream: Captain Mika and Milan Stragarats stood before him demanding his allegiance: Stragarats, gloomy, his gray bristly beard sprouting, his smile unintelligible, like a foreign language. And Mika, smiling, his legs astride, talking as he did on the day they met.

"Wise people live on the Sava . . . !"

He spoke cheerfully and simply, but with an odd wink, as though catching the eye of someone in the distance, behind Zeko's back. This gesture confused Zeko; it was unpleasant and a little insulting. Even so, he liked Mika and would have liked to communicate it to him in some way, but he could not while Stragarats was there.

And Zeko was turning and twisting something, but could in no way solve it or disentangle it, so that in the end everything became both painful and awkward and he woke up with a strong feeling of relief.

Milan's story about Captain Mika continued to haunt him for some time. But then he forgot all about it—both the story and the apprehensions it had brought him. But from time to time, as the two of them sat in front of Naum's café, blinking in the strong sun, his eyes would rest on Mika's round shaven head; and then he would realize, not quite knowing why, just how much he liked Mika. And if it involved risk, he would be willing to take it. And anyway, the risk could not be that great. The fact is that men like Stragarats are a great evil in our lives. And whenever one thinks about him one feels uneasy.

Another of Stanko's neighbors was Ivan Istranin, a carpenter, an expert boatbuilder, who lived there with his wife, Mariyeta.

This was, as Stanko put it, "a difficult case." They were both refugees from Istria. Mariyeta was older than Ivan, more experienced, and a wild woman. He was a fair-haired, slender fellow with pale-blue eyes. His appearance gave the impression of a fully grown but feeble-minded boy. He worked well and hard; on Sunday afternoons he liked to get drunk; in the morning he regularly attended the Catholic church on Krunska Street.

All through the summer Ivan repaired boats and skiffs, and built new craft. In wide linen trousers and a torn shirt, barefoot, his messy hair covered with sawdust, he and his two apprentices worked all day long but were still unable to fill their orders. Mariyeta lived a life of her own, squandered his money recklessly, changed lovers with each season, and in changing them degraded herself still further. Their marital knot was a prime topic of conversation and an object of ridicule along the water front. Master Ivan dared not lay a finger on his wife, but observed everything and endured everything. If only he could have endured it quietly and with dignity! But no, now he complained to everyone, especially to Zeko and the café owner Naum, and then again defended his wife from the neighbors' gossip. Thus this couple disturbed the peace along the bank, but also provided amusement with their constant scenes, threats, tears, oaths, stormy quarrels, and shameful reconciliations.

And one summer, Zeko's fourth on the Sava, something happened that took Master Ivan's friends by complete surprise. Early one Sunday morning, before anyone else had arrived, Ivan came to the café, ordered a few shots of rakiya, and, with his whole face in a frown, like a man in great trouble, he confided to Naum:

159

"I don't know, by God, I don't know how it is going to work out. That woman of mine is beginning to steal money. By God, Naum, I don't know. . . . It will come to no good end."

"Well, well," Naum responded, but this reserved and neutral "well" was modulated in such a manner that no one could tell whether he had said it to condemn Mariyeta or to express pity for Ivan, or whether he condemned them both and, along with them, this world, all of which is "no good, but no good."

That same day, toward evening, after lying in wait for a long time, Master Ivan surprised Mariyeta as she was opening the chest in which he kept his money, and for which she had had a special key fitted. He caught her with a hundred-dinar bill in her hand. He seized a heavy hatchet lying near an unfinished boat, and with swift, powerful carpenter's blows, began beating and hacking up this woman until he turned her into a bloody heap in the darkest corner of his spacious workshop.

Then he left, started toward Stragarats' house, where under the walnut tree a dozen men were gathered, some dressed in their Sunday best, others in their swimming trunks. Lifting his bloodstained hand high up in the air, he screamed through his tears:

"Call the police, call the police!"

With glasses in their hands, rigid with astonishment, the men watched him silently.

This was an exceptional event, even here by the water, where nothing is terribly important. The neighbors were asked to appear as witnesses before the examining magistrate, and most of the Sava people attended the trial. When they returned home, they would say of poor Ivan: "He is no man!" But they all gave evidence in his favor. And this, in addition to the skill of his Slovenian lawyer, contributed to the fact that he was sentenced to only eight years in jail.

Otherwise, the Sava people did not know of such tragedies. Women quarreled about their children, and men about some trifle in business. They quarreled at work and then made peace over a glass of rakiya. Others, again, quarreled over rakiya and made peace at work.

Only a few paces from the house of unfortunate Ivan Istranin, by the road, was the small wooden shop of Joka, the blacksmith. The shop was narrow, dark, full of smoke, sparks, and the sour smell of tempered steel.

Zeko stopped by every day to watch his friend Joka hammering the red-hot steel with all his weight, as though flinging himself at the enemy. While he worked he noticed nothing, not even the apprentice who was helping him, but only issued orders through his teeth. But as the steel assumed the desired shape under his hammer, gradually cooling and growing darker, the blacksmith would revive and begin to notice people standing around him, hear what they were saying, and even begin to answer some of the questions they asked.

A little distance from the blacksmith's shop was his house, neither bigger nor much better than the shop, full of children, one smaller than the other, each one reaching the other's ear. Milena, his tall, neat wife, kept his house and the children in order.

And when, at twilight, men sat in front of Naum's café and teased the blacksmith about his zeal and his large number of children, he only smiled with embarrassment:

"Let it be, let it be; there is never too much of that."

Down a ways from the blacksmith's, there was the workshop of the mechanic Karlo Zemunats, generally known as Dragi; this shop was also made of boards and was not much larger than Joka's smithy, but its interior was brighter and much more orderly. There was no flooring here either, only damp, uneven earth. The walls, made of fine boards, were imbued with a brown, dirty mixture of machine oil and dust. On one wall Zeko's eyes always stopped at a photograph tucked between the boards, of a woman with a child in her lap, as well as at the cheap artificial rose made of red paper below it.

Karlo's family lived in Zemun. He was an unusually reserved person, who talked only with Mika, usually in private. Such quiet and withdrawn people were not too popular along the Sava, but everyone recognized Dragi as a decent man who could, in his craft, "stand up to any engineer." Even Milan Stragarats accepted this fact, although he always referred to Karlo as a "German creep" when he was not present, and when he was, refused to honor him either with his word or his look.

The Sava settlement ended with a long series of shacks and warehouses belonging to a big fuel company. Here mounds of lignite and layers of beechwood were brought from all over Serbia and unloaded from the Sava barges.

This settlement was dominated by dust and mud, soot and loud noises. It teamed with workers, cart and truck drivers, carriers and Albanians. They were all rough, poorly dressed people, who saw everything around them in terms of possible earnings, and whose every thought, word, and movement were in accord with this quest. They were employed by warehouse owners, contractors, supervisors—strict and zealous in words, but frequently corrupt and unreliable in deed.

Each warehouse ended with two windows through which one could see the traditional pots of flowers and heads of children. These were the flats of the warehouse keepers, who still lived exactly as they had in their distant villages and provincial towns.

There were no rafts here, no greenery, nor a single point that would attract the eye. Captain Mika knew these people, frequented their homes, sat with them and joked with them. Zeko also got to know them, stood them to drinks, visited their small flats. And as time went on, they considered him, as they did Captain Mika, a Sava man.

This was where Zeko found life, the true life of most people, unknown to those who lived in closed and privileged circles of interest, consisting of regular monthly salaries, per diems and bonuses, of stipends and commissions, of lifelong pensions for every civil servant, their wives and children. It was only then that Zeko began to realize the complexities of the world of labor: strenuous, unsettled lives, full of uncertainty, where efforts invested in work were out of proportion to the rewards, barely sufficient to feed and clothe the man and his family, particularly after the necessary payments to brokers, moneylenders, real-estate operators. Nothing was either permanent or secure, no one was taken care of or protected, everything was linked to daily earnings, and all talk and conduct was therefore governed by this concern.

The difference between these two worlds was a constant topic of Zeko's thought. The only person with whom he could have discussed this matter was Captain Mika himself. While it was true that, for the most part, Mika expressed himself in unclear maxims and humorous proverbs, he did encourage Zeko to talk and listened to him carefully.

Zeko not only knew the people on the bank, but also many of those who fished on rafts and in willow thickets, passionate huntsmen, good-natured fellows, grouches, or simply eccentrics, who sat for hours with their fishing rods. He would watch the colorful and noisy heap of bathers, true sportsmen and common idlers alike, who sailed along the surface of the Sava, dispersing in all directions, in search of rest, recreation, new pleasures, or simply following fashion trends. He spent many days and many summers in observation.

Usually he traveled a little farther up the bank, to a small raft which belonged to a Belgrade transport company, deserted when the loading of goods was not in progress.

Zeko sat on the raft, which, resting on small metal barrels, constantly swayed back and forth; a steady gurgle of water was heard from under it. And at times it seemed to him that everything was moving: the river before him, the raft under him, the low island across from him which was like an enormous greenish barge, the city high up looking like a fantastic ship with the Kalemegdan fortress as the prow. He sat there, looking at the river surface, wrinkled and blue-gray under the heat of the sun, gleaming as though made of finished steel, but so silken soft that fishing boats, yawls, rowboats, kayaks glided along it noiselessly. When observed through half-closed eyes, the scene turned into a mélange of objects in constant collision with one another, but flowing past harmlessly.

Sveta, a one-eyed fisherman, arrived in an awkward, tarred boat. Zeko knew him well. He was from the other side of the river, but hardly a day went by that he did not sail along this bank. He sat on the rudder, rowing and steering with the same oar. At his feet was an outboard motor, which could be attached to the stern of the boat. A rusted propeller stuck out high. Sveta had probably found it somewhere, in somebody's shack, or in a state warehouse, and was now taking it to a mechanic in Chukaritsa, who would buy it from him for next to nothing, touch it up, and sell it to one of the numerous watersports enthusiasts. Sveta was fully dressed among hundreds of nearly naked bathers: on his head was a heavy black hat, under his jacket a waistcoat buttoned up to the last button, then cloth trousers, followed by slippers on his bare feet. He was dressed the same way on Christmas. And always black and sooty. "You, Sveta, look as though you had been dropped down a chimney," he was sometimes told, but he only blinked with his one eye, and with his black, callused hand rubbed his chin, his mind on his business, which consisted mostly of stealing and various other doubtful transactions. Stanko, who was infallible in his judgment of everything that swam, rowed, or walked on the Sava, claimed that Sveta would lift "everything that was not nailed to the heavens." It was when he was running away from someone that he had lost that right eye of his. Everyone was familiar with this fact. Stanko's servant would say to Sveta when he found him poking around the cabins in the evening: "Look out, I'm telling you; you haven't got an extra pair of eyes!" Misshapen and gloomy, Sveta was always crawling like a water insect after his prey! What a creature! There was such a curse on him that he looked dangerous and suspicious even when he had no intention of doing anything.

Sveta's boat was followed by a trail of white smoke from his short black pipe, a burning coal which he never took out of his mouth, whether lit or not. "If he didn't hold onto the pipe with his teeth, he would fall into the Sava," Stanko would comment.

Then a bright boat appeared in the narrow vision between Zeko's half-closed eyes. A man was rowing; he wore a linen hat, the skin on his arms and shoulders was red and burned by the sun. A beautiful woman in a blue bathing suit sat on the prow, with her parasol open; she must have been a Russian émigrée.

There was something sad in the effort of this elderly man, who was employing all of his strength to carry his burden. But the gloomy thought disappeared quickly, like a tuft of smoke behind Sveta.

Now his vision was blocked by a small, black ship, the *Krayina*, from whose chimney thick, black smoke belched forth like a cloud, casting its shadow on the bright surface of the water. This small but powerful ship dragged two large, loaded barges. On the roof of the second barge there was a wooden house painted white, and in the window was a flower-pot. From behind the house appeared a young, barefoot woman carrying a large metal pot full of water, which she hurled across the railing into the Sava. She was followed by a little white dog, skipping and jumping.

For a few moments the river was deserted. Only the agitated water following the barges broke the light and struck the eye.

But before the water had even calmed down, an eight-man scull, made of fine Japanese wood, came into view, narrow and almost invisible under the weight of the oarsmen in their white sweatshirts with coats of arms. The scull rhythmically thrust out long oars and glided along like a centipede. The coach sat by the rudder, steering with both hands, a megaphone attached to his neck, through which his coarse commanding voice boomed: one, two, one, two. . . . (Zeko was quickly and unpleasantly reminded of Tigar, his home, and Margarita.) Zeko disliked sportsmen; and he did not like them because he did not know them, or, rather, because he knew them only through his son and his companions.

Sport hardens a man's heart and weakens his mind, thought Zeko, and instead of manliness and fighting spirit, it develops roughness and aggressiveness, in addition to money speculation and intrigue. But what do we need such things for? We have plenty of aggressiveness. And greed.

A skiff passed, lightning-like, long and so shallow that the oarsman appeared to be sitting on water. Two long oars spread and fluttered like two wings. The man wore dark glasses; the color of his skin was brown and it was coated with oil, which made his muscular body glisten in the sun like wet bronze. He was probably some Slovenian, a businessman, thought Zeko.

Then an ordinary white rowboat came crawling, with two pairs of oars; a whole family aboard. Husband and wife were rowing. Two women were sitting on the prow and two boys were leaning over the boat, sprinkling themselves with water and then looking at their reflections in it. There was a large basket of food, from which a big watermelon was peeping, and next to it a wicker basket containing a bottle of wine. The very picture of the new times: the husband, a young man, is a parvenu, his wife a snob and a fashion addict, the two sons at high school, the mother-in-law suffering in the sun in her old age, and the sister-in-law, for whom they were trying to find a husband on the water, since all attempts on land had proved failures. They will stop somewhere at the far tip of the island, eat their lunch in the shade under the willows, and then fall asleep slapping at the mosquitoes.

Thus before Zeko's eyes every imaginable form of Belgrade life passed, curious and unusual, often absurd, but always powerful. The Sava is life, thought Zeko, and life should be organized, not accidental, irrational, and chaotic. He himself did not know how to go about it, but he visualized an order in which all those who lived and moved should be able to find their rightful place.

And Zeko deliberated: What place, for example, should be given to this Stanko, who was passing him at this very moment and covering him for an instant with his shadow. So big, full of life, shrewd, he should not live this way; he should not be moving with the sun from one shady spot to another, nor should he work at random as he does, making just barely enough to support his family, to take an occasional glass of wine and buy tobacco. Lots of things should not be done. Nor should he, Zeko, lie idly like this on a raft under the heat of the sun, and, while drowsing and half dreaming, refashion life and decide just how things should and must be.

Yet he tried to visualize an order, not the "discipline" of which our people like to talk, but a reasonable and creative order in which everyone would find approximately what he needed. And he had a new vision of how the Sava water front itself should look: all the men here working better and living more comfortably. Stanko, and Ivan Istranin, with his unfortunate Mariyeta, and Sveta, and even Milan Stragarats . . . They were all new people, with a definite place in life. All . . .

Suddenly the raft shook, breaking Zeko's thought, scattering the harmonious images in his imagination. The metal barrels sounded like giant bells, and water splashed over the boards as a fast motorboat roared into view.

Startled, Zeko followed this powerful, sleek boat with his eyes. He knew the boat, the *Arizona,* as well as its owner, a Belgian contractor and broker. Next to this young muscular fellow there were two young women, daughters of Professor Kralyevich. They were part of the same crowd to which Zeko's son Tigar belonged. Beautiful, strong young women, musically gifted, full of energy and the joy of life, they lived the senseless life of Belgrade's golden youth, pronounced Serbian words in an affected, drawn-out way, the vowels in the English manner, and the letter *r* blurred and low; they neither finished their studies nor did they get married, and they spent in one month what their fathers earned in two.

The bright powerful boat cut the water lightly, and as it advanced swiftly past Zeko he could see outstretched the brown and finely shaped arm of a young woman, and in her hand, as though blossoming at the very top of it, whirled a Paris scarf of fantastic hues.

Seven years had gone by since Zeko had discovered the Sava, and the eighth season was in progress when another change occurred which further eased his otherwise tormented life.

His sister-in-law's family, the Doroshkis, moved from Shabats to Belgrade.

When engineer Doroshki and Maria had moved to Shabats shortly after the First World War, they corresponded with Zeko for a while. But it did not last long. Maria was the first to stop, because the "children have overwhelmed me." When the engineer came to Belgrade on business, he would call on Margarita and Zeko and tell them in his limited vocabulary about their life in Shabats. Four children were born to them. His income was ample. They lived well and comfortably in a house not far from the factory, with a garden, which Doroshki himself cultivated.

In the seventeen years at Shabats, Zeko saw Maria only once. One winter, Dorosh came to Belgrade in the company's car and took Zeko back with him. When their son Filip, who was the eldest, completed his high-school education, they decided to move to Belgrade. That was in the autumn of 1938.

They managed to find a house on Topchider Hill, on one of those anonymous steep alleys that cross Tolstoy Street. It was a small, old-fashioned house with an attic and a big garden, which the engineer cultivated persistently, like a mole. On either side there were rich villas, constructed by builders of repute, surrounded by extravagant gardens with artistically devised trails, silver fir trees, magnolias, and fancy Japanese shrubbery of unknown names.

Maria had not changed much, except for her figure, which seemed to have diminished in size, slightly but proportionately. Her face was already full of tiny wrinkles which alternately vanished and reappeared when she laughed or talked; on both sides were streaks of white hair, while the shock above her forehead was still black and shiny as though moist. She was as animated and cheerful as before, devoted to her children, but without a trace of that exaggerated and obtrusive motherly concern so frequently encountered among honest and limited city women, as some sort of repressed and distorted coquetry.

Dorosh also seemed unchanged, except that his physical and moral characteristics had become more pronounced. He was even more taciturn, his back more bent.

For Zeko, the children were the biggest surprise of all. During his visit to Shabats, many years earlier, they had seemed to him like a little horde, fighting over the gifts he had brought them. A roomful of children, like little pots and pans, each one of them going through a "phase," young as grass that has only just started growing, and, barely visible, covers the earth with a greenish hue. Nothing either inside of them or outside had a constant shape.

The children were all now going to school. The eldest son, Filip, was tall, bent, and quiet like his father, but with a sharp intelligent look that Dorosh never had. Then came the daughter, Yelitsa, two years younger than Filip. Fair-haired, with brown eyes, slender and strong, she was the best Latin student in her class, the "most interesting of all my children," as Maria put it. The girl had been exceptionally gifted since her early childhood. After Yelitsa came the younger sister, Danitsa, plump and doll-like, devoted more to play than to study. And finally the youngest child, Dragan, who had just finished primary school. Maria ran this "quartet" indefatigably, attending to their needs, whims, wishes, day and night.

The arrival of the Dorosh family in Belgrade meant one more oasis for Zeko, one more shelter open in the winter months when the Sava was not "in business."

Their home was quiet and carefree, except possibly when the children were ill, or upset because of poor grades, or when Dorosh's salary proved inadequate to cover unforeseen expenses. It was one of those families in which worries and difficulties are quickly brushed aside and in which good cheer sets the tone.

Zeko called on them at least once a week, no matter what the weather, usually early in the evening when Dorosh returned home from work. Everything connected with his visits was pleasant: the walk that took him there, the visit itself, and his return trip.

Climbing up the steep road to Zvezda, under the chestnut trees, he would look out at the Sava, with its islands, the city of Zemun on the other side, the plains of Srem, the wide hand of the Danube, which with its raised and illuminated northern bank seemed to him like a big door into the wide world. As he looked around him, he would feel relief, the pleasure of a flight from reality, a moment of brief oblivion, a thing so essential to men of Zeko's nature and position. And when, walking along Tolstoy Street, he finally reached that small, nameless alley on which the Doroshki lived, the relief turned into joy.

In the winter he sat in the kitchen and in the summer on the porch, drinking tea with Maria and Dorosh. In this house, which was furnished much more modestly than his own, everything was somehow simpler and freer. The tea was better, cakes tastier, words more cheerful, and between the words and the mouthfuls of food there was laughter, which Margarita's house never knew. When the children came home, they reported the small problems of school life. Maria sat there, tiny and animated, next to her huge husband, and rested her small hard-working hands on the table.

Of all the children, Zeko liked Yelitsa best; so did Maria, although she would never admit it. But during the first year after their arrival in Belgrade, a change was observed in Yelitsa. During the summer vacation, between the sixth and the seventh forms of high school, she went for a vacation to the seashore with her class. She returned from this vacation sunburned and grown, with a settled, sharper look on her face, and it seemed that the precious chestnut-brown texture of her eyes, which had formerly displayed a variety of colors like a liquid, had now hardened into a fine, sharp crystal. Her full lips had become thinner and paler. The broad Dorosh-like smile, which showed her strong, perfectly regular teeth, was no longer there; her childlike movements and naive confidences had vanished, to reappear as rarely as holidays. She looked everyone straight in the face, her lips pressed tightly, her face motionless. From time to time, as a last vestige of all that had disappeared, something swelled in that soft spot below the windpipe, between her breastbones.

All these changes did not occur, of course, at once, but little by little, in the course of the seventh form. Zeko did not notice the changes until Maria had drawn his attention to them. The little girl whom he loved as his own had with time shut herself off completely, not only from him but from her family as well, and began observing and judging everything coldly and critically. It was only with her older brother that she maintained some sort of intimacy, but even there she had become dry and businesslike. The center of gravity for this young creature had been transferred to some other place, obscure and incomprehensible. All of a sudden it was clear that

172

something had happened which, as though blinded, Zeko had not even noticed.

He brought her for Christmas a leather-bound volume of verses by a well-known contemporary poet. Returning the book to him, she said dryly:

"Thank you, Uncle Zeko. Please do not take what I am about to say personally, but I must tell you that I accept no Christmas gifts, nor do I intend to read such books."

Trying to conceal his astonishment and confusion, he turned the incident into a joke, but without success.

"Well, it doesn't really matter . . . you keep the book . . . anyway."

"What do you mean 'keep the book'? How can I keep it after what I have said?"

And she placed the book on the table as though it had been a strange object found in the street.

Such incidents and conversations grew increasingly common in the Doroshki house. Yelitsa would be silent for a while, while her parents talked, and then she would pick out one of their sentences, break it in two, place two contradictions one next to the other, draw a conclusion, and then toss them casually aside, like pieces of broken glass.

In our families, people talk for the most part as though they were thinking aloud, and these conversations flow like troubled water, carrying with them everything that is vague, insecure, and shapeless in their lives; all of it is distilled and filtered into conversations, which in the majority of cases bring about no solution of any kind, but, rather, accompany a process in which time, circumstance, and what people call chance bring about their own solution.

At the table Yelitsa mercilessly and coldly ripped those family conversations to pieces. Her brother had loud discussions with her, and she drove her younger sister, Danitsa, to tears.

"I really ought to wash my white dress," the young girl would say with a drawl.

"Go, wash it," Yelitsa would retort.

"But I don't feel like moving; I am supposed to go to a concert with my class tomorrow, and I don't feel like it."

"If you don't feel like it, don't go."

"But I must; the headmistress, my friends . . ."

"And what about the concert?"

Danitsa would look confused.

"How do I know what the concert will be like?"

"Your attitude is all wrong. This has nothing to do with your headmistress and your friends, it is you and the concert. You ought to know how you feel about the concert, and then the decision will be easy."

"Ah, come on, you . . . you . . ."

Danitsa would blush, turn her head the other way, and furiously leave the table.

The father would give Yelitsa a reproachful look.

"Why do you have to torture this child with your sermonizing?"

"This is the exact opposite of sermonizing."

A moment of uncomfortable silence would follow, lasting until, one by one, they left the table.

This scene, sometimes sharper in tone, sometimes milder, became a regular occurrence in the Dorosh routine. The only person toward whom Yelitsa never expressed even the smallest sign of impatience was her mother, although with her, too, she was somewhat colder and more reserved. Maria kept quiet, and, often wearing a downcast look, listened to the family arguments.

These were the outward manifestations of the changes in

Yelitsa's character. What had really happened inside the girl was neither quite clear nor quite definable.

But toward the end of the year, the mystery was cleared up. The explanation came from Zeko's own wife.

"I don't feel like going to my sister's any more," she was saying at lunch one day. "Maria is crazy, simply crazy; and he is as weak, God knows, as he has always been; and the children, they are infected with Communism. Dorosh's nephew, that skinny Sinisha, brought it into their house, and that clever bitch Yelitsa has turned both her brother's and her mother's heads. And people are saying now that the whole household is red."

The food stuck in Zeko's throat, and he was seized by a violent urge to protect Maria and her household, especially her children, from the invisible danger, to defend them, to identify with them, even though he knew nothing of the issues involved.

Blushing and stuttering, he resisted her attacks and asserted that Maria was a wise woman and a good mother, and Yelitsa an exceptionally gifted child, who had now reached the "awkward years," when young girls go through crises.

"And anyway, what else can children do but follow their times?"

"What, don't tell me you've turned red, too! Don't tell me you are one of those fellow-travelers, the fools!"

"I am not anything, but . . ."

" 'But, but' . . . you'd do better not to go there too often, because their house is under suspicion. The Mayor's wife said so openly at a party the other day."

"For heaven's sake, Margarita!"

"Don't tell me 'for heaven's sake.' They have uncovered 'cells,' or whatever they are called, and contributions for 'Red

Aid,' and this was in some of the best homes on Rumunska Street. The children of the rich have had too much to eat, and act as though they lived in a gypsy quarter. And their parents don't see a thing, just like that silly sister of mine."

Tigar yawned, and, stretching with all his strength, looked at the watch on his wrist. And Zeko felt the food rising in his gullet and his heart beating from a strong, dark feeling in which there was both fear and fury, and, more than anything, a desire not to be where he was.

· III ·

The international war, which started with the German attack on Poland in August 1939, was of little consequence to Zeko's household. As in many other homes, newspapers were read irregularly and superficially. Zeko looked at the headlines, Tigar occupied himself with the sports section, and Margarita with the advertisements, the wedding and funeral announcements. No one was "involved in politics." That, however, did not prevent Margarita, that first autumn, from buying large quantities of flour, sugar, and various other provisions which "would keep," nor did it prevent Zeko from listening to the foreign stations on the radio, something he had never done before. As a result, he became deeply concerned with the fate of Poland, without even thinking about how or when it all started.

Here, too, Margarita stood in his way. With an angry gesture she would turn off the radio, look at Zeko, and say:

"You are only wasting electricity. If you feel sorry for the

176

Poles, go there and cry with them. As for me, I am delighted that Hitler fixed them!"

At which point she would stretch out her arm, bare to the elbow, and demonstrate the way in which people and nations are "fixed."

And Zeko watched before him that outstretched arm of hers, fat and corpulent, without any visible muscles. They are Margarita's deadly yellow arms—heavy and powerful nevertheless—arms that command and rule, take, grab, but work little and give rarely. There is little that is human in their shape. On the elbows, like worn patches, were callused, dirty-gray spots that reminded one of spots on a camel or a monkey.

Zeko finally turned his gaze from her arm, got up and without comment walked out of the room.

And then for days on end there would be no mention of Poland, Germany, or the war. It was only in Zeko's hidden thoughts, unclear even to himself, and in Margarita's endless and complex calculations, that the war had its impact.

But at the Sava the situation was quite different. In the still strong September sun, the last of the season's bathers were talking, openly lamenting the fate of Poland. The Sava men listened to these discussions with pleasure, although they were more discreet and found it more difficult to express themselves.

When the talk was about German victories, Stanko would drink his wine a little faster, and, wiping off his mustache, drawl:

"Well, men, well . . . !"

Stanko imbued this drawn-out "well" with a special significance, probably not quite clear even to him, but which left no doubt that he was not pleased with the present situation and that he anticipated better solutions.

Stanko's servant was much more outspoken, and expressed

177

himself in terms, not easy to repeat; but if we omit from his speech all its many curses, nothing but the names of statesmen and the states they represent would remain.

These men who gathered at the tables in front of Naum's café or under the big walnut tree were unanimous in their judgments, although they did not express them in the same way.

Captain Mika was more calm and reserved than anyone else, and appeared at all times to be in deep thought, repeating in different tones of voice: "We'll see. . . . We'll see everything."

"What shall we see?" asked Milan Stragarats provocatively.

"We'll see. . . . You know how that song goes. . . .

> "Veka's honesty will be scrutinized
> When they have the child baptized."

"Hm," Stragarats growled, and the rest of them broke into laughter.

In Maria's house on Topchider Hill, the war was also being discussed. Filip and Yelitsa were both taking an active interest in everything happening in the world, but they kept their thoughts to themselves and their school friends, leaving the older people guessing and full of foreboding. Maria was worried, which one could detect in her forced smile, but she said nothing.

And when he returned home, Zeko heard from Margarita the latest episode in her struggle to fill her larder with what she called her "war reserves."

"Now I have twenty-eight pounds of laundry soap. And what soap! Soft as down, the best on the market. If the war were to last for another three years, we'd still have enough."

She was telling this story to her son, who was not listening to her at all, not even with one ear.

And Zeko thought all the more frequently of people who, like Margarita, act and live as though other people would forever be engaged in war, and all they need do is to see to it that they are well supplied and thus able to endure until the others stop their fighting, when prewar conditions will be restored.

So, the first year of the war passed in this house, as it passed in so many others, with little relationship to the war but great concern for the "reserves."

In this state of preparation, Belgrade was awakened on Sunday, April 6, 1941, by the distant sound of sirens, followed almost immediately by the dull explosions of the bombs that the German air force was discharging, without a declaration of war, on the open city of Belgrade.

And it was on that day that, for the first time, Zeko assumed the role of acknowledged master and host in his own house. His opinions were not only respected but acted upon as well.

The sirens started howling early in the morning, but Zeko had been awakened, rather, by Margarita's screaming and the sound of footsteps in the apartment above. Upon opening his eyes he witnessed an unbelievable spectacle. His son stood by the door, in his pajamas and a winter coat, and, from somewhere, a proper military helmet on his head. Kneeling on the floor, hanging on to Tigar's sleeve, Margarita was wailing and crying. She was in her nightgown, with a stole over her shoulders, and barefoot. Screaming inarticulately, she was pleading with her son to locate the gas masks, to which he reacted violently:

"What masks are you talking about? Get dressed and go downstairs!"

The young man pulled himself away from his mother and ran off. Margarita crawled toward Zeko's bed. Her feet entangled in her long nightgown, she was completely beside herself.

"Here they are. . . . Zeko, please, where are the masks?"

Zeko got up, quickly slipped on his clothes, and insisted that she put on some too. Trembling as though she had a high fever, she leaned against him with all her weight, repeating incessantly:

"Faster, Zeko, please!"

Then she screamed suddenly.

"Handbag, my handbag! Zeko! Handbag!"

Zeko found her heavy leather bag, took hold of his wife again, and escorted her to the cellar.

"Don't be afraid! Everything is quiet again, see? Take it easy, take it easy!"

Thus he ended up carrying the frantic woman, and found himself surprised at the sheer bulk of this heavy, unfamiliar body, without will or strength, utterly useless.

The cellar was full of noise and confusion. Men and women were shouting and arguing with one another, the children, awakened before their accustomed time, were crying.

As soon as she saw her son with a helmet on his head, Margarita dropped Zeko's arm, and started screaming again.

"Michel, Michel," she cried, while Tigar, without looking at her, said quietly but roughly:

"Sit down and shut up!"

At that moment the first bomb exploded, followed by a series of explosions, which overlapped each other, making it impossible to distinguish them. It sounded as though the earth were boiling over like a volcano, and the whole house tumbling forward in heaps.

One explosion was quite near, and shook the house as if from below, and the blow therefore appeared perfidious and exceptionally unkind. Their teeth chattered.

"They've hit the station," said the superintendent of the house in a calm, almost humorous tone of voice.

Astonished, angry looks were directed toward him. He was sitting on top of a suitcase, looking gloomy and worried, in complete contrast to the flip tone of voice in which he had identified the target of the last bomb. Nervous and reproachful voices flew in his direction.

"Shshsh!"

"Keep quiet, you fool!"

The echo of this hit had not quite receded when another series of explosions shook the city. The cellar lights went out, the air filled with dust. It seemed as though the hill on which Belgrade stood was bursting and collapsing.

For one instant Zeko felt a touch of panic himself, but quickly recovered his senses and became even more keenly aware of them. He felt his whole body quivering, and a shudder went up his spine, freezing into his body. But his brain and all his senses were functioning rapidly and sharply.

In the relative calm that followed they could hear, as if it were an echo of the last cluster of explosions, the clear sounds of an apartment house that was crumbling to pieces, caving in on itself. It was a breath-taking sound, like a series of consecutive explosions deep within rock. These sounds brought to Zeko's mind a picture of a military formation which, set in ceremonial rows, one next to the other, hailed a leader passing swiftly before them with their indistinct and consecutive Hurrah, hurrah, hurrah!

While Zeko was thus in thought, a confusion of frantic voices and commotion rang out in the darkness and dust of the cellar.

"My children," screamed one woman.

"Oh, oh, oh," whimpered another one softly and persistently, like rain.

"I pray to You. . . . I pray. . . ." wailed a weak, tearful man's voice.

181

From somewhere in the cellar, Margarita's voice could also be heard. She was squealing without a word, like an animal that can defend itself only with its vocal cords. And in this voice, Zeko detected something inhuman, something that inspires embarrassment rather than pity.

Someone lit a match, but it was extinguished instantly; they all shouted at the careless man, and screamed about the danger of poisonous fumes. At that point someone produced a flashlight. A stream of light, pale and turbid from the rising dust, passed across the disturbed people.

Zeko took advantage of the light and, crossing over those who were lying or kneeling on the floor, started toward the exit. He removed the iron bar and managed to open the door and go outside. The superintendent followed him. Zeko was surprised to see the familiar staircase and the door of his own ground-floor flat; inside everything was in its place. There was only a little chipped plaster and a bit of glass from the broken window.

The superintendent stood there like a condemned man, wiping his tears and sighing artificially. When Zeko looked at him a little more carefully, he realized the man was completely drunk. He asked him to bring his tools and to climb with him to the roof.

Zeko marched first with a short shovel on his shoulder, and the superintendent followed, stalling and trembling.

When they reached the attic, the superintendent paused and stuttered:

"If . . . if they come again?"

Zeko looked down at him, from where he stood on the steps to the roof, and went on alone.

As soon as he opened the attic door, he felt the dust in the dry spring air. Walking out on the roof, he scanned the city and found himself in an unknown region. Instead of the familiar roofs, he was confronted by a transparent curtain of yellow whirling dust; high up he could discern a deep-blue sky, but below him there was no trace of the earth. The eye could see nothing, and the ears resounded with unusual sounds, minor explosions and dull thuds, as though men of giant proportions, using gigantic tools, were banging something together in the foggy space all around.

Zeko surveyed the terrace; there were bits of earth on it as well as chips of wood propelled here by the explosions, but there was no trace of any unexploded bombs or other doubtful objects. On his way down, Zeko found the superintendent exactly where he had left him sobbing on the stairs; he passed him by as one would pass a weeping child, and descended into the cellar.

He was covered by a stream of light. All eyes were turned to him and from all sides there were questions. It was at this point that Zeko gained the reputation of a man who was not afraid.

During a brief lull between the first raids, Zeko walked all the way to Zvezdara to report to his military command. But he could not find anyone. The command had evidently deserted.

There were more air raids and more mad flights downstairs, and more screaming around the house, but Zeko himself no longer went down into the cellar. He sat in his deserted flat, without thinking much of food or drink, alone with his new thoughts. He was so preoccupied that the sheer force of his thought held him back in moments when fear might have engulfed him and driven him into the cellar.

Thus life began under the German occupation in fire-damaged, plundered Belgrade.

It took Margarita a long time to get over her fear and the

many illnesses which she alleged she had acquired during those few days spent in the cellar. And Tigar, too, was now tame and withdrawn. But one day, Margarita's cousin came from Zemun, gesturing wildly, full of praise for the Germans, for the life in the so-called Independent State of Croatia, in which Zemun was included. As time went on, Margarita and Tigar began moving around Belgrade, buying things, especially food, crossing frequently over into Zemun.

Men in uniform came to their house (Zeko would then lock himself up in his room). Tigar became active in the municipality; he wore a green ribbon around his right arm as a badge of honor. Margarita was buying objects of decidedly doubtful origin to get rid of dinars, which were losing value.

One day Zeko went down to the Sava, but there was hardly a single trace left of the life he had once enjoyed there. Everyone had disappeared, except for Milan Stragarats, who was sitting under the same walnut tree, darting the same proud, fierce glances at everything around him. He was the first to mention Captain Mika, saying that he had probably hidden in a rathole during the crisis. His spiteful laughter echoed along the deserted bank. Everything looked alien and strange, as though the houses had actually been moved around. The following summer the bank came to life again, but new craftsmen and workers were engaged in the workshops and in the warehouses, and it was the Germans who were sunbathing on the beaches and on the rafts.

Anxious to get away from his own home as often as possible, Zeko went to Tolstoy Street quite frequently. But there, too, he encountered confusion and silence. Yelitsa and Filip were either out of the house or in the attic, and when he ran into them, they passed him with a cold, absent-minded greeting. Their father, who had never been eloquent or particularly sharp, had become dumb with fear and did not know where to turn. Maria was full of anxiety about her children. She never talked about it, but her concern was reflected in the dull look in her eyes.

Never had Zeko wanted so much to talk with people, and yet no one felt like talking.

And when he met his old acquaintances, they would greet him with a question:

"For God's sake, man, whatever is going on?"

That's how it is, Zeko thought to himself. We all ask one another questions, but no one wants to answer them, or will not, or dare not.

One Sunday, early in the morning, he ran into a friend on Sarajevska Street and asked him what was new; his friend, wide-eyed with astonishment, said:

"Nothing is good, my friend, that's what's new. Go to Teraziye Square and see for yourself."

The man continued on his way; and instead of going home, Zeko started toward Teraziye, the city's main square. He did not speculate as to what he was about to see, but everything inside of him urged him to continue.

At Balkanska Street, Zeko joined an excited but undemonstrative crowd heading up to Teraziye. The crowd was composed mostly of men, many of them young. Since it was an unusually hot day, they wore no jackets, thus exposing their bright shirts with their sleeves rolled up just above the elbows.

When Zeko reached Teraziye, he saw an overflowing river of people moving through the square. The procession looked as though it were part of a long funeral march. It was only when Zeko followed the glances of the men around him that he saw at the top of a steel lamp post, high up where it branches out into two arms, a rope suspended, and from it a man hanging; and beyond him, at the next post, another

185

rope and another man; and so on down the whole length of the square. He lowered his eyes and thought of going back the way he had come, but then he realized that return was not possible, that he must continue with the procession, that he should see everything. And he passed by and he saw everything, although in those moments it was not clear to him where he was going or what he was looking at. It seemed to him as though the asphalt were heaving under his feet and, together with this crowd of people, carrying him forward irresistibly. And at the same time his eyes moved from one lamp post to another, from one man to another: he observed they were all in peasant clothing. . . .

So that was what happened at Teraziye.

The dead men stood out clearly in the still air of that brilliant summer day, from their bloodless heads, which seemed small and short above the rope, to their toes, which reached out as if feeling for support. With equal clarity Zeko saw the tables spread out before the Café Atina, with beer and rolls on the tables, and he saw the guests, German soldiers and an assortment of civilians sitting there. At the base of the lamp posts sentries stood in full military gear: firm Germans, motionless and hard, as though made of steel, of stone, of some even tougher unknown material. And it seemed to Zeko all along that the movable carpet, on which he had stepped when reaching Teraziye, was carrying him involuntarily toward one of those foreign guards with whom he would inevitably collide, a collision which, whether accidental or not, would have meant real trouble in Teraziye. He was quite near the sentry, very near, even nearer. . . . But as he sensed all of the hardness of that armed man, and all of his own weakness, he realized that he had somehow slipped past him with the rest of the crowd. He had passed within inches, it is true, but passed him all the same; the same crowd that had pushed him perilously close to the sentry was carrying him away. It was only then that he sensed how tightly his teeth were clenched and how rigid his fists. He wanted to move faster, but could not remove himself from the procession because of the people going in the opposite direction; some irresistibly grave need, like a painful duty, drove him to cast another glance at the hanging men. As he was walking, he turned his head and saw two of them, from the rear, framed by the façades of the buildings and the streets full of people.

He started moving faster. The crowd was thinning out.

Without thinking, he started toward Topchider Hill. His need to talk with someone was like a thirst. And as people passed him on the street, it seemed to him only natural that they might all sit down on the grass by the road and talk about what they had seen.

He found Maria busy preparing lunch in the kitchen, talking with two peasant women who were taking their time because it was Sunday. The children were not at home and Dorosh was attending to his luxuriant eggplants, sweaty and silent, as though hoping, big as he was, that he might disappear with them.

As often happened on Sundays, Margarita had gone to Zemun for the day with her son, and had left lunch for Zeko which he would heat up himself. He would have given a great deal not to have eaten alone today, but today, of all days, Maria did not ask him to join them, and he felt too embarrassed to bring it up. He took his leave and started down the hill.

Apparently no one wanted to talk. Compassionate exclamations and desperate movements, that was all.

And Zeko thought to himself: It is when a great disaster strikes a people, when they are most tormented and when the need for mutual help and solace is essential, that, because of the torment itself, people are least able to offer help and comfort one another.

Zeko's empty house received him in strange silence. Only within these four walls did he become clearly aware of what he had witnessed, as if in a dream, that morning at Teraziye. The scene came to life again and with it the anxiety he had felt.

Of the food that Margarita had left him, he ate only a little cheese, fruit, and bread. His agitation grew. The solitude of a summer afternoon in a cool, deserted flat seemed endless, unbearable. He felt the blood beating in his wrists, in the nape of his neck, as though this agitation were infecting his whole body, even the objects around him. Overcome by fatigue, he lay down. Lying on his back, with his eyes wide open, he looked up at the white ceiling above him, and felt that it was vibrating, slowly, but visibly and constantly; the sofa under him was dancing in the same rhythm.

Zeko jumped up and passed through the rooms. Everything around him was agitated and infected with the same excitement.

He went into the kitchen, whose window faced the hill on which stood the neighboring house. He stared at the steep bare slope which blocked the view, and found the same excitement vibrating there too.

Zeko thought of going back to Teraziye, as if he could settle accounts only there, at the source of his agitation. But this idea was only a reflection of his unrest, rather than a practical solution. How could he possibly go there, alone as he was, and in this excitement, which so tormented him and drove him from one place to another?

No, there is no way out and no solution. They are killing people! People are being killed, while some sit in outdoor cafés, eating and drinking, right there underneath the gal-

188

lows, and others withdraw into their homes, so as not to see or hear or know. He had also been like that, but he could no longer separate himself from what he had seen. It was all inside of him. Vainly searching for a solution, he was looking out of the kitchen window into the gulley below and across to the steep slope which rose like a wall, blocking light out of the kitchen.

He noticed furthermore that along the wall of his building, below the window, there was a narrow ledge, designed by the unknown architect for God knows what purpose. This ledge disappeared into the ground, and then reappeared again on the slope across the way, and there it widened into a crude terrace, conceived but never developed. This terrace stood about fifteen feet above the ground, covered with moss and stunted shrubbery for lack of sun.

The ledge was one of the many strange forms produced by our Belgrade architects in the early twenties, when building was done fast, recklessly, without much thought or planning, using whatever was there, or close at hand, with a speed imposed by the desire to own. It was a period characterized by huge, impatient appetites, an unevenly developed sense of responsibility, an insane squandering of energy and materials.

Zeko suddenly climbed up on the window sill and, holding onto it, lowered himself to the ledge, and crawled along it, step by step, until he was able to reach the vertical rain gutter with his outstretched arm. Holding on to the gutter, he reached across the gulley to the ledge on the other side, managing to touch it with the tip of his toe. It can be done, everything can be done, he thought to himself, and leaped with all his strength away from the building and found himself on the other side, on the terrace, where he discovered he could both stand and sit.

He cleared away the earth and gravel that the rains had

washed onto the terrace over the years, and sat down. He felt his blood pounding, his eyes hazed by the heat and the physical exertion to which he was not accustomed, but this concrete shelf, sticking out like a swallow's nest, and hovering above the gulley, did not vibrate like the walls and the ceiling of his own flat. Perhaps he had reached a point at which he, too, would be able to calm down.

Dubiously, he studied his position. The neighbor's walnut tree was towering over his head, and above the roofs of old low houses on Sarajevska Street, a narrow, distant view opened up, which gave him a glimpse of the confluence of the Sava and the Danube and the sharp profile of Kalemegdan at the far end. Everything was novel; never before had he observed the city from this peculiar angle. He had lived in this house for so many years, but the possibility of crossing over to this lovely, quiet, and protected spot had never occurred to him. And all that it had required was a release from fear and petty proprieties, and a somewhat more daring step spanning the empty space that separated the two ledges. Such decisions are not big, but, made at the right time, they can sometimes save the soul.

Zeko sat there for a long time contemplating his new position. But not even the sudden novelty of his situation could sustain his peace of mind for long. It lasted only as long as the fatigue and excitement caused by his exceptional exertion. The memory of what he had seen that morning came rushing back, and with it the unrest from which he had fled, as well as a stern personal reproach: how childish it was to believe that one could escape from this agony through such boyish exploits as leaping over a gulley.

The unrest followed him. Of course it followed him! And it was calling him by his name, from afar, in a low voice becoming closer and more distinct: "Zeko, Zeko . . ."

Then he heard the kitchen door opening, and indeed Margarita's familiar sharp voice echoed across the gulley.

"Zeko!"

Thus the scene at Teraziye, with all its gruesome details, was for an instant transferred in its entirety to this small terrace. Zeko straightened up, his whole body trembling. Margarita appeared at the kitchen window in the sharp light of early evening. She was wearing a hat, and her face was white with the powder which had disappeared from the wrinkles around her mouth and eyes, and coagulated around the nose and the ears.

"Zek . . ."

And the woman stopped, the unfinished word still in her mouth, her eyes bulging with astonishment, her arms raised. With her right hand she made a superficial attempt to cross herself.

"In the name of the Father . . . Zeko!"

This aggressive figure and its angry surprise robbed Zeko of the last vestiges of his brief composure, and he was once again overcome by trembling.

In his breast he felt the sensations of Teraziye: the rumbling noise of the trams, the murmur of the crowd swarming below the doomed men, and the bread and silverware on the tables in front of the Café Atina. And the surprised Margarita trampled through the whole scene, calling out his name.

And at the kitchen window, the woman was wildly throwing up her arms and stuttering:

"What the devil . . . how did you ever get . . . there? What are you doing there?"

Shaking from head to toe, Zeko felt both a passion to defend himself and his inability to do so. It was as though he were dreaming about a furious argument with evil and malicious people, in which he was making an inhuman effort to express, as loudly as possible, his justified fear and scorn, but could not find the voice to shout or the strength to deal a blow. He leaned toward the kitchen window, and, waving his hand furiously at Margarita, screamed in a low, hoarse voice:

"Leave me alone, all of you! Go there, see the gallows, leave me alone, I tell you, all of you!"

His voice was hardly audible, but his face was red, his eyes aflame, the movements of his hand threatening.

Margarita drew back a little from the window, and the man on the little terrace jumped from one foot to another, because there was no room for the long strides with which he wished to drive away his painful excitement. Finding no relief anywhere, his voice betrayed him completely. He tried to strengthen his words, changing their intonation, sharpening their expression.

"Leave me alone, I tell you. You are buying butter and cocoa all over Zemun while people are being hanged in the heart of Belgrade. That's a shame! Shame! If we were humans, we would go to Teraziye and scream loudly: Down with the gallows! Down with bloody Hitler . . . !"

"Ze . . . Zeko!" screamed Margarita, waving her arms like an orchestra conductor who angrily tries to soften the tone of a trumpet player, but the man went on shouting in a weak, frantic voice:

"Get out, occupiers! Down with the murderers! That's what we should be shouting . . . yes . . . and not . . ."

The woman fled from the window and one could hear the kitchen door slamming after her; Zeko was silent, for he had lost his voice. Worn out by the excitement, he sat down, leaning like a sick man against the slope behind him. With his eyes shut, he breathed heavily, his whole body trembling.

In this narrow space, enclosed on all sides, it was growing

dark. The silence was complete, the silence of a Sunday evening in the summer.

Margarita reappeared in the kitchen, but sheepishly, her face distorted with fear, her lips trembling.

"Zeko, Zeko!"

She called to him softly, pronouncing his name gently and caressingly, as one might call a frightened animal. Zeko did not respond, but when she stopped calling him, he suddenly rose, flung his leg out above the gulley, and, with one leap, jumped skillfully across, onto the ledge on the opposite wall, climbed through the window and into the kitchen. Margarita looked at him as if he were a monster, but nevertheless remembered to close the window behind him instantly.

What happened that night in their flat, no one could hear or see, and the times were such that even the most incredible argument between Zeko, Cobra, and Tigar was possible and credible.

It was unlikely that anyone had either witnessed or overheard the scene between Zeko and Margarita. However, she believed the danger to be of such proportions that she had to take into consideration even the most remote possibility that Zeko's threats were overheard and undertake all the necessary measures.

She lost no time. The following morning, the superintendent of the building was instructed to tell one tenant on each floor that Mr. Zeko was "seriously ill." When asked what the trouble was, the superintendent was to answer: "Nerves. . . ." He said this as though pronouncing a foreign word. Wishing to make it clearer, he, for his part, would accompany this word with a gesture: the forefinger of his right hand drawing circles in the middle of his forehead. The tenants waved their hands compassionately.

The high fever which Zeko developed lasted for only three days. Margarita did not dare call a physician for fear that Zeko might be seized again by another fit of fury and start shouting the same threats. Instead, she consulted her sister, Maria, whom she had not seen in a long time. She told her the whole story and asked her to try to persuade Zeko not to create such scenes again, for these days whole families were shot for incidents of less consequence.

Maria was extremely concerned and wanted to call a doctor immediately, but Margarita opposed this. While talking to Zeko, Maria decided that there was no longer any need for medical attention.

Everything ended well. Zeko was soon up again. When the tenants ran into him, they greeted him with compassionate curiosity, and then that, too, was forgotten.

Zeko's unusual fit and his high fever left no visible traces. Nor did the routine of life at home change significantly. And yet, the strange spectacle on the little terrace meant, in its own way, the weakening of Margarita's position and the strengthening of Zeko's. As a result, both the wife and the son started treating Zeko with a little more courtesy, which is not to say more warmly or more cordially, but with the same care people show when they pass by a spot where it is said there is an unexploded grenade.

Zeko was no longer employed. Several times Margarita had tried to convince him that his pension was inadequate, and that he should get a job with an occupation authority, but he brushed aside these suggestions with such determination that she did not have the courage to bring the matter up again.

She was increasingly involved in the task of insuring the family's food supplies. Her fear of everything that was real or substantial, of what could be, as well as of what might never be, was growing. And Tigar proved himself more of a parasite and idler than he had ever been, indifferent to everything that was not related to his muscles and his personal comfort. In addition, he was timid and lacking in skill of any kind, forcing his mother to look after him as she would after a baby.

Zeko was between them. He was no longer afraid of anything; his needs were few; he looked at them as if they were adolescents; to everything they said he reacted with a smile, and rarely honored them with a word. And when he felt bored or uncomfortable, he would leap through the kitchen window and out to his territory. This spot was Zeko's wartime discovery. There he would think with pleasure of the decline of Margarita's authority and the extent to which he had broken free. Although he and Margarita were separated by a distance of only a couple of yards, they were in fact separated by much more—by Zeko's courage and skill to cross the distance. Inspired by this small feat and the slim possibility of danger involved in it, Zeko meditated about danger and courage. The thing was to find the danger, penetrate it, and thereby free oneself. Nor was this process as risky as may appear, because danger lies in wait and strikes everyone equally (however contradictory and incredible this may seem), both those who run away from it and those who hang on to it.

The capacity to control fear is commendable, but basically it is a useless business and a losing battle, for truly there is more fear in us than strength, which invariably gives out in any case, leaving us only our fear. And what fears we humans have—of epidemics, illnesses, and new discoveries, police measures (even those that do not and cannot relate to us), our own thoughts at night, whose roots are not in the external reality but in our own weakened nerves. Thus it became clear to Zeko that fear could be destroyed only at its source. Man's very ability to feel fear must be removed, as troublesome tonsils are pulled from a man's throat.

These thoughts were so diverse and new that Zeko felt a slight giddiness as he sat at the edge of his little terrace, a new fear resulting from the lack of fear, as though these thoughts about the elimination of danger constituted in themselves a danger, at least for such a small man as he. And, indeed, this thought weighed on him like a burden which he had to carry, and under which his whole body shuddered. From time to time, he was full of fear, but he did not pause, he did not surrender. For when a thought becomes fixed in a man and finds support in his character, it determines the ultimate size of the man. The fear in him diminished, and he himself grew.

· IV ·

From the terrace, Zeko saw the lights of Zemun, the city which was now part of a "hostile foreign country," in the hands of the *ustashi*. He saw the Sava, which was always described by Captain Mika as a noble river, and which now formed the borderline between the two unfortunate states, with their poor governments, "Serbian" and "Croatian," which existed on hatred, ignorance, and most ignoble impulses, and by the will of the great fascist powers. He followed several airplanes crossing the skies and the barges being towed so slowly up the Sava, working for the enemy occupation forces.

He was gazing about him, immersed in his usual endless contemplation, when Margarita once again broke her way into his chain of thought, startling him by her presence and forcing him to think about her and matters relating to her.

The angry voice of his wife, arguing with the maid, reached him from the kitchen. Ah, Margarita and her maids! Her whole nature found expression in this relationship, reflecting the insatiable and indestructible need of her social circle—to rule, command, and humiliate weaker people.

For years he had watched Margarita with her maids. Occasionally he had tried to interfere, but he had always withdrawn.

It is true there were girls who were not good workers; some of them stole things from the house and then vanished with money advanced them. But there were others: hard-working girls who would leave Margarita's house after only a few days, not to cheat her, but because it was impossible to live and breathe in this house, let alone work for a modest salary, on Margarita's food and in her company.

And Zeko could understand so well what it meant to be dependent on Margarita, to work under her supervision. She was not satisfied with mere completion of the housework, but pestered the girl from morning to night with her unnecessary, stupid remarks; she penetrated the girls' souls with her lynx-like look, trying to find out what they thought, with whom they associated, what relatives they had. She opened their mail, rummaged through their belongings, and burrowed through their mattresses. She could not forgive eighteen-year-old girls because they liked to take evening walks with their boy friends, because they would not eat leftover cabbage, because they laughed and sang, or were sad, because they had their initials embroidered on cheap blouses, because they liked to have their teeth repaired, because they loved somebody or were pretty, and generally because they had an existence outside their working hours and beyond Margarita's needs.

197

Margarita was capable of talking for hours about how vicious, ungrateful, and bad all the servants were. She could recall a whole gallery of girls who had passed through the house in a little over two decades. There were some whom she would never forget.

At one time she had a short, anemic girl from Srem who stayed with them for only three days. On the third day she was cleaning the corridor and Margarita followed her, pointing to every crack in the parquet floor, issuing endless warnings and instructions. Suddenly the girl stopped cleaning, declared that she no longer wished to serve in such a house, and asked to be paid whatever was due her. Margarita angrily refused to pay, because, as she said, the girl had not given her proper notice, and ended by calling the girl a "whore."

"Okay. I may be a whore, but what kind of a lady are you, using such language? Even if I couldn't get a job anywhere, I wouldn't work for a viper like you. I'd rather starve. . . ."

Margarita threatened her with the police, jumped up and down in the corridor, pouring forth abuse. At one point the girl screamed as though she were having a fit of hysterics, picked up the broom, and threatened Margarita, who fled to the kitchen. Thrusting the broom aside she said:

"A broom isn't good enough; a pistol would be better for you. And one of these days you'll get it!"

The girl left, and Margarita reported the matter instantly to the police. Ten years later she would still tremble whenever she talked about it, and she talked about it often, her eyes bulging with anger as she repeated:

"That rag threatening me with a pistol, if you please! With a pistol! And what's more, when I reported the matter to the police, they smiled at me, if you please!"

One other case came back to Zeko with equal vividness. The girl was tall and fair, with sad eyes and good bearing.

When she came to work, she brought with her a wide black apron. She put up with Margarita for one day, and then went home, leaving the black apron. And she never came back or called. The horror of that one day was evidently so great that she had fled, as if from a plague, without looking back. She had given her mistress a gift, not only of one working day, but an apron too.

And Margarita told this story to everyone, without realizing that it revealed as much about her as it did about the maid.

So it went, from year to year, from maid to maid.

And now again she was quarreling with a girl who had been in the house only a few days, and warning the poor creature that nothing was easier in wartime than for someone to end up in a forced-labor camp; for this was war, and with the Germans there was no nonsense. The threat was a new one, but the quarrel was always the same, and had been for the past twenty years.

And Zeko was thinking of this wife of his, who was blocking every view and disturbing every thought. Ill-tempered, waspish, her hands always restless, she was constantly straightening something out, on her or around her. She accompanied every single word with disproportionate and unnatural movements of her hands. Her face had the expression of a murder victim and the murderer alike. She wore this frown, this savage look, on her face all day; she went to bed with it, and since sleep could neither mellow it nor change it in any way, she got up and entered a new day with the same savage expression, reflecting a sorrow deprived of any grandeur, an affliction which will never encounter either understanding or compassion. But much worse and much more painful than her gloomy expression was her smile, which was like a flash of lightning in gray twilight, a spasm of thin, bloodless lips, a game of wrinkles that had no dignity. Looking at this unsuccessful attempt at a calculated, stillborn smile, Zeko thought of the smiles of peasant girls on a Sunday afternoon, or of simple-minded old men who carry the very light of the sun in their smiles and of old women with hundreds of wrinkles around their animated eyes.

Zeko looked at his wife, comparing her to the once strong girl whom he had desired, and whom, at an evil moment, he had managed to get, all of her and forever.

Zeko thought about other homes and other married couples in his circle of friends. He realized that his own case was exceptionally difficult, but not exceptional; the number of families in similar straits was huge, as was the number of wives with eccentricities similar to Margarita's; only in Margarita's case these eccentricities had assumed monstrous proportions. And in making these observations, he frequently asked himself endless questions about the purpose and origin of these creatures who call themselves ladies. Why, Zeko asked himself, can't these housewives do their job with gladness, rather than with ill-will, grumbling and storming? Why is it that so many women, with good husbands, healthy children, and relative financial security, hiss around the house like furies and wretches, abuse the maids, beat the children, snap at their husbands, answer the telephone gruffly, and argue at the market like fishwives?

And Zeko asked himself: What was it in society that so quickly turned these young women into bitter, cold housewives with dry hearts, short intelligence, sharp tongues, mistrustful looks—in short, sworn enemies of all that was noble and beautiful? Surely it was not illness, for, distorted as they were, they outlived their victims, lasting long enough to enjoy a good old age. Nor was it poverty. Only one explanation remained. The trouble was a social curse: a willful and lasting devotion to everything that was selfish and mean in mankind, and lowest, most insignificant and petty in life. There, that was the explanation. This curse was in turn a logical product of the social system and the erroneous education of women.

Ah, there was no end to the chain of Zeko's thoughts! He had been watching his wife for days and years, and she had been eclipsing the rest of the world, just as now that hateful and unnecessary argument in the kitchen had broken the thread of his quiet meditations, which had of late become so essential to him. With Margarita's appearance, Zeko's expansive, disorganized, but lively meditations—reorganizing the world, its states and its wars, its family and social structure—vanished like tiny figures in a big spectacle.

And finally, when he had successfully shut Margarita's voice out of his life, and even her very existence, he asked himself why so many people in this society lived without a purpose and without dignity. Why do they deceive and humiliate one another in life and butcher and devour one another in war?

He was not successful in finding answers to these questions, and understood that it was impossible for a man sitting isolated on a forlorn terrace to reach an answer, as it had proved impossible when he had lain alone, some time ago, on the raft on the Sava. But he was equally unsuccessful in brushing them aside. The incongruity between the unsolved questions and Margarita's noise around the house grew increasingly blatant, and Zeko would leave his shelter and his home to go to Tolstoy Street.

Indeed, one positive consequence of Zeko's desperate outburst and the illness that followed it, was Margarita's diminished opposition to his frequent visits to Topchider Hill; what is more, she would send him there herself to let his "nerves" relax in the silence and greenery—but in fact she sent him away so that she would not have to see him on his terrace. It seemed a constant threat to her.

And he would go.

The first time he went to Tolstoy Street after his illness, Yelitsa had met him with more warmth, and talked with him as she had not done in a long time, accompanying the conversation with an occasional blinking of her eyes, as though she were looking into the bright sunlight, trying hard to pick out something in the distance.

Zeko was confused and happy.

And Filip came and shook Zeko's hand with awkward youthful cordiality.

But on the very next day they passed him by with only a brief greeting, or so it seemed to him. Nevertheless, it was clear to Zeko that his place was there, in that small house on the hill, and if a solution existed, he would find it there. And he went to Topchider Hill frequently and talked with Maria and Dorosh, and with the children, whom he not only liked but was beginning to understand.

· V ·

The claim that between 1941 and 1944 Belgrade was the "unhappiest city in Europe" is perhaps not altogether valid, but it is true that it was a scene of unparalleled evil and baseness and, at the same time, of greatness as well as of acute suffering. Of all this the house on Tolstoy Street had its share.

Engineer Dorosh himself, big and good-natured, had withdrawn more and more into himself. He appeared to be aging rapidly, as though his huge body was showing traces of what had hit the world itself.

Maria had not changed, except perhaps for her glance, which of late moved faster and reflected something of the intensified anxiety and concern whose cause and origin was known only to her.

And the children had become the most puzzling and the most important part of the household.

Filip was a second-year law student, quiet like his father, determined and persistent like his mother. Since there were no lectures at the University, he spent his time at home, constantly busy with something, which, as far as Zeko could gather, had no specific shape or any tangible results. Yelitsa had developed into a strong girl, not very tall; she graduated from high school and "was not doing anything," although, like her brother, she was busy with something all day long. The hard and forbidding traits that had suddenly appeared in her character and behavior three years earlier subsided, mellowed, and finally disappeared altogether. A smile appeared on her face when she talked, but a new and more secure smile, her eyes were more gentle, her whole bearing more natural.

Danitsa, too, had grown and changed, and no longer resembled the soft, spoiled little girl who found it so difficult to get accustomed to the Belgrade school. Dragan was small, lively, and dark, the image of his mother. Since schools were closed he was passing a rather unusual childhood. When his mother and sister nagged him to study, he asked himself bitterly what strange times these must be "when there is no school but we study harder than ever."

The number of children in this household grew: a regular visitor was a certain Sinisha, a law student. Thin, tall, and myopic, he had an elongated face which carried a mature, stern expression. Another law student who visited often was the stepson of a Chukaritsa tinsmith. His name was Milan, but in his football days he had been called "Reserva," and this name stuck.

Other young men also came; some were students, others, judging by their appearance, were workers. But they did not stay long, often coming only to the gate, and they were never introduced to the family.

It was during the first summer under the occupation that Zeko re-established his friendship with the children. The relationship between these young people and this older man varied in its degree of warmth, but it constantly grew and developed.

They listened together to the radio in the attic, taking the usual precautions employed when listening to a foreign station. But the children made no extensive comments in Zeko's presence. After listening to Radio Moscow, Filip and Reserva would exchange a few words. Zeko took no part in this. As soon as he heard the news he would join Maria in the garden or in the kitchen to tell her briefly what was happening on the front lines and in the world. In time, this procedure became an established ceremonial. But Dorosh was so cautious and timid that he asked that they spare him the details and give him instead only the major outline of "how our side was faring at the front, well or badly." That was all. Soon it became the established custom to tell him one and the same thing at all times: "It's going well!"

Dorosh would raise his thin, long arms above his head, signifying that he, too, wished "our side" well, but was still afraid of trouble.

Months passed, days, nights, hours, and minutes, each of which, in its own right, appeared endless and unendurable. Zeko spent more and more time at Topchider and less in the house he called his own. In fact, in time, he began to feel at home only there and more like a guest downtown. As the times grew increasingly complex, Zeko's friendship with the children developed further.

On the way up to the attic to listen to the radio, Zeko would catch the last words of a discussion that had been in progress among them, or some joke or an allusion to something that was unintelligible to him. Nothing was said before him openly, but less was concealed than before.

Once Filip said cheerfully in the course of a discussion: "Don't worry, with Uncle Zeko we can speak openly. . . ."

These words inspired in Zeko a feeling of great and unknown pleasure.

In his talks with Maria, Zeko often brought the children up, but Maria never entered a discussion about their plans and activities. However, when any of the children were mentioned, she lifted her head a little higher, as if to hear better. That was all. And Zeko wanted to tell her how much he respected and understood these young men and women, how he hated what they hated, and liked what they liked, that he was anxious about them and would like to help them—he did not know how—but perhaps there was something they could not do or did not know how to do, to expose himself to danger instead of them or . . . ah, if he had such difficulty in merely assembling his thoughts, how could he even hope to express them clearly?

This inhuman but heroic age did for Zeko what decades of barren life could not do. It accelerated and completed a process which Zeko himself had initiated several years earlier on the Sava. He had become conscious of many things some time ago, but it was not until that year that he finally came to realize how lacking in true manhood his life had been, how few of the human obligations he had fulfilled. In this war the fronts were everywhere: in the battles themselves, in society as a whole, in the house in which he lived, and in his own soul. Confronted by this dualism, it was not difficult to make a decision. But he understood much more fully what he opposed than what he favored. He wanted not merely to think about events, but to exert some influence on them, to work at a job in which he could be of some use, and in a direction he considered wholesome. He became aware that spasmodic rebellions, and even the boldest outbursts, like the one that took place the summer before on the day of the hangings in Teraziye, were nothing more than personal ordeals and helpless spasms. He realized that his awareness must lead to action, and that action must have a definite aim, that courage itself must serve some end in order to bear that name, and that the nature of things which courage serves determines its true value and its true meaning.

Resolutions and decisions were not easy for a man who had for so long accepted life as it was given him, reacting to it only with his fuzzy thoughts and insecure feelings. But in the fire of war everything blooms faster, ripens more quickly, and brings fruit more frequently. Zeko saw his way to the future through the eyes of children—young men and women who could be his sons and daughters. But what did it matter? The most important thing was to do away, once and for all, with a barren and undignified life, and to walk and live like a man.

Zeko wished to confide in Maria, who was so close to him. But he never quite succeeded in doing so, for every time he started to talk, he would stumble and blush—since, as sometimes happens, according to a strange logic of human feelings, he was ashamed of what was most beautiful in him. But everything was finally expressed, if through bashful and awkward hints, thanks to Maria, who herself spoke little but had an unusual quality: the ability to listen and understand.

Always under the impression that he was mistaken and un-successful, inconsistent with himself and unintelligible to others, Zeko became in time both clear and intelligible, which brought him closer to those for whom he cared most.

In the spring of 1942 Zeko began to help the children in their work, without asking questions about the purpose or the size of the job, or about its ultimate meaning.

He became a little better acquainted with Sinisha, who lived on Svetosavska Street, with his father, a retired school principal. Sinisha was undoubtedly the leader of all these "children," perhaps of some large group as well, but one could learn little about his work from others, and he himself said nothing.

Thin and tall, he had an exceptionally naive and unob-trusive manner about him, always giving the impression that he had just arrived and was now about to leave. And it seemed to Zeko that everything about Sinisha was accidental. His green myopic eyes were usually lowered, and he approached people as though looking at them not with his eyes but with his whole body; and he saw everything, or, to put it more clearly, he knew everything he wanted to know. He spoke as softly and as lightly as he moved, as though not attaching im-portance to words, and as though whatever he said came to his mind that very instant; and his manner was coated with an irony which frightened Zeko a little but attracted him a great deal.

So it was that when he finally came around to asking Zeko for a favor, he did it with his usual offhandedness:

"If you'd be willing, Uncle Zeko . . . and if it wouldn't be inconvenient . . ."

And Zeko protested against the thought that such a task might inconvenience him.

Zeko's skill with a pen proved useful. He masterfully copied documents, signatures on identity cards and certificates, and did these jobs with his usual conscientiousness and patience.

He started out by working on certificates by which people gained exemption from the Compulsory Labor Service. When the collaborationist government organized this program, counter measures were taken to enable young men to get out of it. At the Central Fire House on Bitolska Street, where the actual recruiting was in progress, there were long lines of men waiting for their physical examination. It was soon discovered that it was possible to smuggle out physical-fitness forms from the tables at which the examining commission was seated. These forms were then filled with the names of young men, enabling them to move about in the city without fearing the police who were on the lookout for people without proper Labor Service documents.

It was on these forms that Zeko performed his first services for Sinisha, copying from the original the signatures of the physician and the head of the commission.

While working on his first assignment of this nature, Zeko put down his pen for a moment and remained motionless, lost in thought, looking down at the forged document. He studied his hand as though seeing it for the first time, that hand that had started writing and drawing so many years ago, and for so little purpose. It was pleasant to sit in this way, with one's hand engaged in this little labor; and he would have liked to go on working on these good and honorable forgeries until he was exhausted.

That was how Zeko started, and he continued to copy and touch up many other documents which had been slipped into the engineer's house in different ways and slipped out, fully revised, with all the necessary seals and signatures. The sheer amount of this material made Zeko aware of how large was the number of people serving the same cause.

Later on Zeko was put on other jobs. Since his appearance suggested a substantial and regular citizen, he could frequently be used to deliver materials and correspondence. The telephone in his house, which had been entered under Margarita's name, was used for the communication of news and messages.

However small and insignificant all these services and jobs might have been, they were of great importance to Zeko, because they gave him a feeling that he was alive, that he was heading in the right direction, that he was doing something and being useful. This was not the Sava, where he had found a friend in Captain Mika and seen life as it really was and with all of its problems. Nor was this his little terrace, from which he addressed rebellious and vain protests and on which he had spent hours in helpless meditation over things of no real use in this life.

Zeko felt calm and proud, although this calm was not undisturbed, nor his pride either.

On his way down the hill from Tolstoy Street, looking at the city in the darkness and at the skies above it with large, clear stars, which through the swinging branches of chestnut trees seemed to be burning in the wind, he was often overcome by doubt and cowardice: those old, complicated feelings of inferiority or of nonexistence, which sometimes assumed the appearance of over-all hopelessness and despondency.

He would recall the silence with which the children, and even Maria, sometimes greeted him, the conversations interrupted when he entered a room, and the cold, mocking look in Sinisha's eyes. These things wounded his ego, which can happen to a man when he is at his weakest; the belief that he would never become one of them, that he was nobody and nothing, as he had been before, a man without clear aims for whom there was no room in the larger community because he could not measure up to it, because he had neither the strength nor the character to give substance to his good intentions.

He experienced fear, too, not so much the fear of the police, but, rather, the fear of the unusual, of movement and of change. At such moments an endless series of painful questions would arise. What was the nature of all this activity? Was this only some isolated, youthful movement behind which nobody really stood? What did they want? Where were they going?

He could not always answer these questions, and yet he knew that in spite of everything, he was with them. And he understood that if, in an undertaking of this kind, one were to wait until all fears were silenced, he would have to wait a long time.

But there were also evenings when, on his way back to town, he was possessed by a vague but powerful feeling of self-confidence: he was a worker with a good job, a useful friend among friends, and linked not only to the children, but to all those who stood invisibly behind them.

With such varied and conflicting thoughts and moods, he frequently walked down the hill, looking at the same clusters of stars in the northern skies of Belgrade, in different seasons and in different lights. These walks went on for weeks and months and years. And as the years passed, the moments of depression and doubt were increasingly rare. At the same time he was acquiring a knowledge of events in the world and their relation to the work he was doing, and he no longer thought of himself and his own moods as often. He looked out on the dark city with its few stifled, milky pools of light and at the skies glistening above, with the Big Dipper, whose handle, pointed upwards, cut deep between the small clusters of stars.

People at work, Zeko thought to himself; he knew some of

them and was helping them. This thought gave him a new tranquillity, and with it he fell asleep and slept soundly.

This calm was not to be left undisturbed.

In the summer of 1942, Filip disappeared somewhere in the vicinity of Belgrade. He had been taking small trips, with a bag over his shoulders, to nearby villages "in search of food," as they put it euphemistically in those days. One time he did not come back. Immediately afterward two gendarmes arrived at Dorosh's home in the company of an agent of the Special Police, and searched the house. The agent gruffly stated that he knew only too well the meaning of such "disappearances," that this house would be watched for evidence of Partisan activity, and that the mother and the father would be responsible for the son. They came once again, at two o'clock in the morning, and made another search of the house. But that was all.

Zeko never asked what had really happened to Filip, nor where he had gone. Maria did not talk about it, and the children lived as they always had; but their friends' visits were less frequent and more discreet. They continued listening to Free Yugoslavia on the radio, and Zeko continued doing his little "favors." The material was no longer prepared in Dorosh's house, but a little farther down the street, in a wooden shack in which an older woman lived.

One could reach this house almost completely unnoticed from Tolstoy Street by crossing through two neighboring vineyards and the virtually invisible openings in fences between them.

The other center was the house of Reserva's stepfather, but Zeko was not sent there often, and when he did go, he would not enter the house, but only the shop below.

Zeko knew of one more pickup point, and that was by hearsay; it was in a lumberyard on the bank of the Sava. This contact was maintained by a fellow known as Vule, a fair-haired, vigorous young man from the vicinity of Uzhitse; always smiling, he seemed rash, spoke breathlessly, and moved quickly. Zeko found him pleasant but a trifle overwhelming, and whenever he met him he thought to himself: He is one of those who would spare neither himself nor others.

Thus the house on Tolstoy Street was "relieved" and, as it appeared to Zeko, forgotten by the police for one whole year. But the next November both the house and Zeko suffered a heavy blow.

One morning Danitsa telephoned Zeko from a neighbor's house, and asked him to come to Tolstoy Street. When he arrived he found the house in a state of unusual confusion. Danitsa said it first: "They took Yelitsa away last night."

Zeko felt as though everything had suddenly stopped and frozen: air, time, sounds, and blood. He could hardly hear what they were saying.

Three Germans and an agent of the Special Police had come at three o'clock in the morning, made a search of the house, and ordered Yelitsa to get dressed. They cut the telephone wire and took the telephone with them, as well as the radio from the attic. But they allowed the family to put together a package with some clothing and a little food.

Yelitsa kissed everyone, as though leaving for the station, and entered a green Gestapo car. It had exceptionally strong headlights and a searchlight next to the driver's window.

Zeko examined the house, where traces of the search were still evident. He paused by the little table where the radio had been kept, and saw, in the corner where the telephone once stood, a wire that had been roughly cut with a pair of pliers. All of Zeko's attention was concentrated on these details, as though in them he might discern the meaning of what had happened.

He left the house to deliver some messages for Sinisha. Finally evening came, and, left by himself at home, he was forced to face the horror of this event, and in so doing experienced a pain he had never before known.

"They've taken away the child," he repeated to himself, dully, mechanically, as the pain echoed within him, producing a form of suffering unlike the many he had endured in such abundance throughout his life.

For days he did not think of food, could not sleep, and found that his repulsion toward Margarita and Tigar had assumed almost physical proportions. Sinisha had cautioned him not to repeat anything of what he had seen and heard on Tolstoy Street, but this warning was superfluous, for he would not have done so anyway.

He could hardly remember the time when he had paid attention to Margarita's words and had searched in her face for an opinion of his behavior. The war had become the measure of all things for him; or to be exact, the war as seen through the eyes of this incredibly small but important segment of Belgrade—the "children" on Tolstoy Street. And in the past few days the focus had been reduced to the thought of Yelitsa and what had happened to her.

Zeko began to suffer from hallucinations. He would hear Yelitsa's voice; he would awake from his sleep, roused by the same admiration and kindly affection which he had always felt for this girl. "A positive man," Yelitsa had said, bending her tongue a little while pronouncing the letter s. In the middle of the night such expressions frequently came to Zeko's mind, instantly followed by a spasm of pain.

"The comrades are fighting." How often the word "fight" had resounded in him, shaking him to his very roots. He heard it pronounced as she had pronounced it, simply and solemnly, like a child, if a creature so conscious of her own strength could still be called a child. Hearing it from her, the word had gained substance for him; and it was further developed by his image of Filip and Reserva sitting on the train, acting as if they were, like other people of Belgrade, merely out in search of food, as they would tell the police. And it consoled him to think that he was so close to the struggle itself.

At night he would suddenly wake up full of fear that they might be torturing the child at that very instant; he perspired in his freezing bedroom as though he himself were under torture.

How can this young woman, a Communist, so good and beautiful, be locked up in a dirty, stuffy room, hungry and beaten, while the Margaritas and the Tigars walk freely in the sun, breathe fresh air, and live comfortably? This brutal contrast alone sufficed to show which side was the right one in the present division of the world.

And the longer Yelitsa stayed in prison, the more Zeko realized that the problem transcended purely personal considerations, involving the girl and her parents. The center of gravity of his thoughts was shifting from personalities to general causes.

In this tragedy, as in other misfortunes of the war, Zeko found consolation among the family on Tolstoy Street, who were, this time, in as much need of comfort as he himself.

He came to understand the full depth of Maria's character. No tears, no confusion, no useless words. Her pale face had acquired a deep yellow tone and her eyes would lose themselves increasingly in vague contemplation, from which she would break out the instant Yelitsa was mentioned.

But what was really surprising was that on these occasions, Dorosh, the timid giant, displayed a great deal of dignity and presence of mind.

Danitsa also exhibited courage, as did her brother Dragan,

who observed everything around him with his dark eyes, so like his mother's. They both seemed more subdued and serious.

They were all deeply shaken by Yelitsa's imprisonment, but as if by silent agreement none would exhibit the least sign of weakness. And this behavior was, in itself, their strongest link with the girl whom they loved so much and for whom they felt such sorrow.

They talked of Yelitsa only when absolutely essential, and only in practical terms. Once a week they put together a package for her containing food and clean clothing. Dorosh and the children saw to it that the food was there, but the preparation and delivery of the package itself was Maria's task, and she allowed no one to help her. She took this particular job upon herself, and wanted to do everything alone, as she had once given birth to her alone and fed her from her own breasts. The children would help her carry the package to the concentration camp at Banitsa; once or twice, when the weather was exceptionally cold, she allowed Zeko to accompany her.

The winter was bitter and windy. Maria walked with her short but firm stride, turning her black hood to one side to protect her from the wind, leaning against the force of it. Zeko walked alongside, carrying a red thermos and a box of apples, while Maria was holding onto the bundle of food. He slipped on the ice in his oversized winter boots, his step producing a dull echo, as if in accompaniment to the monotonous and firm rhythm of Maria's walk.

He tried to start a conversation, but in vain. His words disappeared rapidly in the wind, and Maria, after a first brief response, lapsed into silence. It was obvious that, while on the road to Banitsa, she did not like to talk. Zeko felt superfluous and confused.

Some distance from Banitsa they could see its large gate and the long queues of people, mostly women, waiting with packages. They were stamping their feet, blowing into their fingers, nervously shifting their bundles and boxes about.

Maria took the thermos from Zeko, thanked him briefly, and told him to go home. He hesitated for an instant, but she repeated her request in a commanding, almost harsh tone.

She took the parcels and walked off without a word. He stood still for a moment.

The big gate was closed, and on either side there were smaller, narrow doors with steel bars, and next to them small niches in the wall for the guards. Two long lines stretched in front of those doors. The queue in front of the right-hand door was the longer, curving well across the road. Maria joined this queue.

The acceptance and inspection of packages had not yet started.

With a feeling of painful confusion, Zeko finally tore himself away from this spectacle and started for home. On the verge of leaving, he caught some sounds, broken by the wind, from the queues in front of the left-hand door. Several women were arguing with an old man, accusing him of spitting in their presence. The women all talked at once, and their words could hardly be distinguished. The small old man, dressed like a peasant and covered with soot, answered the women angrily. Only the last bitter, hoarse words reached Zeko: "It seems to me that now I would spit in God's own face."

Zeko turned around and started on his way back along the road, which was hardly visible in the snowy whiteness, marked only by the tracks of sleighs and carts, like bruises.

On his way back, he was no longer carrying anything, but he felt weighted down nevertheless, as if all the parcels and bundles, all the torments and burdens of those who stood waiting before the gate were in his arms.

Winter was coming to an end; February was warm with the deceptive signs of spring, the south wind on the earth, and fiery sunsets above Bezhaniska Kosa.

One day Maria came back from Banitsa, her package in hand; the guards had refused to accept it, nor had they given her any clue concerning Yelitsa's fate. And for the first time Zeko saw tears in Maria's eyes, or, rather, only a swift, brief reflection of tears, which appeared and vanished almost at the same moment.

On Maria's next visit the package was accepted, and this happened several more times, until, one day, she was firmly turned away.

Someone at the Red Cross told Maria that eighteen women prisoners from Banitsa had been taken to the railway station one night, and from there shipped to a concentration camp in Germany. The names of only fifteen of the women were known. Yelitsa's name was not among them, leaving the faint hope that she was, perhaps, one of the three nameless travelers.

· VI ·

In February a new phase of the war began, signified by the sudden fear that Allied aircraft might soon begin to bomb Belgrade, and by the innumerable preparations which a city takes to protect itself against attack from the air. For months regulations had been appearing in the newspapers, carefully instructing the population in the necessary protective measures. Public shelters were expanded; cellars were being examined, cleared up, and fortified; new ones were being built specifically for German personnel. In the streets one could see people buying dark paper to black out their homes, a measure ordered by the authorities under the threat of the most severe punishment.

One day Sinisha casually asked Zeko what he would do in the event of an air raid. The question surprised Zeko.

"What would I do? Well, the same as ever."

"You are not thinking of leaving Belgrade, Uncle Zeko?" asked Sinisha, lowering his shortsighted eyes.

"No," answered Zeko, wanting to add: "No, not if I am needed here," but he felt embarrassed and said no more.

"Not even if it gets to be pretty thick?" asked Sinisha in his usual ironic manner.

"No, I don't think so," Zeko answered softly.

"You are brave, Uncle Zeko."

Sinisha immediately changed the subject and started talking in a humorous vein about other things.

That was all. But Zeko sensed that he was now under some "obligation" in case of an air raid, and this feeling made him calmer, indeed rather pleased with himself.

In February and March electricity was suddenly cut off. In two or three cases a siren was also heard, a long-drawn-out sound signifying the "first warning," not to be confused with the short peals which people compared to a dog's howl, and which announced "immediate danger."

The minute the lights went out, there was a sudden rush of noise and commotion in Zeko's apartment. Margarita started howling, moaning, and screaming with excitement, asking utterly senseless questions, and making unreal proposals. She did everything in a bustle and a heedless flurry, looking in vain for the flashlight which was in her pocket and collecting objects to take with her into the cellar.

At such times Tigar was as mortified as a frightened animal, telling his mother to hurry up, not to yell needlessly, until he began to raise his own voice.

As she was about to leave for the cellar, she would begin shouting orders to Zeko; to put the fire out, to open the windows.

And once the mother and the son had finally descended into the basement, Zeko would finish his supper alone, in the dark, and then, having put out the fire in the kitchen stove, he would jump out onto his little terrace with quick, experienced movements.

From there Zeko looked into the darkened sky and saw the blackness interrupted by streams of light from the German searchlights, moving in great arcs like the needles of a giant compass, ill-fatedly measuring the great space and then disappearing high against the clouds.

From time to time Zeko could hear the hurried steps of soldiers on the nearby streets, and the roar of automobiles as the soldiers rushed to get out of their path.

These were solemn and wholesome moments for Zeko; he could once again contemplate the problems of fear, courage, war.

If the alarm lasted a very long time, Zeko would return to his room, undress in the dark, lie down and go to sleep. And the following day he would have to listen to Margarita's admonitions, which, like most things she said, were helpless and sad. This helplessness was the clearest proof of the internal disintegration, not only of Margarita, but of the circle to which she belonged. They were finding it increasingly difficult to find any orientation in the changing environment.

The air raids themselves began on April 16, 1944, Easter Day, around ten in the morning.

Zeko was getting ready to go out, not on business, but simply to get away from Margarita, who was reprimanding the latest maid, a small rosy girl, named Filomena.

The bells were ringing in the Belgrade churches.

The sound of the bells receded in the vast space under the immense vault of early summer sky hovering above the city.

Then the siren was heard, overwhelming the distant, pale moans of the church bells and breaking the tranquillity of the holy day. This was the "preliminary alarm," several long and extended whistles, beginning and ending with a metallic sigh. With the sirens appeared Margarita, her face distorted with fright. She was fussing about the house, falling against different objects, against Zeko and the maid, calling them by their names as though she did not see them. She was collecting necessary and unnecessary objects, but shouting only unnecessary words.

Zeko tried to calm her down, to explain to her that the sirens were only a warning. But as he was talking, the siren bellowed again, this time announcing immediate danger. Margarita was scared out of her wits, but her tongue was still alive.

"Ah, bandits! Bandits! Michel! Where is my child? Michel! The key, the key to the small suitcase, Filka, why are you standing there? Why are you staring so stupidly?"

Amid the general confusion, the rushing and shouting, and with the help of the frightened Filka, Zeko managed to get the distraught woman into the cellar. Tigar was already there. He had been playing table tennis and had gone directly into the cellar, unconcerned about anybody or anything else. His mother, in tears, looked at him tenderly. She tried to put her hand on his back, but he shook her off with a brusque movement, and sat motionless, speechless, bent, immersed in his own worries. One could get nothing out of him at such moments, not the slightest movement, sound, or look, as though he needed all his powers simply to preserve himself and his own body. And while Zeko was searching for a seat, any seat, for Margarita, whose legs were about to give way, Tigar remained in his place, motionless, as if he knew no one.

As soon as he had found a place for his wife, Zeko abandoned the cellar. Mounting the stairs, he could still hear her weak, injured voice, imploring him to take care, although she herself, by that time, no longer had the slightest idea what it was she wanted him to do.

Reaching the empty flat, he opened all the windows, and then went into the kitchen and jumped across to his little terrace. He could hear the radio announcing that "heavy enemy air formations were flying above Montenegro and Serbia."

From the railway station below, the sharp and prolonged whistle of a locomotive could be heard, but that, too, stopped abruptly, and then there followed the complete silence characteristic of cities that are waiting for an attack.

Zeko looked out at the view that opened before him from the little terrace. On one side this view receded in the light mist above the Danube islands. On the other side it was clearly bounded by a cluster of houses against which was silhouetted the Zemun station. And directly in front of him he could see the Belgrade station, with a row of railway cars in front, and the Sava river bank, and then, raising his eyes, the top of Kalemegdan and the confluence of the Sava and the Danube; and there at the confluence, the islands, backwaters, and bays glistening in the sun like the pieces of a broken mirror.

The silence was strange enough, but equally strange was the city's horizon, which was deeper and clearer, as though it had assumed a new expression anticipating the new dangers.

The silence was broken by the faint sound of the antiaircraft batteries, concentrated in a suburb east of the city. The uneven cannon fire spread circularly and was finally heard in that very section which, until so recently, had stood dumb and motionless.

Into this vibrating and solemn atmosphere penetrated the faint but constant noise of motors. Protecting his eyes with the palm of his right hand, Zeko looked upward, but he could see nothing. He lowered his eyes, which were full of tears caused by the intensive glare of looking almost straight into the sun. Then he spotted at a reasonably low altitude several small, white planes. Approaching from the west, they flew over the station, near the Sava bridge, and then rose, like sea gulls, who, flying low over the surface of the sea, suddenly arch upward into the sky. Zeko counted them: eight—and a ninth flying in solitude behind them. At first he thought they were German planes, but suddenly he saw, in the distance, two railway cars springing diagonally from the ground, as horses do when they rear up on their hind legs. A cloud of black earth and dust rose with them. Zeko realized immediately that they were Allied planes, not German, and shuddered at the thought that a dream was coming true. The railway coaches crashed back to earth; black smoke poured from them, and its column grew increasingly higher and wider. The silver-white planes flew on above the Sava, racing upward, and disappeared from Zeko's vision.

The last one came into view, a bright-red spot glowing on it, as though it were adorned with a flower. And when it was above the river, little balls popped out of it, like huge flakes, at first two of them and then a third. This plane, too, vanished from sight, and those white flakes rocked and swayed in the skies and, carried by the wind, sailed softly away from the direction the vanishing planes were taking.

The smoke from the railway coaches rose higher and higher, and its center grew red with flames.

Stiff with excitement, Zeko completely forgot where he was, who he was, and knew only one thing: at long last the enemy was being beaten and destroyed—the enemy who had become the center of his thoughts and of all his hatred.

The flak stopped. The three white drops in the skies descended slowly, opening up into parachutes, disappearing one by one from Zeko's sight, falling somewhere behind Bezhaniya.

Zeko was thinking with wonderment how much it all resembled a game in the middle of a summer day when the defense batteries again opened up, all of them at once. At almost the same moment, a series of bomb explosions was heard, five or six in a row, and with the explosions their strange echo, the rumble of the buildings as they caved in on themselves. But all these sounds were overwhelmed and subdued by the roar of the aircraft themselves, like a steady thunderstorm advancing above Zeko's head.

The cumulative effect might be compared to the sensations produced when two wild beasts clash with one another, and, turning into one, produce together the most shrill and horrible howls, amid the dust and broken greenery whirling around them as they execute the quickest and most perfect movements.

At this point Zeko lost consciousness, but only for a split second; a moment later he was alert again, bristling with curiosity.

He threw his head back and turned his eyes toward the clear sky above him, shielding them with his hands. The air seemed to be trembling, and the earth below was still vibrating from the joint impact of the explosions and the demolitions which followed. And everything trembled in Zeko,

223

too, mechanically and uncontrollably, as though he were riding fast on a cart along a rutted, stony road.

In uneven rows, at the height which Zeko for some reason or other estimated at "more than thirteen thousand feet," many charcoal-colored bombers were moving along at a speed that seemed slow and timeless. Zeko counted: four, seven, eleven, sixteen, twenty-two; and then on both sides of this formation, new clusters appeared, confusing him completely and upsetting his calculations. The skies seemed covered with the aircraft swarming in from all sides. And above this black ceiling, like little fishes in the water, the fighter planes glistened, silvery and barely visible.

New bomb explosions attracted Zeko's attention, this time from the Zemun side of the Sava. At the Zemun airport, pillars of earth were still hovering in the air, along with chunks of concrete from the runways.

And almost immediately afterward the formations disappeared in the skies, heading northwest. Only their roar remained, and then an echo of that roar, and then silence. Somewhere in the distance three last volleys of artillery fire were heard, and then two more, and then one, like the last drops of rain after a downpour. The silence was universal and absolute. From the Zemun airport rose a uniform wall of black dust.

Then Zeko realized that the dust was reaching him; and he could feel it in his eyes and under his tongue. For the first time he was frightened, and fleeing from a danger that had already passed, he retreated quickly from the little terrace.

He walked through the apartment, into which dust was making its way, heading for the cellar. On the way, he suddenly overcame the fright which had chased him away from the terrace.

Standing on the top stair, he had an excellent view of the

mass of human bodies, in a variety of positions, clustered in the cellar below.

Once, years earlier, he had visited the Belgrade Mental Hospital to see a cousin, a student who was a schizophrenic. The hospital physician took him to the common room where the patients were kept in the daytime.

The mass of tightly packed people in the half-lit cellar reminded him vividly of that long-forgotten experience.

He saw people sitting, lying, standing up in a dozen curious positions, women lying prostrate, with deathly pale faces, their foreheads covered with wet rags. He saw men sitting with their elbows on their knees and their faces in the palms of their hands, and others standing glued to the wall with their backs, and their heads thrust back, as though chained. He saw couples in passionate embrace, and others who had decisively turned their heads away from one another. A whole maze of contorted faces and looks, as though frozen in cataleptic positions.

From this maze two arms rose toward Zeko, and behind them was Margarita's face, with an invisible expression, her voice tearful, broken, but still demanding:

"Zeko . . . What's going on, for heaven's sake?"

Confused by the exceptional circumstance and wishing to say something, Zeko said:

"It's all right, everything is quiet. . . ."

At that instant, a solitary but powerful explosion occurred, probably a delayed-action bomb. And immediately afterward, there was silence again. In this silence, hands, fists, and hateful looks were addressed to the man on the basement stairs:

"Shut the door! . . . Fool!"

"Idiot! We'll lose our lives because of him."

"It's calmed down, my foot!" said someone in a deep and ironical basso, ending this nervous rebellion, in which women's voices had uttered rough words which had, until then, existed only in their thoughts.

Women were sobbing more loudly, and over all those voices hovered Margarita's martyr-like and drawn out "Ahhh!"

Zeko fled. In the corridor he ran into an engineer, a third-floor tenant, who was coming down the stairs from his flat, excited and almost cheerful. He asked questions and answered them himself.

"Did you see it? I saw it all. I think Groblyanska Street really got it. The Baylon Market, definitely!"

The engineer took Zeko's arm. Unaware of what they were doing, they went out into the street.

There was not a soul anywhere. The silence was as on a mountain. Somewhere high up there was a buzzing noise, a thin, constant, monotonous noise, as though part of the silence.

They walked up to Kneza Milosha Boulevard, and watched as a broad and homogeneous cloud of yellow dust rose above the southeast part of the city. Then the siren sounded from atop the Albania Tower, with a long uninterrupted sound, then another one, from Chukaritsa, and then a third, from the Danube.

The danger was over.

Zeko instantly started for Tolstoy Street. Full of anxiety he hurried up the hill. People who had just left shelters were passing by him. They were all talking loudly and with excitement. Some of them laughed, but this laughter was neither healthy nor good. Many smelled of alcohol.

From the hill, one could easily see burning railway cars in four different locations at the station. Zemun had disappeared under a heavy cloud of smoke and dust, as had southeast Belgrade.

No bombs had been dropped on Topchider Hill, and yet

Zeko did not feel at ease until he saw the familiar little house, untouched amid the early spring greenery.

Inside the Dorosh home everything seemed in turmoil. The engineer and Danitsa were terrified of air raids. The girl's eyes were filled with fear, and from time to time her whole body would shake, as if with a nervous spasm. And Dorosh, pale and silent, was gathering odd objects, going through papers, and from time to time was saying, half aloud, as though threatening someone:

"Ah, not me, I am not going to stay here and wait for new bombs. No!"

Maria and Dragan were calm and self-possessed.

From the hill, Zeko went to Svetosavska Street to see how Sinisha was making out and to find out whether there was anything for him to do. Sinisha received him with his usual short and obscure jokes, but he was more animated than usual. When Zeko told him what he had seen of the air raid, Sinisha repeated several times:

"The Allies have done it, Uncle Zeko, they have!"

He asked Zeko if he would, that very day, survey the city to estimate the damage as well as to check on certain specific houses to find out whether they were hit, and, if hit, who was killed in them. He told Zeko not to bring the report back to him, but to take it to Topchider Hill, from where Vule or one of the children would bring it down to him.

Zeko visited the bombed-out parts of the city, inspected the ruins and their many painful scenes, and returned, exhausted, to his home at twilight.

There he found Margarita and Tigar discussing where they might find a better and safer shelter. She greeted Zeko with reproaches for having left her, for not having taken care of his house and family, and for loitering instead on Topchider Hill. She claimed that she knew, for a fact, that Belgrade

227

would be leveled to the ground that night, and, forgetting the reproaches and admonitions with which she had showered him only a moment before, she kept asking Zeko where they should flee.

"Nowhere."

She looked at him, frozen and dumb with hatred and fear, and in a tearful voice mumbled unintelligible words, and then suddenly the residue of her earlier fury reasserted itself; she jumped up and down in front of him, banging her fist against the table and screaming:

"What do you mean 'nowhere'? By God I am going to run to the end of the world. You get killed, you fool, you've always been a fool, but my life is precious to me, more precious than anything else in the world. I . . . I . . ."

She again broke into helpless tears.

Finally, Zeko managed to slip away and he locked himself in his room. For a little while he heard voices and commotion around the house and he could see, in front of his closed eyes, demolished homes and bodies wrapped in torn rugs carried out of the destroyed houses. At last he fell asleep, exhausted by the long walk and the numerous impressions.

At dawn he was awakened by banging and screaming around the house. He got out of bed. Margarita was fuming and asking several questions all at once. Where should they go? What kind of vehicle should they get? What should they take with them? And what could they do with those belongings which they would have to leave in the house?

Still burdened by the sights and sounds of the day before, Zeko paid no attention to the woman, who, healthy and whole, in her undamaged house and her nicely furnished apartment, was in a deeper lament than those whom he saw yesterday standing near ruins in which everything they possessed had been destroyed.

228

"Zeko! Zeko!" Margarita screeched from time to time, but Zeko did not respond, as though Zeko were not his name. She was packing things feverishly, as though blind, gathering all sorts of trifles, throwing all her weight on them. Suddenly her arms grew limp, her eyes filled up with tears, and she lowered herself to the floor, and just sat there, where she happened to be, next to an open suitcase. But then she rose, called Zeko, who again did not respond, and went on packing, now crying softly, like an unhappy little girl, and then again scolding and cursing like a whore.

Tigar was constantly under her feet, subdued and full of caution. As on the day before, he did not say much. His eyes were full of fear, and when his glance collided with his mother's, they would gaze at each other stiffly, like two lost creatures, until he lowered his eyes and she went on crying, pretending to be packing.

There was no trace left of their "efficiency," of that arrogant self-possession which once made them seem almost omnipotent.

When broad daylight came, Tigar finally agreed to go out in search of a car, a fiacre, or a horse cart. Seeing him to the door, with tears in her eyes and her lips trembling, Margarita shouted to him:

"Go to the Germans, go anywhere, pay as much as they ask for, but don't come back without something that will get us out of here!"

There was not a moment of peace in the house that morning. Margarita was packing, crying, worrying all her worries at once: about the house, the furniture, their flight to safety, pronouncing loudly every thought that came into her head, only to contradict it the next moment. She made telephone calls to every conceivable source of help, and when there was no answer from some number, because the telephone connections had been severed in the bombed part of the city. she wept again, and in fury spit into the receiver.

Zeko sat in the middle of the room, eating his breakfast. Tamed and helpless, his wife looked at him with fury, but also with awe and respect.

"You are lucky, you are, to have such nerves . . ."

And Zeko went on eating peacefully and felt that for the first time after more than twenty years he was sitting at his own table, enjoying the food he was eating, paying no attention to Margarita, and not feeling the slightest dread of her.

And when she began stringing illogical sentences together, in which her overweight personality and her miserable property assumed the importance of life itself (in both this and the "other" world), he quietly interrupted her.

"You are not what matters."

And as he proceeded to explain to her what was on his mind, not sparing her feelings, but with no anger either, Zeko looked straight into her eyes and realized that those eyes, of which he had been so terrified for years, even when she was not around, were not in fact unusual eyes. There had never been anything in them before, and there was nothing now. And when he came to think of it . . . Ah, he found it both humorous and sad, but it inspired neither laughter nor pity in him, for he was conscious only of his liberation.

Tigar finally arrived with a horse cart, and the senseless and furious argument with his mother resumed. Zeko tried to help them, offering several suggestions which they subsequently followed, an altogether unprecedented situation.

It was decided that they should go to Zheleznik, to stay with the peasant who delivered their milk. When Zeko said that he would of course stay in town and take care of the house, they were elated.

Now everything went faster, more efficiently. Even so, Margarita paused at every door in the house, crossed herself, and managed to find time to scold the superintendent, who was helping with the luggage. Calling to Zeko, she shouted:

"Take care of everything . . . shut the windows . . . there are some cookies in the green box, don't open any of the others. . . ."

Finally they left. Zeko helped them settle in the cart. Margarita let out a screech every few minutes, thinking that she had forgotten something which was invariably found in one of her pockets. Finally she seated herself in the cart, surrounded by suitcases of all sizes and bundles of all shapes. She was next to the driver, who was telling her, as one would an ignorant child, where to put her feet so that they would not dangle over the sides. And Tigar was perched high in the cart, sitting on a long mattress which had been thrown over all the suitcases. He wore his usual perplexed expression, immersed in his own problems.

Zeko watched them from the front door, and when the cart started, he waved as if to children leaving for a May Day excursion.

Returning to the flat, which gave every appearance of having been plundered, Zeko spent some time putting away scattered objects, shutting gaping wardrobe doors, putting everything in its place.

When he was through, he washed his hands, settled into a comfortable armchair, heaved a sigh of relief, quietly enjoying his new freedom. Suddenly he remembered that he had to take a message to Topchider. He looked at his watch and jumped up. It was ten o'clock.

When he reached the end of Kneza Milosha Boulevard, he saw that all the traffic was heading out of town, and that none seemed to be going into it. He heard the first siren as he reached the road to Dedinye. It was followed immediately afterward by the signal announcing immediate danger. Zeko quickened his pace, his whole body perspiring. Automobiles full of Germans passed him at tremendous speeds, all in the direction of the suburbs of Dedinye and Topchider.

Near the Zvezda crossroads a young peasant woman caught up with him. Over her shoulder she was carrying a yoke, with empty milk cans on one end and a bundle on the other. Her face was burning with excitement as she walked with that rapidity characteristic of peasant women of this region: bent forward a little, moving her legs from her hips, and swaying with the shape and weight of the burden she carried. She asked Zeko whether the siren was the "dangerous kind" or "just a warning."

"Hurry up, hurry up! It would be better for you to get off the road and into some grove," said Zeko with a confident voice, as if he knew how things were going to develop.

"Oh, God damn them all . . . all of them. . . ."

Although she was upset, she seemed to be smiling; but one could not be sure. Her healthy, strong mouth and her straight white teeth assumed a form which, without any effort, resembled a smile.

The antiaircraft batteries started up from somewhere near the Danube. Walking still faster, Zeko turned toward Tolstoy Street. The peasant woman followed him and turned off the Topchider Road too. She caught up with him in front of the Doroshki house, asking him if she could take shelter there, for she did not know how to manage alone.

The house and the garden were deserted. Zeko called out, and Maria answered from the basement.

She was sitting with Dragan in the candle-lit cellar. Dorosh and Danitsa had left the house early that morning with the countless others who, expecting a new air raid, had taken shelter somewhere in Koshutnyak and Banovo Hill.

They were pleased to see Zeko, and asked the peasant woman to sit down. With a sigh of relief, she removed the yoke and wiped off her perspiring brow with a kerchief.

It was quiet and cool in the cellar. The candle was burning straight. The sound of antiaircraft guns was heard in the distance, muffled and faint. Immediately afterward, the noise intensified, and added to it this time was the roar of the approaching aircraft, heavier and more powerful than the previous time. Almost at the same instant explosions could be heard, accompanied by an unusual whistle and a crash which rocked the ground in the cellar and the house above. The cellar door shook as though someone were trying to force it open.

Zeko stood on the bottom step of the staircase; next to him was Dragan, holding on to Zeko's hand. As soon as the thundering began, Maria jumped from her chair and stood next to the child.

His teeth clenched, his eyes open wide, Zeko saw everything around him quite clearly, although the flame of the candle was flickering wildly.

The peasant woman started moaning loudly, and then dropped her head against her knees, her hands folded under her chin. And in this position, like a child in the womb, she sobbed and sobbed.

Maria stood upright, her hand on the boy's shoulder, glancing at Zeko from time to time, as though seeking confirmation of her thoughts. When the candle cast a full light, he could see Maria's eyes, set in her still face, radiating a strong, dark-blue flame, such as he had never seen before either in her or in anybody else. And when the boy raised his eyes toward him, his serious and curious eyes, Zeko saw in them the reflection of the same deep-blue light, only shorter and weaker.

Zeko thought acutely of death, which seemed so close, and

of the possibility of annihilation, knowing that a shallow cellar under a weak house was not much protection, even from a small explosion. He desperately wanted to stop the dull roar of the engines above their heads, and the thunder of the explosions and the banging of the doors, and the creaking and the dancing of all loose objects in the cellar and in the house itself, up there, above their heads. Holding the boy by the hand, it seemed to him that he had become manifold, linked to all the "children" whom he had come to know over the past three years, linked in an endless struggle involving life and death, seconds and inches.

That day the Allied air forces made three assaults on the German armies that had settled in the "city and fort of Belgrade."

The third one was the heaviest. Air pressure pushed through the closed door like a strange cold wind through a light curtain. Their clothing shook and their skin tingled. The candle went out. Dust made the air heavy. The peasant woman was crying.

But then suddenly everything was calm. They relit the candle, opened the door to air the cellar, and went outside; the peasant woman did not move, her body still in the same strange position.

Finally the "all-clear" siren was heard. It was already well into the afternoon.

When they gathered on the porch in the sunlight, they were pale and dusty. The peasant woman, her eyes downcast, was silent, as though ashamed of herself. She was slowly recovering, and after she had washed her face and had had a drink of water, she suddenly regained her old appearance, speech, and bearing. Ruddy and smiling, she threw the yoke over her shoulder, and, vigorously thanking everyone, left, shouting: "Ah, God damn them one and all . . . !"

Zeko lunched on the porch with Maria and Dragan. The boy ate with gusto and talked with animation. A little later Vule came by with an account of the day's bombing. He was more excited and more impulsive than ever. Zeko gave him the information he was supposed to relay to Sinisha, arranged to meet again in his own flat, and went off, addressing Dragan as "my old war buddy."

When he reached Zvezda he found the city covered with smoke and fires. Below him, on the Sava bank, the shacks were burning from Senyak all the way to Chukaritsa. He noticed that Stanko's green bathhouse, caught in the flames, had broken off and that the river had carried it into the middle of the stream. "This too will pass!"

When he reached Kneza Milosha Boulevard he found the first traces of bombardment. Zeko's house remained untouched. But below them, on Sarajevska Street, there was heavy damage and huge craters gaped in the middle of the street filled with water from broken mains.

Zeko's flat was full of dust, earth, pieces of wood and rocks from the explosions. The water system, telephone, and electricity were cut off. Life went backward, as though it had suddenly moved in space and time. Everything was rough and primitive. One had to go in search of water, fix something makeshift for light, all things that had once come as though by themselves.

By the time he cleaned up, it had grown dark. He lit a candle and went into the bathroom. While he was washing his face, scantily using the water from the pots in which he kept a reserve supply, he was startled by a knock on the door. It was the superintendent of the building, who could hardly stand on his feet. He was stammering, his tongue thick in his mouth:

"Mr. Zeko, I simply can't take it any more. My wife is

235

leaving tomorrow for Kumodrazh. I don't know what to do. Believe me, that siren is worse than anything in the whole world. Never mind the bombs. As soon as it starts my knees give out, and when it's over—I'm half dead. Terrible! I don't know what to do."

Zeko had a hard time sending him away, but succeeded in postponing the discussion until the next day.

He slept like a log. When he awoke it was already daylight. He got dressed and went downstairs to see the superintendent and found that he had already left. The stairs were crowded with people leaving the house, with suitcases in their hands and blankets over their shoulders.

Outside, the streets were also full of people, on foot and in carts, all moving in the same direction, toward Topchider.

Zeko watched the endless procession a long time. They were in mobs, crushed together, fleeing like sheep in search of some place where bombs did not fall. There were old, bent men and ancient women who were crawling; there were young, healthy people who were sitting in carts, with a bottle of rakiya in their hands and a bundle next to them; there were mothers who were pulling their children by the hand, reminding them sharply to walk faster. It was a restless anthill in which details repeated themselves, merged, and then disappeared.

And through this throng passed German soldiers in cars or on motorcycles, making their way without difficulty, as though through shallow water, looking neither one way nor the other.

By ten in the morning the streets were deserted. The windows on the upper floors of abandoned buildings were wide open.

Standing alone in the middle of a square Zeko looked excitedly in all four directions, feeling that everything on this

236

unusually warm day seemed strange and infinitely long, endless, and without a name.

And then he started down the street, toward his home. Before he entered the front door, he glanced at a handsome old-fashioned one-story house across the street, where the widow of a civil servant lived with her son and daughter-in-law. Her legs were paralyzed and she had been sitting by the window all day long for years. Zeko was bewildered to see her bloodless face, lit by the sun behind the windowpanes. Her son and daughter-in-law and the maid had probably gone away, too, leaving her alone.

Zeko paused, as though embarrassed, and then, not knowing why, took off his hat and awkwardly greeted this woman whom he knew only by sight. The white, old face with dark eyes smiled sadly and almost imperceptibly, as though from a great distance. And Zeko quickly disappeared into his empty house.

There was no resumption of the air attack for several days.

Life began to revive. In three days the occupation newspapers resumed publication. The telephone started functioning again, and then electricity became available. The repair of the water supply took a longer time. But even so, life was unusual and limited. In the early morning people left in droves, reaching the outskirts before nine o'clock. The city remained almost deserted until late afternoon.

· VII ·

The number of assignments grew.

One day Sinisha came to see Zeko at home, the first time that had happened. With his nearsighted eyes he looked carefully around the apartment.

While pacing about, he suddenly asked Zeko:

"Do you know a certain Mika Jorjevich, known as Captain Mika?"

Zeko was surprised and pleased. An image instantly arose in his mind: the Sava, many years ago, and Milan Stragarats pronouncing Captain Mika's name ("A Communist, and how!"), spitting in the grass as he did so.

"Yes, I know him, I do." And not knowing what to say next, Zeko added cheerfully, "He's a good man."

"Good . . . ? Not bad. The chief thing is that you know him personally."

As usual, Zeko withdrew a little before Sinisha's irony, but Sinisha continued, unaware of anything. He told Zeko that Vule would come and fetch him, and that he would take him where necessary, and that the rest he would learn when necessary.

On his way out, Sinisha made a gesture to Zeko as though wishing to embrace him, but without touching him, and asked him quietly and in passing, casting his eyes around the room:

"Do you stay here during the air raids?"

"Here."

"And you take it well?"

"Well, yes," Zeko answered slowly, afraid of Sinisha's irony.

"Not I," said Sinisha quickly.

"You?"

"No, I don't. But you are brave, Uncle Zeko."

There was a smile on his face, but a smile that excluded his

238

eyes. It affected the lower portion of his face, giving it an expression of childlike innocence.

So they parted.

Vule arrived two days later around seven in the morning, strong, ruddy, with his face all washed and fresh, his long hair still wet.

He asked Zeko whether there was anyone else in the flat. Zeko replied that there was no one. Then Vule asked whether Zeko would be alone that evening too, and Zeko answered affirmatively. Vule said he would come and get him as soon as night fell. He said he would try to obtain an *ausweiss* or two, the permit issued by the station authorities to those who arrive after the curfew because of late trains. Zeko wanted to know a few more details, to be a little better informed, to arrange certain things together with him, but Vule, who was in a hurry, rash and smiling, assured him that everything would be all right. And he left as abruptly as he had come. Some of his characteristic unrest lingered in Zeko's flat.

As the day progressed, Zeko's mind was brought back to this conversation, and each time he grasped the fact that he would have to join Vule that evening, he was quite bewildered.

In the afternoon, the skies grew overcast, and a tremendous rainstorm broke. It poured so hard that the view from Zeko's flat was blocked in every direction. And when the rain finally did stop, the skies remained low and gloomy, and darkness came over the city well before the accustomed hour.

Zeko was sitting in the big front hallway of his apartment, reading, although he could no longer see too well. He was about to get up to turn the light on when from behind the main door he heard someone trying to fit a key into the lock. He jumped up. Before him, in the early twilight, stood Tigar.

239

He had on a long raincoat, a French beret was on his head, a leather briefcase in his hand.

Without greeting his father, he explained that he had left Zheleznik just a short while ago, traveling on the back seat of a friend's motorcycle, and that he wanted to take some things he and his mother needed.

He did not take off his coat, but proceeded to go from one room to another, banging the closet doors as he went. He opened the dressers, collected things, and placed them in his leather case.

The air was close. Zeko was trembling inside; his son's presence, and the manner in which he was moving around the house, infuriated him. But Tigar was in no hurry. Zeko began to lose his patience. Suddenly it occurred to him that Vule might arrive and find Tigar here, although Zeko had, that very morning, assured him that there would be no one in the house. Vule might misunderstand Tigar's presence, and Sinisha, in turn, might doubt his reliability. Trembling at the thought of this possibility, Zeko leaned against the door.

Tigar reappeared in the hallway, and without any explanation attempted to pass his father on his way to his room. Zeko put his hand on the doorknob and spread his arms, barring Tigar's way. Only then did Tigar take the trouble to explain that they needed the electric bulb in Zeko's room. Zeko did not hear a word of this. He felt the blood rushing into his head, concentrating in his eyes. He pushed the young man's hand away from the doorknob and said hoarsely, his breath short:

"You have no business in there."

"Don't be silly!"

"Get back!" thundered Zeko, giving him a push in the chest, using all his strength.

It seemed to Zeko that everything was shaken from its foundations—the apartment, the furniture, the two of them, and that everything would crash to the ground—but nothing happened.

"What? . . . Why? . . ." Tigar was stammering in his confusion, his head lowered.

Zeko started breathing again. Everything around him resumed its normal place, and he discovered, to his surprise, that every man was capable of striking and defending himself.

He looked at his outstretched hands as if he had never seen them before. He wanted to grab some hard object from the table, but not finding anything, he only yelled, by now quite hoarsely:

"Get out, get out, you scoundrel!"

As though he had seen an apparition, Tigar's eyes were wide, his great strength suddenly disappeared. And he vanished, opening and closing the door behind him inaudibly. The swaying hallway around Zeko stopped its motion and regained its twilight composure. From the street he heard the sounds of the motorcycle being started up in a series of small explosions.

Half an hour later Vule arrived. He carried a small shabby, black-market suitcase, which Zeko instantly recognized. In this same suitcase, three months ago, he had carried nine pounds of sugar from Despotovachka Street to Chukaritsa, and in the sugar there had been buried a material quite unfamiliar to him.

Vule explained quickly and breathlessly the first portion of the evening's assignment. They would leave instantly, but not together. Vule would leave first. They would meet by the tunnel behind the Gospodarska Tavern. If it were too dark to make each other out, Vule would whistle "like a peasant." (He began whistling, laughing at his dissonant Uzhitse tune.) Then along paths that Zeko knew well, they would reach the river bank in front of Naum's café, which he also remembered well. There they would meet whomever they were supposed to meet, receive what they were supposed to receive, and return immediately by two different routes. Vule had not been successful in getting the *ausweiss,* but that did not matter, because it was more than likely that they would return well before the curfew.

Zeko felt uncomfortable about the *ausweiss;* indeed, he was generally disconcerted by Vule's carefree attitude, but said nothing. In addition, he kept wondering what connection there was between their "expedition" and Captain Mika, about whom Sinisha had spoken, and whether, indeed, Zeko would see him that same evening. But he would not ask questions.

Vule was the first to leave, and started down Sarajevska Street; a little later Zeko left, going by way of Kneza Milosha Boulevard.

The night was pitch dark. Like the rest of Belgrade, the street was not lit, and the windows were blinded. Only the lamps, equipped with special shields, cast a small dull light on the worn granite pavement. The skies were still overcast following the afternoon rain so that the street with its wartime lighting resembled a long, dark cellar with a low ceiling.

From time to time a military car moved down the street, with its dimmed lights, from which, through thin slits, two weak dots of light penetrated, like candles for the dead in a dark room. Pedestrians were infrequent and could be recognized only by the sound of their feet. There were two kinds of steps; the well-shod step of the German occupation soldier, and the fast but cautious, or tired and frightened step of men belonging to a conquered nation.

A ghostlike night. It was in turn cold and stifling hot. How much better, and how much easier it would be not to be walking at night into danger, but to have remained instead in one's own room, quiet and secure! Zeko caught himself entertaining such thoughts, but only for a moment; they disappeared just as swiftly and imperceptibly as they had appeared.

Not a single one of his earlier fears and doubts again crossed his mind. The steps of the German soldiers in the dark did not frighten him, but, what is more, only convinced him that this was the right and the only possible way. He felt like singing, so happy was he to be following this road; he could laugh at these well-shod, stupidly arrogant steps, steps which he knew led inevitably to ruin and shame.

In the badly lit squares Zeko could occasionally see intense women with sacks of smuggled food on their backs. Are they mothers, carrying wheat and lard from Zharkovo and Zheleznik to keep themselves and their children alive? Or are they merely blackmarketeers? Let them be! So long as they do not walk with that iron inhuman step, with its false confidence, that same false confidence with which the black army has tried both to intimidate the conquered nations and to give heart to itself. And perhaps, in this same darkness, there are people like himself, and like Vule, walking the streets, following similar assignments. And Zeko drew himself up at this thought; it seemed to him that, in the dark, he and they, all of them on their various assignments, could somehow sense each other's presence.

There was no fear left, and not a trace of hesitation.

And again the steps of German soldiers were heard, a lone sentry or in groups: tup-tup, tapa-tupa, tup-tup, but they could no longer confuse Zeko, for, in spite of them, he heard inside of himself an army of steps, which moved, in this same darkness, dumb and invisible, and for that very reason beyond defeat; which will make an end to all fear, to all the blackouts, and prevent these feet from crudely oppressing the earth which belongs to all men.

And Zeko walked softly but securely, as though it were broad daylight and as though he were marching in a procession with dear and familiar friends. Here and there the street was torn up by bombs and there were holes fenced by boards. The darkness was so thick that, to find his way, he had to use his hands.

He paused when he had reached the Gospodarska Tavern. The darkness was absolute, like a barrier behind which there was no life. And again he felt unrest, but now it was shapeless and quite helpless. Stopping only for a moment, he quickly oriented himself and started off to Chukaritsa at a somewhat slower pace.

Passing through the tunnel under the railroad tracks, Zeko waited for Vule's whistle, but there was not a sound anywhere. Leaving the tunnel he turned to the right, onto the narrow familiar path.

He walked for a while and then stopped to listen once more. He heard nothing and decided to go back to the crossroads. At that same instant he heard the signal—the low, indolently drawn-out tune. Zeko gathered his lips to reply with the same whistle, but at that moment he heard a man's voice thundering in the dark!

"Halt!"

Someone was yelling from the road, and the tunnel reverberated with the command and multiplied it with its echo, so that Zeko did not hear the command, nor the voice behind it, but only a rumbling which made it seem as if the whole concrete mass of the tunnel was breaking and tumbling.

From the dark a flashlight beamed, carefully circling around the tunnel. At that same moment a shot was fired, fol-

lowed by two or three more shots. And then several more. But
Zeko could no longer count, for by that time he was running
along the soft earth in the direction of the Sava. At his back
the shots continued to whistle, producing a strange sound
reminiscent of some forgotten episode in the Balkan War.
Zeko was in complete darkness, but he had the odd feeling
that he could be seen by the whole world. Again the shots
echoed, mixed with the sharp sounds of a whistle, now somewhere on the right, and then again farther away. Breathing
heavily as he ran, Zeko was busily devising ways of sidetrack-
ing his pursuers and getting away not only from the scene of
shooting, but from the café in which they were expected.
(Captain Mika flashed through his mind.) And if the patrol
continued chasing him, he would lead them away from
Naum's café as far as he possibly could.

He thought he had left the bushes and that he was on the
familiar cart path which ran along the bank. He crossed the
path.

Only two more shots were heard, but they were quite distant, and then there was silence. Zeko's heart went on beating
excitedly and he was losing his breath. Trying to get off the
road on which they would easily find him, he decided to go
down to the river, and, going from raft to raft, and from shack
to shack, get to the railway tracks, cross them at some deserted
point, and thus reach Kneza Milosha Boulevard. He thought
of everything: the approaching curfew; the lack of any trace
of his at the scene of the shooting; Vule and his suitcase; and
at the same time he was penetrating the darkness with his
eyes, and feeling the earth with his feet, looking for a path
which would lead him along the bank. He hoped to find the
old raft, the one mounted on metal barrels; if it were still
there, he would go right down to it.

From the distance he again heard the sentries' whistling, a sound as sharp as a threat. If he could only find the path! A path as near to the river and as far away from the café as possible. With the tip of his shoe he finally felt the edge of the river bank, but at the same time he realized that the ground under his feet was giving way, and that he was sinking, together with the earth that was crumbling under him. Desperately feeling for the river bottom with his feet, and trying in vain to hold on to something above him with his hands, Zeko was disappearing, still not believing that he was disappearing. But everything was pulling him to the bottom: the darkness, the earth, and the water, which, as a result of the recent rains, had overspread its banks, and had become unusually deep at that spot. And he sank without a trace or a sound.

A few days later, the following notice appeared in the newspaper *Novo Vreme*:

> My mentally deranged husband, Isidor Katanich, left our flat on the 23rd of this month and has not been home since. He was wearing a gray suit, a soft black hat, and brown shoes. If anyone knows anything about him, please contact the office of this newspaper. Margarita Katanich.

No one ever responded to this notice and nothing was ever heard of Zeko. The Sava carried a good many bodies in those days, many of which disappeared in the willows and shallow water, or else washed up on the bank by the Danube. They were buried by peasants who made no announcements and sent in no reports.

Vule managed to get away that night; two days later he was in touch with his comrades at Despotovachka Street, who did their best to find out something about Zeko's fate. That summer their activities were broadened, and developed a quickened pace and new courage, contributing to the general liberation that was fast approaching.

They mentioned Zeko often, and mourned him as one of their own.